A NEW FAMILY AT PUDDLEDUCK FARM

DELLA GALTON

Boldwood

First published in Great Britain in 2025 by Boldwood Books Ltd.

Copyright © Della Galton, 2025

Cover Design by Alice Moore Design

Cover Images: iStock and Shutterstock

The moral right of Della Galton to be identified as the author of this work has been asserted in accordance with the Copyright, Designs and Patents Act 1988.

All rights reserved. No part of this book may be reproduced in any form or by any electronic or mechanical means, including information storage and retrieval systems, without written permission from the author, except for the use of brief quotations in a book review. This book is a work of fiction and, except in the case of historical fact, any resemblance to actual persons, living or dead, is purely coincidental.

Every effort has been made to obtain the necessary permissions with reference to copyright material, both illustrative and quoted. We apologise for any omissions in this respect and will be pleased to make the appropriate acknowledgements in any future edition.

A CIP catalogue record for this book is available from the British Library.

Paperback ISBN 978-1-83656-628-1

Large Print ISBN 978-1-83656-627-4

Hardback ISBN 978-1-83656-626-7

Ebook ISBN 978-1-83656-629-8

Kindle ISBN 978-1-83656-630-4

Audio CD ISBN 978-1-83656-621-2

MP3 CD ISBN 978-1-83656-622-9

Digital audio download ISBN 978-1-83656-625-0

This book is printed on certified sustainable paper. Boldwood Books is dedicated to putting sustainability at the heart of our business. For more information please visit https://www.boldwoodbooks.com/about-us/sustainability/

Boldwood Books Ltd, 23 Bowerdean Street, London, SW6 3TN

www.boldwoodbooks.com

For Sue Baker, who has inspired me and helped me so much, with love and thanks.

1

Phoebe Dashwood stood at the top of the darkened stairs, listening. The noise came again, the tiniest of cries that faded off to a whimper. She glanced at the lit face of her smartwatch. It was 3 a.m. She'd had around thirty-eight minutes of sleep since the last time she'd been woken. Not that she was counting.

The annoying thing was there was probably no need for her to be awake now. She wished she could stay asleep, but she couldn't. Her mind and body were totally attuned to the tiniest sound. It was as though in the last six weeks she'd become an entirely different person. She supposed she had. She'd gone from being a smart, organised and capable veterinary professional, owner of her own vet practice with four staff working for her, to being a mother. She'd known it wouldn't be an easy transition – the world and his wife had a view, a somewhat smug view, as far as Phoebe could see, on the shock of new parenthood – but she'd thought she was prepared.

That illusion had been smashed on day one. Becoming a mother was by far the hardest thing she'd ever done. Looking back, she likened herself to someone who'd just learned to swim a width at the local pool thinking they'd have a stab at swimming the English Channel. It didn't matter how many pep talks you gave yourself, or how much back-up and support you had, at the end of the day you were alone, floundering in a dark sea.

Well, not quite alone. The creak of a floorboard in the old farmhouse alerted her to Sam's presence, and she turned to see her partner emerge, yawning, from their bedroom. Gorgeous, dependable, dear, kind Sam. She couldn't imagine life without him.

'It's my turn, isn't it, Pheebs?'

'I was awake anyway, and you were snoring. I didn't want to disturb you.'

'It's cool.' He rubbed his eyes. 'Although it's a bit early for their next feed, isn't it? Were they crying?'

'I think so. Something woke me anyway.'

They went together across the dim landing and Phoebe pushed open the door of the spare bedroom. The familiar warmth and smells of the room hit them as her eyes adjusted to the velvet darkness.

Sam squeezed her hand. 'Thank God there's only three of them.'

'I know.' Phoebe leaned over the open-top crate and saw that one of the puppies had crawled blindly away from his littermates and was snuffling around on the newspaper, trying to find his way back to them. Hence his cries. With no mother to suckle them, the pups were more vulnerable than usual and more reliant on each other for warmth and security.

'Do you think we should move them into our room?' Phoebe murmured. 'Then we could virtually feed them in our sleep.'

'Nice idea, but I think if we did that we'd just double the time we're up. They'd wake Lily up every time they were hungry and she'd wake them up every time she was hungry. No, I think they're better off in here. I'll get the bottles to do their feed, it's only a little bit early.'

'I'll help you.'

'No, it's fine. You go back to bed. Keep your strength up for Lily's next feed.'

Phoebe smiled and the smile turned into a snort at the ridiculousness of their situation. 'We must be totally bonkers, Sam. Taking on three orphaned puppies when we've got a newborn baby of our own. I'm so sorry. I didn't think it through, did I?'

'You just did what you always do. You agreed to take the pups because you're the kindest, loveliest, most compassionate woman I've ever met.' He curved an arm around her shoulder. 'Now, be off back to bed with you. I'll sort out these babies while you go and sort out ours. Try and get some sleep.'

For a moment Phoebe leaned into his arm, drawing strength from him. She wished she could stay there. She felt overemotional and weepy, which she knew was down to lack of sleep and hormones, with maybe a small slice of guilt.

She shouldn't have taken in the pups, but it was hard to say no when the woman who'd brought them in with their mother, who'd been past saving, had clearly been at her wits' end. Phoebe knew the pups would have died too if she hadn't agreed. It had been a case of 'say yes, and think about the consequences later', as it so often was when you oversaw the running of an animal sanctuary.

Even so, it had been a crazy decision. She and Sam were only just keeping things on an even keel as it was. She might be on maternity leave from her practice, Puddleduck Vets, and they might have a manager in charge of the rescue, Puddleduck Pets, but that didn't remove the heavy weight of responsibility she felt for it all.

From their bedroom across the landing, Lily began to yell and Phoebe gave herself a little shake. Her baby, who was all the more precious because she'd lost the first baby she'd carried, needed her. Enough of this self-pity.

By the time Phoebe got back to the crib, Lily was crying fitfully, as if she'd somehow become aware that both her parents had gone AWOL. Her little red face was screwed up in distress.

'It's OK, my darling. Mummy's here. It's all right, my baby.' Phoebe scooped her up in her sleep sack and held her tightly until her crying eased. 'Are you hungry, little one?' As she spoke, she carried Lily over to the bed. She'd decided to breastfeed her from the outset, because there was a very strong tide of opinion that proclaimed breast was best. This also seemed to be accompanied by a lot of smugness, Phoebe had found. Or maybe that was just her exhausted, somewhat jaundiced view of the world, right now.

Because breastfeeding wasn't the lovely, bonding, natural routine Phoebe had always envisaged. It was flaming hard. They had persevered and it had got better, but if anything, lately it had been getting worse again. Apparently, the six-week struggles weren't uncommon, but that didn't make her feel any less of a failure. Lily didn't always feed very well and often seemed as though she was still hungry.

Phoebe was beginning to wonder if she had enough milk for her baby. She glanced at the breast pump on the dressing table and winced. That had been a disaster too. It was hard enough getting a decent amount out of her useless breasts to keep Lily satisfied, let alone using that torture implement as well. Her nipples were sore as hell and Phoebe was convinced they weren't up to the job.

Cabbage was the answer apparently. Someone had said that cabbage leaves would soothe the soreness. But Phoebe couldn't remember if you were supposed to cook the leaves or leave them raw. When was she supposed to have time to cook flaming cabbage, let alone go to the shops and buy it?

That was something else to look up on Mumsnet or ask the health visitor – her worries about the quantity of milk she was producing, not cabbage. Mumsnet was the quicker option. Except that whoever she asked, she got a different opinion. There were plenty of people around her to ask too – her best friend, Tori, had a little one who'd be two in December, and her brother and sister-in-law, Frazier and Alexa, had twin four-year-olds and a fourteen-month-old. They all seemed to have coped perfectly fine.

Alexa was the archetypal earth mother. She made everything to do with children and babies look effortless. Alexa her sister-in-law, not Alexa the virtual assistant, although the computer was definitely an earth mother too with her calm as a cucumber, self-satisfied voice. Alexa the virtual assistant sounded way too pleased with herself if you asked her a question about babies. As if everything was entirely simple. There had been several times when Phoebe had been tempted to throw Alexa on the floor and stamp on her.

Even Tori, who'd always proclaimed she was the least maternal woman on the planet, seemed to cope fine with little Vanessa-Rose. Phoebe had never heard her complain. It was clearly just Phoebe who couldn't cope with her precious, precious daughter.

In her arms, Lily arched her back and refused to even try to latch on, and Phoebe felt a tear drip down her nose and land on her baby's soft downy head. She had never felt so useless in her life.

'I'm sorry, my darling. I'm sorry if I'm not doing it right.'

Her overtired brain whirred. Maybe it was because she was

an older mother. She was thirty-eight. But lots of women had babies later than that. Tori was thirty-eight too.

Maybe she was trying too hard. Maybe they should get some formula after all. It was something else to put on her list to discuss with Sam. Along with who they might be able to find who could help with the feeding of the orphaned puppies. There must be someone who'd help.

Every four hours day and night was a hard ask, but it shouldn't be that difficult to find someone. There were plenty of volunteers at Puddleduck Pets. Phoebe racked her brains over who might be suitable. She thought briefly of her grandmother, who until recently had owned and run Puddleduck Pets. But Maggie was seventy-seven, and her health wasn't brilliant. It wouldn't be fair to ask Maggie.

Phoebe ran through other possibilities. Maybe one of the practice staff – they all loved animals – or Natasha, who was the full-time manager of the sanctuary. Alongside every name there were reasons why it wouldn't work. Or maybe she was just too tired to think straight. Phoebe suspected that might be the case.

This was day three of four-hourly puppy feeding and a baby who barely slept. She lay back on the pillows with Lily in her arms. She would work it out in the morning when she could think straight.

* * *

When Sam came back into the room, he saw that Phoebe had fallen asleep on her back on their king-size bed with Lily sprawled on her chest. He wished he didn't have to wake them. He stood for a moment looking down at the woman he loved most in the world and his new daughter.

The love he felt for them both was so fierce that it hurt. He'd never imagined he could feel like this. He'd never imagined fatherhood would be so hard either.

If you'd have asked him to pick the one thing in the world that would make him supremely happy, he would have picked this. He'd loved Phoebe for as long as he could remember. Their mothers were best friends and Sam and Phoebe had grown up together. He'd been over the moon when Phoebe had agreed to marry him – not that they'd got round to that bit yet.

Although Lily hadn't been exactly planned, Sam had always wanted his own family too, and let's face it, neither he nor Phoebe were spring chickens. But prior to becoming a dad, Sam's life had consisted of working at Hendrie's Post Office and Stores, run by his mother, giving riding lessons at Brook Riding School, which was in the New Forest half an hour from Puddleduck Farm, and riding his own horse Ninja, as well as living with Phoebe, Roxie, their hyperactive dalmatian, and Snowball, his black fluffy cat. This was before you counted any of the dozens of animal waifs and strays that lived at Puddleduck Pets.

He'd thought life had been busy before Lily's birth, but he realised now that he hadn't known the meaning of the word 'busy' back then. Lately, all the days seemed to blur into one another. He'd cut down his hours at Hendrie's Post Office. Luckily Ma had insisted on it, although it hadn't been their original plan. Their original plan had been that Phoebe would look after Lily in the day until she finished maternity leave and Sam would do the nights, helped by Phoebe expressing her milk.

It had looked so simple on paper, but nothing had gone according to plan. They both did the nights. Phoebe had cried when she'd tried and failed to use the breast pump and she told him she couldn't sleep anyway so what was the point in her not feeding Lily directly?

Sam had given up doing any riding lessons. Trying to teach

kids when you couldn't stop yawning wasn't a good look and fortunately Ninja wasn't at livery at Brook Riding School any more. He was stabled here at Puddleduck Farm, so Sam didn't feel obliged to teach lessons.

He missed it sometimes. The pink horses. The yellow spotted dogs. *Pink* horses. *Yellow* spotted dogs. Oh my God. Sam realised, with a small start of shock, that he'd actually dozed off on his feet and he'd started to dream. Luckily the bedroom wall had been behind him, solid and real, and he hadn't actually fallen over. Good grief, he didn't remember ever feeling this tired in his life.

He crossed softly to the bed. What were the rules about sleeping with your baby? He seemed to remember it wasn't good. Horror stories of crushing them accidentally jolted him properly awake. Very gently he lifted Lily into his arms and carried her back to her crib. To his relief, she didn't wake. She just punched out with a tiny fist in her sleep. He'd got all the way to her crib and laid her in it before she opened her eyes, saw his face and began to cry softly. His heart sank as he picked her up again and rocked her in his arms.

'It's OK, sweetheart. Daddy's here.'

It was another fifteen minutes before she was sleepy enough to put down again without her eyes springing open.

Sam laid her in her crib and tiptoed back to the bed. It was 4 a.m. With a bit of luck he could get in another two hours of sleep – or unconsciousness, as he and Phoebe had taken to calling it. He covered them both over with the duvet and closed his eyes. It would be OK. Tomorrow was Wednesday. Well, technically today was Wednesday, but tomorrow would be Wednesday proper. The sanctuary's quietest day – if there was a quiet day. Nothing much ever happened on a Wednesday in September.

2

When Sam woke up, bright sunlight was streaming through the gap in the faded flower-patterned curtains. On full alert, he reached for his phone and stared bleary eyed at the numbers. Eight a.m. That couldn't be right. He never slept past seven. Never say never. They didn't have a routine any more. Shit. He was due at the Post Office at ten thirty. There was Ninja to see to, the puppies to clean up, and any other jobs he could do to make Phoebe's life easier before he left her with Lily.

He tugged on his jeans and a sweatshirt. The September mornings were getting cooler, and a few minutes later he was downstairs and standing in the doorway of the farmhouse kitchen where he got an enthusiastic greeting from Roxie, who was all spots and wags. Phoebe was at the Aga, toasting bread in a flat metal toasting rack on the hob which you turned halfway through to brown the opposite side. The delicious scent of toast hit Sam's nostrils and his mouth watered.

'Morning, love. Why didn't you wake me? And why are you using that? Has the toaster broken?'

'Because you need the sleep, and no, but I like toast like this. Maggie always used this rack. I swear it's nicer. It doesn't dry out as much. And the Aga's on anyway. Might as well make use of it, the price of gas, these days.'

Sam crossed the flagstone floor of the big old kitchen to Lily, who was lying on her back on her play gym on the floor. He crouched down to speak to her.

'Hello, gorgeous.'

Lily blew bubbles at him, and his heart melted.

Phoebe took a plate of buttered toast over to the huge old wooden farmhouse table. It could seat twelve and had been in situ for as long as both Sam and Phoebe could remember. When Maggie had handed over Puddleduck Farmhouse to Phoebe and Sam she had refused to take it with her, saying they'd need six men to carry it, and where would she put it in her nice new bungalow anyway?

'I've had an idea about the pups, Sam. I'm going to call Jade Foster at Duck Pond Rescue. I think she might take them. She's younger than we are. She's probably got more stamina.'

'And she hasn't got one of these,' Sam said, tickling Lily's tummy. 'That's a great idea.'

'She can only say no.' Phoebe handed him a slice of toast. 'Cherry jam?'

'Perfect.'

He straightened up. 'Has madam been fed?'

'Fed and changed. The pups are fed too but I haven't done a clean.'

'I'll sort them out before I go to work.'

'Thank you. I've got a catch-up meeting with Max and Seth this morning. Seth wanted a chat about an anomaly.'

Seth Harding, who'd once been Phoebe's boss, but who now

worked part time for her as his retirement job, and Max Jones, who was her junior vet, were holding the fort while Phoebe was on maternity leave.

'What kind of anomaly? Is everything OK?'

'I think so. Seth said it was nothing to worry about but he wanted to put me in the picture about something. Don't worry, they're not overstepping the mark. I told them if there were any problems I need to know.'

'All right. Well, hopefully it's not a problem.' Sam knew as well as Phoebe did that Seth, who lived in a tweed jacket and flat cap, was the master of understatement. If there was an outbreak of Foot and Mouth, Seth would probably call it an anomaly – or a minor mishap!

'OK. You're right about this toast. It's really good.' He looked at her, taking in the dark shadows beneath her eyes. 'Are you OK, honey? You will keep me posted if Seth's anomaly turns out to be anything serious.'

'Course I will. Give your mum and dad my love.'

Soon after Sam had left for Hendrie's, Phoebe strapped Lily into her front-loader papoose – those things were a godsend – called a delighted Roxie, who had definitely had her nose put out of joint since the arrival of Lily, but who was immensely good-natured about it, and went out of her stable-style back door into the bright autumnal day. The air held a hint of coolness and smelled of the countryside which was all around them.

It was lovely being able to walk to her practice, which was less than a minute on foot from the house through a yard which had gates leading off it that opened out onto the various pathways and fields of what had once been a dairy farm run by Maggie and her late husband, Farmer Pete. When Pete had died just before the couple took retirement, Maggie had turned the farm into an impromptu animal sanctuary, which had become more official across the years.

It had been Maggie who'd persuaded Phoebe to set up her own veterinary practice here four years ago. Maggie, who'd always hated the label Gran, had persuaded her to convert an old barn into the spanking new practice that was Puddleduck Vets. Sam's dad, who was a kitchen fitter, had helped with the refurb. Sam and Phoebe hadn't been an item back then. Phoebe had been sworn off men at the time, and Sam had just come out of a relationship. It was funny how things worked out. For the longest time Phoebe had thought Sam was too much of a good friend for there ever to be any chemistry between them.

Not that there was much chemistry around with a newborn on the scene. With one arm around Lily, safely tucked up in her papoose, Phoebe pushed open the glass reception door of Puddleduck Vets and checked there were no dogs in the front section of the waiting room before ushering Roxie in ahead.

Marcus, her youngest member of staff, was behind reception just to the left of the door, beavering away on the computer system.

'Hey, boss.' His face broke into a grin. 'Good to see you, and the little one. Is she behaving?' He stood up to see as Phoebe got to the desk.

'Depends on what you mean by behaving. She's not giving her mum and dad much sleep. Are you, my darling?'

'I bet.' Marcus looked fondly at Lily. 'Gorgeous though, isn't she?'

'She is. Although I think I might be biased.'

Marcus wasn't your average youngster. He could be intense

and was much more serious than a lot of twenty-something lads. Which also made him incredibly reliable and conscientious. For a long while he'd even insisted on wearing a suit to work every day, and calling everyone Mr or Mrs. But he'd loosened up a lot since he'd started dating Natasha, the sanctuary manager. They both adored animals; they were perfect for each other.

The door that led through to the back of the surgery opened and Seth popped his head around it. He gave her a beaming smile. 'Ah, Phoebe, I thought I'd heard your voice. Have you come for that chat?'

'Yes, please, if you've got time.'

'Perfect timing. Max is doing morning surgery but he'll pop in between appointments if he can. How's the gorgeous Lily? I swear she gets bigger every time I see her.'

'She certainly gets heavier. Shall we come through to the back? We should probably make the most of her being quiet.'

'Roxie can stay in reception with me,' Marcus said, giving the delighted dalmatian a treat. 'You sit yourself down there, girl.'

She plonked her bottom down instantly in the felt dog bed – Marcus was brilliant with animals, and that was before he'd done an animal behaviourist course and taken up dog training as a sideline.

Phoebe followed Seth through to one of the back rooms, which was lined with built-in crates for patients who were either recovering from or awaiting surgery. As far as she could see it was currently empty. At the far end of the room in a partitioned-off area was a tiny office-cum-dispensary. Jenna, who helped to cover reception as well as being Phoebe's vet nurse, was making up a prescription. She came out to coo over Lily briefly, before turning back to what she was doing.

'So what's this anomaly?' Phoebe asked Seth curiously.

'It's easier to show you, lass.' He strode towards the corner of the room and opened the door of the biggest crate, which they kept for the larger dogs. Phoebe followed him, realising that it wasn't empty after all, but contained an oblong box about three feet long with a glass door.

'It's a vivarium,' Seth said in explanation. 'It's temporary. We needed somewhere heated for this little fellow.' He pointed and Phoebe bent curiously. She'd expected to see a reptile of some description – very occasionally one was brought in, although they usually referred them on to an exotic animal vet. They didn't really have the experience to treat them in house. But instead of a reptile, Phoebe found herself looking at a circular, pale, almost white-coloured bundle of prickles. It was small enough to fit in the palm of an adult hand, and looked like a spiky conker case, but it was the wrong colour.

'What on earth is that?'

Seth leaned over the vivarium. 'I'll show you.' Very gently, he scooped up the prickle ball and brought it out. Phoebe had been right about it fitting into the palm of his hand. Seth wasn't a big guy physically, he'd been a jockey in a previous life, but there was plenty of room for the little creature. Seth manoeuvred it expertly until Phoebe could see amongst the prickles a tiny dark pointy snout and two black button eyes and she realised she was looking at a hedgehog, although it wasn't like any hedgehog she'd ever seen before.

'Oh, my goodness, is that a baby?'

'Nope. He's fully grown. Meet Bumble. He's an African pygmy hedgehog. Cute, isn't he?'

'Wow, yes. He's absolutely adorable.' Phoebe leaned in for a closer look and Lily mumbled, as if in agreement. 'What's wrong with him?'

'Nothing contagious, don't worry. I wouldn't have brought

you two back here if there was.' He met her gaze. 'No, he was just suffering the consequences of an owner who didn't know how to look after him.' He put the tiny hedgehog carefully back into the vivarium and straightened.

'As the name suggests, he's not a native and he has to be kept at a temperature of somewhere between twenty-two and twenty-six degrees, which means of course he needs a heated enclosure and he can't come outside to play unless it's a nice warm day. And we haven't had many of those lately.'

'No, we haven't. Oh dear. So had he got too cold?'

'Yes, and he'd started to go into hibernation. Which can kill these little fellows as they don't have the fat built up to survive it.'

'You've done your research obviously.'

'I have. I know a lot more about APHs now than I did two months ago which was when we saw the first one.'

Phoebe nodded, glancing down at Lily, who'd gone to sleep, her little face serene. Phoebe wasn't surprised, she'd had precious little sleep last night, and Lily loved being close. Still, at least it meant she could have a proper conversation with Seth.

'So why had the owner got him?'

'She bought him for her six-year-old daughter. She'd seen pictures of them online, thought how cute they were, and figured he'd be the ideal pet. Cheaper, less trouble to keep and more entertaining than a kitten or puppy. Wrong on every count, of course.'

Phoebe felt her heart sink. People who bought pets without doing any research into their care weren't a new thing but usually the pets were hamsters or guinea pigs, and it was harder to go wrong with one of these than a hedgehog that wasn't even native to the UK.

'Unfortunately, Bumble here isn't a one-off,' Seth continued.

'I've had a word with some vet friends and apparently these chaps are becoming a popular pet. They're not cheap but they're easy enough to get hold of. People advertise them online. As you can see they look incredibly cute, and you know as well as I do that not all breeders are reputable.'

'No.' Phoebe remembered a run-in she'd had with a lop-eared rabbit breeder a couple of years ago. Belinda Bates, who'd been in it purely for the money, hadn't cared one bit about who bought her rabbits, and whether they could care for them properly. In the end, Phoebe had managed to get her shut down. But this was a whole new kind of challenge. 'Is it actually legal to keep them, Seth? I thought you needed a licence for exotic pets.'

'Unfortunately, yes, it's legal, although the RSPCA don't recommend it. To be honest, they make pretty poor pets for kids. They're nocturnal, they need specialist care, and they're prickly, of course. They're not necessarily all that sociable either. So you might find your little hedgehog curls into a tight ball of prickles every time he sees you.'

Phoebe sighed. 'Oh, gosh. And you said Bumble here isn't the first?'

'No. The first one I saw had a weight problem.' He raised his bushy eyebrows. 'They're prone to obesity because they don't get enough exercise. In the wild they'd hunt all night and they can cover miles doing that. They're not going to be doing much hunting stuck in a vivarium.'

'What happened with that one?'

'I called a chap I know who's a specialist and he was able to point me in the right direction on feeding, etc. I got Marcus to pull a fact sheet off the internet for the client about diet and exercise. You can get them exercise wheels – similar to what you'd get for a hamster.'

'Sounds a good idea.'

'Yeah. It's better than nothing.' His face shadowed. 'To be honest, it worries me that people want to keep wildlife as pets at all. You wouldn't keep a fox as a pet, or a badger.'

'I couldn't agree more.'

'I knew I'd be preaching to the converted, and I'm sorry to bother you with it, lass. You've got enough on your plate, but I wanted to keep you in the loop too. I've been talking to a couple of vets on a forum and there's a growing trend on keeping these little hedgehogs.'

'How long's Bumble going to be here?'

'That's the bit I wanted to talk to you about. The owner doesn't want him back. She's asked that he be put to sleep. She can't afford to heat her house apparently, let alone a vivarium.'

Jenna, who'd obviously finished her prescription, came across the room to join them. 'We told her we'd try and rehome him and she said fine.'

'But obviously we wanted to ask how you felt,' Seth finished diplomatically.

They both knew perfectly well she'd have agreed instantly, but it was nice to be asked. Phoebe said out loud, 'Of course we must try and rehome him, and it's fine to keep him here until we do.'

Lily chose that moment to wake up and start to grizzle and Phoebe bent to soothe her, knowing the time for chat was over.

'Thanks, both. Sorry, I'm going to have to sort her out. But I'll have a think about this, and we can catch up again in a couple of days. He's fine in here, and if we need the space he can come in the house.'

She met Max on her way out of the surgery. 'Phoebe. My apologies. I got sidetracked.' Her junior vet, who was blissfully unaware he was also the practice heartthrob thanks to his Hugh Grant voice and rugged good looks, looked out of breath.

'I got delayed with Mrs Philips. She's only just left.'

He'd only just escaped, more like. Mrs Philips was one of Max's biggest fans. Phoebe suppressed a smile, then having promised to catch up with him and Seth again soon, she headed back to the house with Roxie at her heels.

Snowball, Sam's cat, who'd just returned from a night's hunting, twined himself around her legs as she opened the door. He turned his nose up at her offer of cat biscuits for breakfast and curled up in Roxie's basket by the Aga instead.

'You don't mind being up all night, do you?' Phoebe addressed him as he blinked sleepily. 'But you've got the luxury of sleeping all day.'

Phoebe loved the menagerie she and Sam had acquired between them, not to mention Maggie's menagerie outside, but God she was tired. In between the daily routines of seeing to Lily, and the puppies, and getting an update about what was going on at Puddleduck Pets from Natasha, she thought about the plight of poor Bumble.

Having a vivarium taking up precious space in the recovery area was a problem they didn't need, but in one way it was a good distraction. The last few weeks had been a blur of exhaustion and her focus had been, understandably, almost entirely on Lily. But when Seth had been talking, she'd felt her brain engage. Looking after animals, saving lives, it was what she'd been trained for, what she lived for. The plight of the pygmy hedgehogs was sad, but it had felt really great to have an animal problem to focus on.

An image of the hedgehog's tiny little face, amidst a mass of white prickles, popped into her mind. Its total vulnerability had tugged at her heart. It was an amazing thing, Phoebe thought with a slight sense of wonderment. When she was pregnant with Lily, she'd wondered if having a baby would affect her deep love of animals. Whether she'd somehow feel less love for them when she had her own flesh and blood child to care for. But it hadn't been like that. She'd quickly realised that love wasn't something that needed to be measured out. Or if it was, it wasn't finite. You could always find another big bucket of love.

3

Phoebe decided to talk to Sam about Bumble. He was very grounded and sensible. But first she needed to sort out the orphaned pups. She phoned Jade that afternoon and was delighted when the younger woman recognised her voice immediately.

'Hey, it's lovely to hear from you. How are you? How's everything at Puddleduck Farm?'

'Busy as always.' Phoebe took a deep breath and decided it was best to get straight to the point. 'This is terribly cheeky, Jade, but I was wondering if you could help me out with something. Please say no if you can't.' She kept her fingers firmly crossed behind her back as she glanced at Lily, who was supposed to be having her afternoon nap but hadn't really settled. 'We've just been landed with a litter of two-week-old puppies. The mother died unfortunately, so they need hand-feeding every four hours and I'm not able to do it at the moment.'

Lily began to yell in the background just as Jade was answering. 'Don't worry. We should be able to take them. We can have them in the cottage for a bit. Was that a baby I just heard?'

'Um, yes. That's Lily. She was born six weeks ago. She's keeping us very busy at the moment.'

'Oh, that's amazing. Congratulations. I didn't even know you were pregnant.'

'It wasn't exactly planned. But we're delighted. She's an utter sweetheart. Sam's besotted. He's a very hands-on daddy. Sam does a lot of the night feeds because I'm with Lily all day. I don't think she ever sleeps. But I can't ask him to look after puppies as well. Although he'd probably say yes.' Phoebe decided not to mention that they'd had them for a few days already – it felt too much like admitting failure.

'We're fine to have them. What kind of pups?'

Phoebe felt relief swamp her as she answered. 'It's hard to say. There's two brindle and white and one brown. Mum was a brown spaniel-type cross. Not sure about Dad.'

'We'll come and pick them up,' Jade said. 'It's no problem at all. We can come about five if you like. I'll lock up early.'

'Thanks so much, Jade. I owe you one, big time.'

When Phoebe disconnected, Lily was still crying and she wasn't far off joining her. But with tears of relief. Oh, my goodness, she hadn't realised quite how much she'd been hoping Jade would say yes. Thank goodness for lovely people like Jade.

'Now then, my darling.' She picked up Lily. 'What about this nap then?'

Lily stopped crying. She clearly wasn't sleepy at all. Phoebe cuddled her. 'Playtime it is then,' she said.

* * *

Jade arrived just after five as she'd promised. As Jade and her partner, Finn, approached the glass doors of Puddleduck Vets,

Phoebe went out to meet them with Lily, happy in her papoose. They both stopped to coo over the baby.

'She's gorgeous,' Jade said. 'You're not working, surely?'

'No, I'm on maternity leave. But I pop in now and then. Sam and I live in the house on site anyway. I just saw your Land Rover pulling in so I thought I'd come and say hi.' She blinked. 'Thanks so much for this, Jade. Sam and I could just about manage puppy feeds as well but it'd be a struggle, and I didn't want to ask my gran. Maggie thinks she's still a spring chicken but she's the wrong side of seventy-five and she's supposed to be stepping back from the animal side since we moved into Puddleduck Farm.' She grinned. 'The puppies are in the house. Follow me.'

A few moments later, the three of them stood looking down at the tangle of brown and brindle pups who'd been asleep when they arrived but had become aware of the humans and were now waking up and mewling blindly.

Phoebe saw the look of tenderness on Jade's face as she leaned into the pen. 'Gorgeous little ones. Why did their mum die?'

'Lack of nutrition from what I could see, and she wasn't that young, bless her. The woman who brought them in didn't hang around very long. Said they weren't hers. We didn't ask too many questions. What's the point? People lie anyway, don't they? But it was nothing infectious, I did check that.'

She exchanged glances with Jade. 'At least she brought them in,' Phoebe added. 'Even though it was a bit late.'

Finn carried the box of pups out to the Land Rover and placed them gently in the animal transporter. Jade took the rest of the bits and pieces Phoebe insisted on giving them. 'There's enough formula milk to last them until they're weaned,' she told them. 'If you bring them back when they're old enough I'll do the worming and inoculations too. I don't want this to cost you anything. Apart from sleep,' she murmured, suppressing a yawn. 'Thanks so much again.'

'It's our pleasure,' Jade said, and gave Phoebe an impulsive hug. 'You look after yourself and this little one. Don't go back to work too early.'

'Oh, I shan't,' Phoebe said. 'I can't risk falling asleep halfway through a consultation. You will keep me posted on their progress, won't you?' She blew a kiss in the direction of the puppies. 'They haven't had the best start.'

'They'll be absolutely fine,' Jade promised as she and Finn climbed back into the Land Rover. 'We'll take very good care of them.'

Phoebe waved them off with a deep sigh of gratitude.

'That's another problem solved,' she told Lily softly. 'All we need to do now is to sort out Bumble.'

Lily blinked sleepily at the sound of her voice.

'One very cute little pygmy hedgehog,' Phoebe added, smiling down at her daughter. 'How hard can it be?'

Sam was delighted about the rehomed pups, but more reticent about the pygmy hedgehogs when they discussed it that night in the Aga warmth of their kitchen after dinner, which had been toast – same as breakfast – although with cheese this time to ring the changes. 'I think you've summed up the problem there. They're very cute.' He got out his phone and tapped a few buttons. For a few moments he was silent. Then he turned his phone round to face her. 'I just counted twenty-four adverts on Pets4Homes selling one or more very cute little pygmy hedgehogs.'

'Oh, good grief. That's unbelievable.' Phoebe leaned in for a closer look. 'How much are they selling for?'

Sam did a quick scan. 'Anything between a hundred and three hundred. It's obviously a lucrative hobby. They can't all be breeders.'

'No, they can't. And I guess they must sell them or they wouldn't be doing it. I'm amazed so many people want them. I'm also amazed we haven't had more in. Although Seth did say Bumble wasn't the first.'

'Yes, but if you think about it, they're not as expensive as getting a getting a dog or a cat. Well, they're not if you don't include the vivarium, and vivariums aren't that expensive, especially if you don't realise they've got to be heated all the time.'

'No, you're right. And that's part of the problem. People just don't realise what they're taking on.'

'What did Seth say about it?'

'He thinks it's a matter of education. If people knew all the ins and outs they might not be so keen to rush out and buy one, but the problem with that is that we don't tend to find out in advance that a client's going to buy one. We only get called for advice when they're ill.'

'Yes, good point.' Sam paused for thought, his eyes serious. 'Well, maybe the situation's not as bad as you think. It doesn't sound like Seth's seen that many. What did Natasha say? I'm assuming none have come into the rescue?'

'I haven't had a chance to catch up with her yet. But no, I don't think so or she'd have said. I'll speak to her tomorrow about Bumble. Maybe he could go on our monthly rehome newsletter.'

'Good idea. If it's any consolation, I've never even heard of anyone getting one. I'll ask Ma about it tomorrow. She's never mentioned them either.'

Phoebe nodded. Hendrie's Post Office and Stores was the hub of Bridgeford and a hotbed for all the local gossip. Sam chatted to customers all day long in the shop, it was part of his job, so it was definitely the kind of thing he would have heard.

'How is your ma?'

'She's fine. She was asking after Lily. She wanted to know if you needed any help with anything. She said she'd love to see her.'

'Does she fancy doing a couple of night shifts?' Phoebe quipped, before adding quickly, 'I'm joking about the night shifts. But tell her she can visit any time, of course she can. My mum and dad keep offering their help too. And Maggie does.'

'Maybe we should let them help,' Sam said softly. 'Instead of saying no all the time. Now she's in more of a routine.'

'I'm not sure she is in a routine, really. Unless you count random sleeping and wanting to play a routine.' Phoebe glanced across at Lily, who'd actually been asleep for half an hour in her Moses basket and was now snoring softly. The picture of a happy baby. Phoebe knew she should wake her up or she'd be wide awake by bedtime, but she couldn't bring herself to do it.

She felt her eyes fill with tears. 'I've been useless at the whole routine thing.'

'Honey, no, you haven't. You feed her at the same times every day, that's a routine.'

'Yes, but half the time she doesn't want to feed. She just arches her little back and cries.'

'That's not your fault.' Sam leaned across and gently wiped a tear from her face. 'The health visitor told you that.'

'Did she? I don't remember. I was thinking I should speak to her again soon and ask if I can change her onto formula milk. I don't think I'm cut out to be a breastfeeding earth mother.'

'Surely that's our decision, not the health visitor's. We can change her over any time. It would be easier too if I could feed her. I could do the nights then without waking you. You've got her all day, after all.'

'Yes, but you work all day, Sam, it doesn't seem fair. We agreed I'd do the nights.'

'You can't do every night and every day. That's definitely not fair.' He smiled at her. 'Let's try it tonight. We've got formula milk on standby. We can make some up and try it, and hey, at least tonight it's just Lily and not three squalling puppies as well. Did you tell Jade what she was letting herself in for?'

'She knows. She's not silly. Even if she did go all misty-eyed when she saw them.' Phoebe managed a smile despite herself. 'And she's got that nice Finn to help her. He seems a decent bloke. I wish we were nearer to Duck Pond Rescue. I think Jade and I could be good friends.'

'You've certainly got plenty in common.'

'We have. And talking of friends, I should touch base with Tori and ask her about the whole feeding thing. I don't remember her having any problems at all, but maybe that was just me looking at the whole new mum thing through rose-tinted glasses.'

'Or maybe she just didn't tell you about her problems. Maybe she was doing what we're doing and telling everyone she knows that everything's hunky dory and blissful.'

Right on cue, Lily started to yell, and they exchanged glances.

'She's got a fantastic sense of timing.' Sam made himself heard above the din. 'I'll see to her. And I'll make up the milk. You go and phone Tori.'

Phoebe took his advice and she grabbed her mobile and escaped to the room at the front of the house, which they kept tidy for guests, but hardly ever used because most guests sat in the kitchen, which was huge and warm and animal-friendly and muddy-boots-friendly.

Maggie hadn't used the room much either for the same reason. Phoebe felt as if she was doing something a little bit forbidden as she pushed open the door, beckoned Roxie in with her – the dalmatian had also been keen to escape the din – and headed for one of the two brown corduroy sofas that sat at right angles to each other. Even the terracotta and cream cushions were nicely plumped up, and the patterned rug that lay in front of the wood-burning stove didn't have as much as a dog's hair on it.

Phoebe sank onto the sofa and beckoned Roxie up beside her. The dalmatian complied elegantly and rested her head on one of Phoebe's legs, fixating on her mistress with adoring dark eyes.

'You're so good,' Phoebe told her as she called Tori. She decided if she didn't answer, she would stay on the sofa anyway. It was so comfy. A half-hour nap would be wonderful.

Tori answered almost straightaway. 'Hey, stranger. Synchronicity. I was just about to phone you.'

'Were you?'

'Yes, I've missed you. But I didn't want to hassle you. Or wake you up if you were having a kip. I know what it's like with a baby. You grab your sleep whenever you can.'

Phoebe felt warmth stealing through her at the gorgeously familiar sound of her best friend's voice. 'I've missed you too. How are you? How's little Vanessa-Rose? How's Harrison?'

'Never mind us, I want to know about you. How's it going? Do you feel like your eyeballs have been removed from their sockets, dipped in something hot and then put back in again? Or that your entire brain has been given a good shake and none of the pieces went back in the right place? Or do you feel like you've woken up on a different planet where you don't know any of the rules?'

'All of them.'

Tori gave a peal of throaty laughter.

'It's not funny. I'm sure you never felt like that. It's awful.'

'Pheebs, my lovely, of course I felt like that. It was bloody terrible and I wanted to give her back. I would have done if that had been an option.'

'But you always looked so peaceful when I came round.'

'Semi-conscious, don't you mean?'

'No, that's not true. I distinctly remember sitting on your bed while you fed her once, and you told me it was wonderful.'

'Did I? I was definitely lying. But do you want the good news?'

'Oh, yes, please. I really need some.'

'It gets better. The first six weeks are the worst.'

'Are they really? Or are you just saying that because she's six weeks old?'

'No, I'm not just saying it. I promise. Cross my heart and hope to die. It gets better because you adjust and you get into a routine and they settle.'

'I can't breastfeed,' Phoebe interrupted. 'I'm sure you didn't have any problems with that.'

Something that sounded like a snort came down the line. 'Oh my God, that's so not true. I must have told you that. We had to change onto formula in the end. That helped massively. You don't want to listen to all that "breast is best" bollocks that's spouted. The reality is that less than 50 per cent of new mothers continue breastfeeding past six weeks. Seriously. We ran a feature on it last week in the mag. I'll send it to you.'

Phoebe let out a breath she didn't realise she'd been holding.

'Oh, wow,' she said with something akin to wonderment.

'That's such a massive relief. Why on earth didn't I call you before?'

Tori laughed again. 'Look, I've got to go in a sec. Harrison's just done us steak and chips, but why don't I swing by at the weekend? We can catch up properly then.'

'That would be absolutely wonderful.'

'And Phoebe. Change to formula. And take every offer of help you can get. I bet your mum and Maggie are champing at the bit to help. And I bet you haven't let them.'

'You're right.'

'Invite them round.'

As she disconnected, Phoebe felt as if a huge weight had been lifted from her shoulders. She wasn't a failure, she wasn't unique. She was OK. Everything in the room looked better. From the flat-screen TV to the golden pine French dresser to the slatted wooden blinds at the tall windows. It all looked shinier and brighter and sparklier, and the whole room felt full of hope.

4

Phoebe told Natasha about Bumble the next day and the young sanctuary manager confirmed what Phoebe had thought – they'd never had another African pygmy hedgehog come into the rescue.

Natasha had been amazing since Lily had been born. She had been a volunteer helper since she was seventeen and when Maggie had offered her a full-time job, she'd jumped at the chance. She was now in her early twenties and aside from Maggie, its erstwhile owner, she knew more about the Puddleduck Pets set-up and animals than anyone else.

'So Bumble's our first,' Phoebe said. 'He can stay in the surgery for now, but if they need the space he might need to come up to the house.'

'OK. I'll ask around the volunteers – see if anyone knows someone who'd take him, and I'll report back.'

'Thanks.'

'My pleasure.' Natasha's eyes gleamed. 'I'm sure we'll find him a home. He does look really cute. Leave it with me. And don't go worrying about him. You focus on your little one.'

Not for the first time, Phoebe thought that Natasha was amazingly mature for her age. Last year she and Marcus had bought a house together, a stone's throw from Puddleduck Farm.

Woodcutter's Cottage, which had once belonged to Tori, was a tiny two up, two down at the end of an unmade lane. Phoebe and Sam had lived there for a while too but it had been too small to house their growing family.

'Don't get any ideas about taking him back to Woodcutter's,' Phoebe said now. 'It's way too small for any more animals.'

Natasha giggled. 'You know me so well.'

* * *

Tori came round on Saturday evening as she'd promised. She didn't bring Vanessa-Rose but she did bring wine and also hot chocolate, in case Phoebe had decided to persevere with breastfeeding – she hadn't. Which made life so much easier.

'You're doing great,' she told Phoebe as she let herself through the stable door into Puddleduck Farm's capacious kitchen.

'How can you tell? You've only just got here.' Phoebe grinned despite herself as she took in her friend's glossy red hair, tied up in a French plait today, and sensible brown dungarees, and boots.

'You haven't got your dressing gown on,' Tori quipped. 'Don't you remember that evening when you came round to ours when Vanessa-Rose was very little and I still had mine on at teatime?'

'Mmm, vaguely.'

'And you've brushed your hair.' She stood in the middle of the kitchen with her hands on her hips and scanned the area. 'Also it's relatively tidy in here. My God, you're a supermum.'

'I'm definitely not. I just ate a whole packet of After Eights.'

'Great dessert for keeping up your energy levels.'

'It wasn't dessert, it was dinner.'

Tori waved a hand. 'Eating them instead of dinner is even better. They can be counted as dinner calories. Definitely supermum.'

Phoebe shook her head. 'Definitely not. I don't even like After Eights. I found them in the back of the cupboard. I was looking for biscuits but we didn't seem to have any. I haven't quite got back in my shopping routine. It's tricky taking Lily round the supermarket.'

'Order online. Where is she anyway? Did you decide to have her adopted, after all?'

Phoebe laughed. 'She's with Sam in the other room. I think he's changing her.'

'What a man.' Tori's green eyes were bright with mirth. 'Come here, give me a hug. You look amazing. Did you take my advice about formula milk?'

'I did. Only two nights but it's revolutionary. I actually got six hours' sleep last night.'

They hugged and Phoebe breathed in the scent of Tori's signature wild musk perfume and was reminded again of how much she'd missed her friend. For the next couple of hours, which were interspersed with cooing over a delightfully well-behaved Lily, they caught up on their lives.

Tori filled Phoebe in on what she'd been up to. Tori had verged on being a workaholic before she'd had a baby. She owned and edited the local magazine, *New Forest Views*, which was distributed free to thousands of homes in the New Forest. She'd only ever had one full-time member of staff on the editorial side, a woman called Laura, although she did use freelancers a fair bit.

'I've just taken on a guy to help me with selling advertising. He's good. He's pretty much paid for himself already.'

'Is he on commission?'

'Part commission. The more he sells, the more he makes.'

'Sounds perfect. And how's the gorgeous Vanessa-Rose?'

'The gorgeous Vanessa-Rose is at the terrible twos stage, and she's not even two for another three months. It was a relief to leave her with her daddy.' Tori winked. 'Daddy/daughter time is definitely something to encourage from the start.'

'Harrison's always been pretty hands-on, though, hasn't he?'

'He's pretty good, yes.'

Harrison was Tori's husband. He worked as a groundsman for Rufus Holt, the current lord of the manor, whose estate abutted Puddleduck Farm, although it was quite a bit bigger, acreage wise, than Puddleduck Farm.

In the days before she'd started dating Sam, Phoebe had dated Rufus for a while. It hadn't worked out but the two were still friends. Rufus had sent congratulations flowers when Lily had arrived, and Phoebe had always been close to his son, Archie, who was now thirteen.

Phoebe hadn't seen so much of Archie since he'd been away at school, but he'd done a week's work experience at Puddleduck Vets, back in the summer, and he was planning to come for his official placement with her next year. He wanted to be a vet.

She wondered if he'd still come. A lot had changed at Beechbrook House over the last couple of years. Rufus had surprised everyone by marrying his former nanny, Emilia Gruber, last year. They'd had a beautifully romantic wedding, in a treehouse, within Rufus's own private woodland. They'd had a baby since too, a sister for Archie, who was now about six months old. Everyone had pretended not to notice the slight date discrepancy between them getting married and Francesca's birth. The marriage was undoubtedly a love match. That was evident when you saw them together.

Rufus and Harrison weren't just employer and employee, they were best friends too, having been at school together, and it was partly because of this that Phoebe had always been a bit wary of the tall, slightly morose Harrison. Although she'd warmed to him lately. He was just – as Tori had often pointed out – not the most sociable of souls and he had an incredibly dry sense of humour.

'Harrison is lovely. I'm still glad I married him,' Tori said with a wicked gleam in her eye. 'Having said he didn't want any children he's now angling for us to have a little brother or sister for Vanessa-Rose.'

Phoebe clapped her hands together in excitement. 'Oh, wow, are you going to?'

'Not at the moment we're not. Maybe when Vanessa-Rose goes to school, although if I leave it until then I might not fancy the idea of going back into the nappy changing, sleepless nights arena.' She rolled her eyes. 'I've told him I'll think about it.'

It was one of the happiest evenings Phoebe could remember, and it made her realise how stressed she'd felt lately. They laughed a lot and, even though Tori only stayed until just after ten, Phoebe felt like she'd had a week's holiday.

'You two need to do that more often,' Sam said as they got ready for bed. 'We should make sure one of the grans babysits at least once a month.'

'Bring it on,' Phoebe murmured. 'We can speak to them all.' Maggie and Eddie were coming round for a visit tomorrow, and her parents and Sam's in the next few days. And now she felt slightly less exhausted and a lot less of a failure, she was really looking forward to seeing them.

* * *

When Phoebe woke up the next day, the bed was cold. Sam had said he was riding Ninja early and she hadn't even heard him leave. Presumably neither had Lily because she slept through until Phoebe went to wake her.

'It seems a shame to wake you up at all, little one,' Phoebe murmured as she stood at her daughter's crib, looking down into the baby's peaceful face.

Lily must have heard her voice because she moved in her sleep, before blinking open her eyes and yawning, and then stretching out her arms.

Feeling a rush of love, Phoebe picked her up. It was amazing how much better she felt after a third fabulous night's sleep. She must remember to call Jade today and see how those puppies were doing.

She and Sam had staggered the grandparent visits. Her parents were coming later in the week, Sam's would come next weekend, and Maggie and Eddie were coming today, just after eleven, which meant Phoebe had time to sort out Lily, and also to touch base with Natasha and walk around Puddleduck Pets and see how everything was going. Sam had promised to be back from his ride so she could chat to Natasha without Lily.

Phoebe knew she'd never have coped without her young manager, who oversaw the paid part-timers, two of whom covered her time off in the week and the numerous volunteers who came in to help out.

* * *

The forest had always been Sam's happy place. There was something about trotting along a sandy path through the trees, listening to the rhythmic thud of his horse's hooves, the sounds of birdsong and the rustle of leaves through the trees that soothed the soul. It was the best soundtrack in the world, even though he was pretty tired.

It was huge, this parenthood thing. Much bigger than he'd even imagined. Being responsible for this tiny baby girl who was 100 per cent reliant on them had been a massive adjustment.

Aware that his horse was blowing slightly with exertion, Sam squeezed the reins to slow his pace. Ninja wasn't competition fit any more. Sam didn't have the time to keep him that way. 'Whoa, boy, steady, boy. Steady, steady, that's it.'

Ninja tossed his head against the feel of Sam's hands, and his bit chinked against his bridle as he slowed his pace and they came back to an energetic walk. Sam took a deep breath of the cool morning air. This was a great time of day. He had the place to himself. And he loved the solitude. Sometimes it seemed as though it was the only part of his life that had remained unchanged over the last year.

Everything else, even his job at Hendrie's, was different. He and Ma had different conversations. She never asked after Ninja or whether they were doing any competitions – there was no time for competitions any more. She never asked how Sam felt or whether he was OK.

Sam reminded himself sharply that the world didn't revolve around him any more. It revolved around Phoebe and Lily. As of course it should. He adored them both and yet... sometimes he had a blast of euphoric nostalgia for his old life. The one where the biggest decision he had to make was whether to go out or stay in for supper.

Ninja shied at something in the hedge and Sam was almost unseated. He gathered his reins, knowing his horse was picking up on his tension. 'Steady there. It's OK, boy. It's all good.'

He'd wondered lately if perhaps he should give Ninja up. Sell him on to a home where they'd have more time for him. Ninja was wasted sitting in a field with no equine company and sporadic exercise. Ninja loved to compete. He always knew when they were going to a show, not just on the morning itself, but for the days leading up to it. He'd prance around his field, tail held high, looking like the champion he knew he was. Sam had loved it too. The adrenaline, the preparation, the early-morning drives in the horsebox to a showground, the meeting of friends on the show circuit, the camaraderie of it all.

God, what was he thinking? That had been his old life, his bachelor life. Of course he didn't want that back. He blinked away the images, coming back to the peaceful green presence of the forest. Coming back to now.

The first hints of autumn were beginning to touch the trees. There was the odd red and yellow leaf, and the bracken dotted across the forest floor was beginning its transformation through bronze to autumn gold. In another month the forest would wear the blazing reds and golds of its autumn apparel. There would be shorter days and cooler weather, misty mornings, bonfire smoke and barbecues. The forest would have metamorphosed into a new season. Everchanging. The old would be dying, getting ready to make way for the new.

The circle of life. Change was inevitable. Sam felt a shiver run through him. He wasn't yet ready to give up his horse. However sensible it might be. He thought he'd been prepared for the all-encompassing changes that had swept through their lives like a tsunami this last year, but he hadn't been. He hadn't been prepared at all.

It was an old cliché that no one is ever prepared for parenthood, but it was so true. He was a dad now and despite the hard work and the broken nights, he loved it. He was still in awe of what Phoebe had given him and he needed to do more to show her how much he loved her.

For a start, not everything had to change. They could still have date nights. It would be easier now they were bottle feeding Lily. He'd never been one for big romantic gestures but he resolved to try harder. A date night, flowers, some couple time if they could rope in the grans. He felt a sense of excitement rising as he turned Ninja's head towards home.

5

Phoebe saw Sam ride into the yard and dismount and take off Ninja's tack. Sweat from the horse's back sent clouds of steam rising into the morning air. Spotting her and Lily, Sam waved. He looked rosy cheeked and not in the least bit tired.

'Nice ride?' she called across.

'Great, thanks.'

Briefly, she envied him, escaping into the peace of the forest. She berated herself. Sam deserved some time to himself, and he got precious little of it lately.

A few minutes later, with Lily safely handed over, Phoebe strolled around Puddleduck Pets. As well as dogs and cats, there were geese and puddle ducks. It was a puddle duck, back in the mists of time, that had given the farm its name, and apparently as long as they had one in situ the place would always be lucky.

Maggie had been very insistent about that, and Phoebe had no intention of arguing with her grandmother. No one who knew Maggie would have been optimistic enough to think they could win an argument with her – not when it involved an animal. Besides which, Phoebe loved the old lady far too much to question something she felt so strongly about.

There were also four donkeys that shared a field with Ninja. Maggie had started the place with donkeys, or neddies as she called them, and had somehow never got round to rehoming them.

Natasha was talking to some volunteers by the kennels when Phoebe caught up with her. She broke off and came across when she saw Phoebe.

'Hey, how's it going? Where's the little one?'

'With her daddy. How are you?'

'I'm good, thanks.' She gestured towards the group of volunteers she'd just left. 'We've been talking about keeping wildlife as pets.'

'Really? What sparked that off? Was it Bumble?'

'No, actually, although I may have some news on him as well. Remind me to tell you that in a minute...' She paused. 'One of those ladies' neighbours has got a barn owl. She found it when it was injured apparently, nursed it back to health but decided not to let it go again and now it lives in her shed. They've just been discussing the pros and cons.'

Phoebe gasped. 'Are there any pros? For the owl, I mean?'

'That's what I said. But the woman won't listen apparently. She thinks the owl's fine chained up to a perch in her shed as long as she feeds it. That lot are thinking of staging a break-out when she's at work. Project Owl Release.'

'Blimey. That's radical.'

'I think it's essential.' Natasha's eyes grew serious. 'It's cruel keeping a wild thing captive. Wildlife need a voice. And if we don't speak out for them, who will?' Her cheeks flushed. 'It annoys me that people keep animals so they can video them and show them off on TikTok just to get views and loads of flaming "likes". And talking of likes, did you hear about that influencer who took a baby wombat from its mother in Australia? Just for a video! That one backfired. She had to leave the country due to the backlash on social media.'

'I saw that on the news. It's sad.'

'Yes, it is.' Natasha flicked a hand through her dark fringe and forced a smile. 'Sorry for dumping all of that on you when you just came out for a catch-up. You caught me at the wrong moment.'

'It's fine. You're right. Wildlife do need a voice. You said you had some news on Bumble?'

'That's right, I do.' She brightened. 'I found a woman who runs a hedgehog rescue. Only on a small scale in her back garden. But she's offered to take him. She's got a shed and a heated vivarium.'

'That's nice of her.'

'Yes, it is. Marcus told me Bumble wasn't the first. That you'd had other APHs turning up in the surgery lately. They're wildlife too, really, aren't they? They're not pets to be shown off. It makes me mad.'

'Me too,' Phoebe confessed. 'And I want to do something about it. I've been thinking a lot about the African pygmy hedgehogs – er, APHs – but maybe it's a bigger issue than just exotic pets. Maybe it's wildlife in general. I was talking to Seth about it the other day. And Sam.'

Natasha nodded. 'I heard about that. Marcus thinks it's a question of education. And he might be right. Because it's thoughtlessness as much as anything. People don't think things through and they can be flaming selfish. As we know with this lot.' She spread her hands out to encompass the kennels and yard. 'They get a cute little kitten or puppy or rabbit without considering the future at all, and then when it becomes a problem they dump it on us.'

'To be fair, there's a lot of nice thoughtful people around as well.'

'Yes, I know there is.' Natasha stuck her hands in her coat pockets. 'That's my cynical head. It's definitely getting cooler, isn't it? Shall we walk round and I can give you an update on everyone?'

'Great.' Phoebe whistled for Roxie, who was sniffing about around the five-bar gate that led towards the cattery, and the dalmatian trotted across.

'We may as well start with the cats,' Natasha said as they made their way past the barn to the cattery block. 'It's been a good week for cats. We've rehomed seven and only taken in two.'

'Seven, that's amazing.'

'Four of them were kittens, but that still counts.' There was a smile in her voice. Phoebe was relieved she was back to her usual sunny self.

'I had a woman come in yesterday who'd lost a cat too, I mean, as in she'd moved house and he'd legged it. She's fairly local. She was anxious to see if anyone had brought him in.'

'Had they?'

'No, unfortunately, but it's possible they will. She left a card with her details on. Marcus said we could put it up on the notice board in the surgery.'

'Of course we can. Has he been lost long?'

'A week so hopefully he'll turn up. She moved from the other side of the forest and the woman who bought her house said she'll keep an eye out for him too. He's a big tom so he might have gone wandering. That's not unheard of.'

'Talking of big toms, how's Saddam?' Phoebe asked after the

half-feral cat who'd been one of her longest and most infamous residents before Natasha and Marcus had rehomed him at Woodcutter's.

'He's having a great time keeping down the rat population in our little bit of the forest. Marcus says I should stop him, but I've never been that fond of rats. Besides which I'm not sure putting a bell on his collar's going to do much. He's far too smart. He gets through cat collars quicker than we get through hot dinners. We often find them hanging on tree branches in the garden. Sam saw him once, rubbing his neck against a tree branch until he managed to hook off his collar.'

Phoebe laughed. 'That sounds like Saddam.'

They went into the cattery block and Natasha ran through the current residents, none of which had been there that long.

'Also, I've got a fundraising idea,' Natasha added as they came out again. 'It's to do with the neddie field. Shall we go there next and I'll show you?'

A few minutes later they were standing at the five-bar gate that bordered the field. In the distance, one of the little group of donkeys, who were all grazing together, raised her head. It was Diablo, Phoebe saw with a smile. He was Maggie's favourite and was known for his escapee tendencies. Phoebe had once found him and the others in Rufus Holt's back garden when the fence had blown down during a storm. It had been her first introduction to Rufus and Archie. Getting the donkeys off Rufus's pristine lawn hadn't been a good introduction either.

Thankfully a lot had changed since then.

Ninja was on the far side of the field, but he'd spotted the humans too, and both horse and donkeys were now trotting across the short cropped yellowing grass to see if there were treats on offer.

'Do you remember when Maggie was planning to convert

part of the neddie field into a secure dog field so she could hire it out to dog owners by the hour?' Natasha asked conversationally.

'Yes, I do. She even went as far as getting the planning permission for it and for the new access gate on the road. She didn't do it in the end though, did she? I'm not sure what stopped her.'

'It was the cost of the fencing, I think.' Natasha ran her hand over the five-bar gate. 'It was astronomical, and she didn't think there'd be enough demand to justify the expenditure. She didn't think she'd be able to charge enough either. She didn't think people would pay much to use a field when they've got the whole forest to walk their dogs in.'

'That's right. I remember.' Ninja had reached them just before the donkeys, and Phoebe stroked his neck, while Natasha retrieved some carrot slices from her pocket.

'Demand's got a lot higher since then,' Natasha continued as she distributed carrot slices to five interested parties. 'I've been talking to a few dog owners lately. Loads of people use dog fields these days for all different reasons.'

'Go on...'

'Romanian rescues with no recall. To be fair, it's not just Romanian rescues, it's any dogs that don't come back when they're called. Or dogs that don't like other dogs because they weren't socialised properly as puppies because of Covid. Or dogs that are scared of other dogs, or dogs that are fine with other dogs but whose owners are worried other dogs might be a problem. There's a lot of those around too.' Natasha paused for breath. 'Marcus says it's usually the owners who are the problem, not the dogs, but the outcome is the same. There are lots of people who don't want to let their dogs run free unless they're in a contained area and they can guarantee getting them to come back.'

'But how much are they prepared to pay for this? That was definitely another one of Maggie's concerns. She didn't think she'd be able to charge more than a pound or two a go.'

'I've checked out the going rate and we could charge at least ten or twelve pounds per one-hour slot. If we get booked up a lot, and I think we would, that could work out really well. Even in the winter there's quite a few hours of daylight. We could advertise to your customers in the practice as well as Puddleduck Pets.'

She sounded so enthusiastic that Phoebe was loath to burst her bubble by mentioning the cost of the fencing. It would take an awful lot of ten-pound slots to pay for that before they started making a profit.

It was lovely standing there in the morning sunshine feeding the donkeys titbits and making plans. She watched Ninja, who'd ambled away again and was grazing a few feet away, the sweat patches where his saddle had been still in evidence on his back.

'It's not as though we use the field much in summer either,' Natasha said. 'We always fence it off temporarily because the grass is too rich.'

'That's very true. I've thought about getting a couple of liveries in,' Phoebe said. 'Maggie mentioned that too. But they'd have to come through the yard, and it's busy enough already without having any more cars in and out. That could be a problem with hiring it out as a dog field too.'

Diablo nudged Natasha's pockets and she gave him another slice of carrot. 'Not if we put in a new access gate on the road like Maggie was planning. If we had a little pull-in area for a couple of cars it would work.'

'You're right. It would. We'd need insurance as well but I could shop around for that.'

'I haven't told you the best bit yet.' Natasha took a deep breath. 'Sarah, one of the owl rescue team I was chatting to earlier, just happens to be married to a fencer. That's what we were talking about before we got onto the owl. And she thinks he'll do it for a knock-down price. They've got two Romanian rescues, Romi and Lunar. They adore their dogs and she was lamenting the fact they have to drive miles to the nearest dog field where they can let them off their leads. They'd love a field locally they can take him. So they've got an ulterior motive. We could do some sort of a deal, couldn't we? A lifetime of free use of the field for their dogs, in return for doing everything at cost.'

'That's a genius plan. Would he really do that?'

'Sarah was sure he would.'

Phoebe nodded thoughtfully as she looked out at the field and visualised how it would be split in two as Natasha had suggested. She was right. If they put in an extra bit of fencing down by the road to create a pull-in for cars, it would work perfectly as a dog field.

'Let's ask him to give us a quote. Feel free to negotiate with him about the free dog field for life deal. And please be careful with Project Owl Release. You don't want to get arrested for trespass or worse.'

Natasha grinned. 'We'll be very careful. I promise.'

6

When Phoebe got back to the house, she found Maggie and Eddie already ensconced at the big old table in the kitchen sipping coffees and chatting to Sam, who had Lily on his lap.

'Finally,' Maggie said, hearing Phoebe and Roxie coming through the back door and turning to say hello. 'I thought you'd abandoned ship. Not to mention your husband and daughter.'

'You're early.' Phoebe consulted her smartwatch. 'It's not even ten forty-five.'

'I couldn't wait any longer. I can't believe it's taken you this long to invite me.'

'Since when have you needed an invitation?' Phoebe countered. 'You usually just turn up whenever you like.'

'I wouldn't dream of it.'

They locked gazes and as Phoebe met the hazel eyes that were as familiar as her own, she burst out laughing. 'It's so good to see you, Gran. And you do know you don't need an invitation, don't you?'

'I *do know* I can't stand the word Gran.'

'How about Great-Gran?' Phoebe heard Eddie chuckle as

she went across the kitchen towards Sam and her daughter, neither of whom had made a sound during this brief exchange, and lifted Lily gently out of his arms.

'Come and get reacquainted with Maggie, little one,' she said, taking the baby over to where her grandmother sat.

She saw Maggie's eyes light up with love and a look of tenderness warm her weathered face.

'She is so gorgeous. She must have most of my genes.' She shot a glance at Phoebe and then she laughed too. 'Great-Gran doesn't sound quite as bad, I have to say.'

'It's the word "great" she likes,' quipped Sam. 'Who wouldn't want to be called great?'

'Less of your cheek, young man.' But Maggie was still smiling as she took Lily in her arms. 'I'm only holding her while she stays quiet. I'm not getting involved with changing her or feeding her or any of that malarkey. I'm better with puppies than human babies.'

'I don't mind being called Great-Grandad either,' Eddie put in, and Phoebe glanced at the old man, who was beaming and also flushing slightly. Eddie never said much. He was fairly deaf so it was hard to know how much of any conversation he could actually follow, but she suspected he didn't miss much either. Maggie had told her once that Eddie was of the opinion there wasn't much point in talking unless you had something interesting to say.

Eddie used British Sign Language, and he and Maggie had developed a version of their own that they often used for private conversations. Like Maggie, he was still mentally sharp as a tack. He might walk with a stick, these days, but other than that he was fit for his age. Maggie put this down to the fact he'd spent most of his life embroiled in the hard graft of farming. As she had herself.

Phoebe told them about the discussion she'd just had with Natasha about the dog field.

'She's a smart cookie, that young lady,' Maggie said approvingly. 'She's right about demand. Lots of people don't train their dogs properly these days. It's definitely worth asking Sarah's husband for a quote. The cost was the main stumbling block I had before and the planning permission will still be valid. It wasn't that long ago. If it could be done on a budget, I think it could be great.'

They segued into a discussion about the cost of things and then into wildlife and people keeping pets they'd once have left well alone like the owl in the shed.

'That's a cost thing too,' Maggie said thoughtfully. 'The price of puppies went through the roof in lockdown and it hasn't come down that much. In the olden days crossbreeds were free – people had a job to give them away. Nowadays the breeders call them some fancy designer name and charge a fortune. It's scandalous.'

Eddie nodded. 'Cockerpoos,' he muttered. 'I blame the Americans.'

'The Americans?' Sam echoed, looking at him. 'What have they got to do with it?'

'He's right,' Maggie said. 'That's where cockerpoos came from. Back in the fifties. They were bred as companion dogs. But these days any old cross gets a fancy name and a fancy price tag.' She frowned. 'Yorkipoos, cavapoos, pekapoos, and don't even get me started on the shih tzu crosses because I don't want to swear in front of junior here.' She winked at Phoebe.

'It's true,' Phoebe said, when Sam raised his eyebrows in amazement. 'About the price tags, I mean. All of those breeds have extortionate price tags. I see them in my surgery.'

Lily, eager to be included in the conversation, gurgled and waved her fists.

'Quite right, darling,' Maggie said, bouncing her on her knee. 'It's outrageous what doggies cost these days. Cats too,' she added. 'Back in the day most cats were moggies, and you couldn't give them away for love nor money. Nowadays you've got your ragdolls and your Maine Coons as well as your Persians and your Siamese, and I hear Savannahs are popular now too. None of them are cheap. It's not that surprising people think it's a good idea to capture a wild bird and keep it as a pet.'

'Do you think it's a matter of raising public awareness, Maggie?'

'Yes, although that's probably easier said than done.'

'We could certainly do our bit in the practice. We're thinking of putting up posters.' Phoebe looked hopefully at Eddie, who did the fact sheets Maggie used for the adoption packs. 'I was hoping maybe if we did some research on the various animals you could do us a poster, Eddie?'

He nodded. 'Can you get an article in the paper too? Your friend's got a newspaper, hasn't she?'

'You mean *New Forest Views* – Tori's magazine. Yes, of course she has. Why didn't I think of that? It must be baby brain.' She tapped her forehead. 'I saw her last night. I'm sure she wouldn't mind. I need to work out what animals to do.'

'You could start with African pygmy hedgehogs,' Sam suggested, and both Maggie and Eddie looked blank.

Phoebe told them about Bumble. 'We've hopefully got him a home, but I think we're going to be seeing a lot more of those little fellows.'

Maggie looked grim. 'It's not new for people to want exotic pets. The Savannahs I mentioned are a cross between the serval, which is an African wild cat, and a domestic cat. They've been in the country a while. Unfortunately.' She shook her head, and Phoebe knew she was biting her tongue not to share her opinion of people who bought exotic animals without knowing anything about their care. Instead, she busied herself making faces at Lily, who responded in kind.

'We could do with a fact sheet on foxes,' Sam murmured. 'I've heard of people getting them so tame they start behaving like dogs. It's never a good idea to get wild animals that reliant on humans.'

'Rabies,' Eddie put in, and everyone looked at him in alarm.

'We haven't got rabies in England,' Maggie said. 'Unless it's a recent thing – I've given up listening to the news, it's too flaming depressing.'

'No, we haven't got rabies.' Sam was shaking his head in bewilderment.

Eddie waggled his index fingers above his head. 'Wild ones.'

'He's talking about wild rabbits,' Maggie said, after a brief signed exchange with her husband. 'And he's right. People do sometimes keep wild ones – why pay for a rabbit if you can just lure one out of the wild?'

Luring a wild rabbit into your garden struck Phoebe as a lot harder work than going to the pet shop and buying one. Rabbits were very timid and they surely hadn't got that expensive, had they? Then she remembered Belinda Bates's lop-eared rabbits. They hadn't been cheap. She cleared her throat. 'Why don't we start with African pygmy hedgehogs, owls and foxes? I'll do some research on the hedgehogs and pass the details to Eddie. Is that OK with you, Eddie?'

He gave her a thumbs-up sign.

'I think your daughter's nappy may need changing,' Maggie said, screwing up her nose and looking at Phoebe hopefully.

'No worries, I can do it,' Sam said.

'I'm guessing this might not be the best time to ask you and Eddie about helping out with babysitting duties then?' Phoebe said to her.

Maggie grinned and dropped a kiss on Lily's head, before giving her back to Sam. 'I thought you'd never ask, love. That's if you're sure you and Sam are happy having a couple of old codgers like us looking after your precious daughter?'

They both nodded, and she looked relieved. 'It'll also give me an excuse to spend more time helping out in the rescue,' she added with a gleam in her eye. 'Full-time retirement doesn't suit me.'

* * *

Phoebe's parents, Louella and James, said much the same thing about helping with Lily when they came by later in the week. It felt like a rerun of Sunday morning with all of them sitting around the wooden table, but instead of coffee they were drinking tea with some M&S very chocolatey biscuits that Louella had brought with them.

'You haven't got time, Mum,' Phoebe said, biting her lip. 'You've got school. The last thing you need is another childcare commitment.'

Louella looked shocked. 'We're talking about my granddaughter here.' She glanced fondly at Lily, who was sitting on her lap. 'I don't see her as a childcare commitment.'

'It's still time you haven't got, though.'

'Your mother hasn't told you, has she?' James looked across at her. 'She's decided to take early retirement from Bridgeford Girls School come Christmas.'

'You never are.' Phoebe stared at her mother in amazement. 'You said you'd never retire.'

'I might do the odd bit of supply teaching to keep my hand in, but yes, your father's right. I've decided to stop teaching on a permanent basis.'

'We've decided one less workaholic in the family would be good,' James added, encircling them all with a gesture. She and Maggie weren't the only workaholics, Phoebe acknowledged. Her father and her brother Frazier also both worked loads of hours in a family law firm.

'That's right.' Louella's pink cheeks coloured up a little. 'I thought I might like to get to know my newest granddaughter a little better.'

Phoebe was amazed for the second time. It wasn't as though her mother was short on grandchildren. Frazier and Alexa had three.

'I know your brother's got three,' Louella said, reading her mind. 'But it's different when it's your daughter's child. Isn't it, my gorgeous girl?'

Lily gurgled in contentment. She looked perfectly at home on her grandmother's lap.

'She thinks she might get more of a look in with this one,' her father said, looking at his wife indulgently. 'What with Jan being the other grandparent and all.'

Phoebe glanced at her mother, whose eyes were twinkling. 'You and Jan have been discussing this, haven't you?'

'We may have been discussing it a little.'

'They've practically got a rota organised between them,' James said.

'No, we haven't,' Louella objected hastily as Phoebe and Sam exchanged glances. He looked as mystified as Phoebe felt.

'I take it you don't know about this?'

'Ma's said nothing to me.'

'We don't want to step on any toes,' Louella continued

quickly. 'We just want you to know the offer's there. Should you need it. There's a few baby and gran clubs in the forest. Music and Movement. Wriggle and Jiggle. I'd love to take her to one of those. It would be fun.'

She looked between Phoebe and Sam. 'You two work full time and Jan and I are both of an age where we feel we'd like to slow down a bit and get to know our granddaughter. If that's something you'd like too – obviously.'

There was a sudden hesitation in her voice and Phoebe said, 'Oh, Mum, of course it is. We'd love you to be involved, wouldn't we, Sam? We want you to be a big part of Lily's upbringing.'

'Yep,' Sam said. 'Although I'm not sure how Ma's going to work any less hours at Hendrie's.'

'I think she's got something in mind, but I'll let her tell you that herself,' Louella said. 'Now I know we're all on the same page.'

'Maggie wants to help too,' Phoebe said.

'What's Wriggle and Jiggle?' Sam asked, round eyed.

'The baby and gran version of dancing, I think,' Louella said happily.

James and Sam exchanged bemused glances.

'Let's have another biscuit to celebrate a plan well made,' James said, getting up. 'I'll stick the kettle on again, shall I?'

'I'll do it,' Sam said, leaping to his feet and passing the plate of biscuits around again. 'And while I've got you both here, I don't suppose there's a chance of having a trial babysitting night so I can take your beautiful daughter out for some couple time, is there?'

'We'd be delighted, wouldn't we, James?' Louella got her diary out. 'When were you thinking?'

'This Saturday coming?' Sam said hopefully, glancing at Phoebe, who was nodding slowly.

'I'm up for that – definitely.'

7

Their Saturday night couple-time date didn't work out quite as Sam had expected because Phoebe kept looking at her watch. Even though they'd only gone to a local pub, he knew she was anxious about leaving Lily.

In the end they'd gone home early.

'It'll be easier next time,' Phoebe promised as they all but ran back into Puddleduck Farm to see Lily, 'but it was a brilliant thought, Sam. Thanks.'

* * *

On Monday morning, Sam found out what Louella and James had meant about his ma working fewer hours as soon as he got to Hendrie's.

His father, who'd usually have been out on a kitchen-fitting job, was helping his mother carry some boxes of stock into the back storeroom when he arrived.

'I can do that, Pa.' He looked at him curiously. 'Haven't you got places to be?'

'Not today, son.' Ian Hendrie set the box he was carrying onto a shelf. 'I'm – er – I'm selling the business.'

'Since when?' Sam felt shock ricochet through him. 'Is something wrong? Are you OK? Is Ma OK?'

'We're both fine. Don't panic.' Ian turned round to face him. 'It's been on the cards for a while. It's been getting less profitable, see. People are pulling their belts in. They can't afford the top-end new kitchens they used to – and as you know, that's where the real profit is. Lots of people don't even have the old kitchen ripped out these days, they just do refurbs and replace all the cupboard doors instead.'

Sam knew this. His father had complained about it before, blaming the state of the economy.

'But can you afford to stop? Can't you diversify?'

'To answer your questions back to front, I could try and diversify but I don't need to – and yes, I can. I've just pulled down a small private pension. Your ma and I decided it was the right time.'

Sam was speechless. He couldn't remember his pa ever doing anything different than working with his hands, going out to customers, heading off early in his van every day, and coming back late every evening, and although he often complained about the long hours, Sam had always taken that as par for the course. Just part of the job. It had never occurred to him that his father didn't like what he did.

'To be honest with you, son, I won't miss it. It's hard graft. It's a young man's game. And it's a young man that's buying it.'

'But what will you do instead?' Sam still felt a bit blindsided.

'Work with your ma in the shop. It'll be a nice change.'

'Um, right...'

'It won't affect you, don't worry. Unless you want it to...' His father looked at him keenly. 'We thought you were planning to cut down your hours. Wasn't there talk of you being more of a hands-on – er – dad – is that the right expression, these days?'

'There was. Yes.' Sam could feel a pulse beating in his neck. That was exactly what he'd told his parents before Lily had come along. It was one of those things that had been a lot easier to say than to actually do. When he and Phoebe had discussed it, it had seemed such a logical and obvious solution. Sam would cut down his hours as a riding instructor, which he loved, and at Hendrie's which was less of a vocation, but what he'd always done, and he'd look after Lily so Phoebe would go back to work full time.

But a logical and obvious solution, planned out with cool, level heads, had nothing whatsoever to do with the reality that had arrived, and now the time had come, Sam felt as if his whole life was spinning out of his control. His whole life was changing and it was all too fast and it seemed that he didn't even have a say in the matter. Even his parents were in on the act.

He couldn't carry on the discussion. He couldn't breathe. He spun round and stormed out of the storeroom, through the shop, which had only just opened and luckily didn't have any customers in, past his bemused ma, and out of the front door onto the main Bridgeford High Street. A few minutes later he was striding past The Crown, one of Bridgeford's four pubs, where the landlord was just putting out the blackboard which said 'Open for breakfast'. The smell of bacon and coffee drifted out onto the street, which would normally have had him pausing, but today Sam barely noticed it.

He hurried past shopkeepers unlocking their doors and getting ready for the day, and past a scattering of early commuters heading for work. Everyone was in a rush, everyone had purposeful strides, everyone knew where they were going. Everyone except him. At least that's how it felt.

He didn't stop until he reached the pavement at one end of the grey stone bridge that gave the town its name, its arches spanning the clear water. Then he paused and leaned over the parapet, his fingers touching the rough stone warmed by the morning sunlight.

The bridge wasn't high; the water was only ten or twelve metres below him. All along the riverbank were houses and restaurant fronts that were as familiar to Sam as the backs of his own hands. Red-tiled roofs on red-brick buildings, and the white tables and chairs and pink parasols at the back of a pub that overlooked the river. He'd lived here all his life, worked at Hendrie's all his life too; he'd never known anything else. He didn't want anything else.

For a moment he imagined waking up every day at Puddleduck Farm, waving Phoebe off to work, being in sole charge of their daughter, taking over the endless routines of feeding and nappy changing, with only the briefest forays into the outside world to struggle with a buggy and a supermarket trolley around the shops. He imagined not having Ninja any more. No more rides through the cool green peace of the forest, breathing in the dappled sunlit air. No solitude, no time to call his own.

He knew suddenly that he wasn't up to the job. He'd never be able to do it. He'd never been good enough for Phoebe, and looking after Lily full time, being a full-time dad, was such an enormous overwhelming responsibility. He recalled the night when he'd fallen asleep standing up in their bedroom and dreaming of yellow spotted dogs and pink horses and he imagined that moment repeating over and over.

What if that happened again? What if he made a mistake with her bottle, did something wrong, put her at risk somehow because he wasn't up to the job?

Sam didn't realise he'd let out an anguished groan until a

passing jogger shot him an odd look, before quipping, 'Don't do it, mate. The water's way too shallow.'

Sam was jolted back into the present, aware of the low rumble of the traffic on the bridge, as the jogger grinned and sped past him.

The guy was right about that. The bridge wasn't high enough either. The most you'd get if you jumped off from here was a sprained ankle. Not that jumping off bridges was or ever had been top of his list of 'things I'd like to do on a Monday morning'.

Blimey O'Reilly, what had got into him? What was he doing? What had even happened just now in the shop? Pa must have thought he was losing the plot, running out like that. Sam gulped in a great lungful of the traffic-fumy air and lifted his hands off the rough stone. He was exhausted, that was the truth of the matter, and it was only Monday. Maybe lack of sleep was responsible for the panic he'd felt in the storeroom. Was still feeling, he admitted to himself, although he now felt slightly foolish as well, standing here on the bridge, contemplating the darkness of a future that both he and Phoebe had been so desperately excited about, just a few short months ago.

Even so, he was trembling slightly as he walked back into Hendrie's a few minutes later. Not an obvious trembling – it hadn't extended to his hands, he was relieved to see as he'd opened the door – but an inside trembling that seemed to have taken over his body. He had to get a grip. This was crazy stuff. He didn't want to worry his parents.

Not that they seemed worried. His ma shot him a keen look as he walked past her. 'Just remembered something I left in the car,' he offered as an explanation, and she nodded.

His pa didn't say anything at all. The Hendries had never been big on talking about their emotions. Feelings weren't something that were discussed, particularly negative feelings. Sam was pretty sure his parents would have been horrified if they'd known what was going on in their son's head.

Now he'd calmed down again he was pretty horrified himself. It was definitely sleep deprivation. It would be OK. He just had to get some more caffeine inside him and get into the routines of the day.

Luckily the Monday morning rush had just started and there wasn't time to think about anything else anyway, let alone have an uninterrupted discussion. By the time he left that evening, his father had gone out somewhere, and the only reference his mother made to him selling the business was to say, 'So, what do you think about Hendrie's being a full-on family-run operation then, son?'

'I think it's great news, Ma. Dad's not getting any younger and it'll do him the world of good cutting his hours down.'

'And I'll have more time to see my granddaughter growing up. I'm thinking I might join a choir too. Did you know there are mama and baby singing groups? I could take Lily.' For a second, he saw the same sparkle he'd seen in Louella's eyes a few days earlier.

'That sounds brilliant, Ma.' He patted her arm.

'You can cut your hours too, if you want to, Sam. We can set up a new rota to fit in with childcare.'

Sam swallowed. 'We can. That would be great.'

* * *

'I didn't think your dad would ever retire,' Phoebe said when Sam told her that night. 'Although I can see his point about it being a young man's game. He's sixty, isn't he?'

'Sixty-one, same as Ma. It was a shock to me too, but you're right. It had to happen sooner or later.' He had a curious expression on his face, Phoebe saw, more worry than relief, but she carried on talking. 'So, that's what my mum meant when she said they could help us out with childcare. That's going to help a lot. We should talk about me going back to work.'

'What, now?'

'Well, no, I don't mean I should go back to work right now. I'm not planning to go back for a bit, but I'm thinking I could do a staged return. I don't know, maybe I could go in one day a week in October.'

'That soon?' He shifted and didn't quite meet her eyes.

'Well, yes, Sam, especially if our parents are planning to help. I don't mean I'm actually going to do much in October, but I'd really like to get on top of what's going on with regard to any new clients we have. Also at the moment we've had to hand over most of the farm call-outs to Marchwood, because Seth's covering my work at Puddleduck Pets. And that's costing us money.'

She knew she'd already told him this, but maybe he hadn't taken it in. Marchwood was Seth's former practice. Marchwood and Puddleduck Pets still did each other's out-of-hours cover, but giving them all the farm work as well was extra.

'Seth's itching to get back to the farm animal side of things,' she added when Sam still didn't speak.

'Yeah, I bet,' he said at last. 'So one day a week in October then, and I'll still go into Hendrie's for four.'

'That's what I'm thinking. Then at the beginning of November, all being well, I'll go in two days a week, then in December I can increase it to three depending on how things are panning out, and by January, February, I can go back full time and you can cut down your hours accordingly.'

Sam was nodding slowly.

'I mean, if that's all OK with you?'

'Yeah. Of course it is.' A muscle twitched in his cheek and she had the feeling he wasn't as on board with all this as he was saying. Maybe he was worried about finances. She was just about to ask him when her mobile pinged with a message, and, distracted, Phoebe reached for it.

It was from Natasha and was headed up 'Great News'.

Curiously, she opened it.

> Are you free for a quick chat? Fence man's come back to me, and I think you're going to like his quote.

'I just need a quick chat with Natasha, Sam. Is that OK?'

'Go for it. I need a pee.'

From upstairs, Phoebe thought she caught the sound of a thin wail.

'I'll see to her,' Sam said. 'You speak to Natasha.'

When they caught up again twenty minutes later, Phoebe was so excited she'd forgotten Sam might be worried about finances.

'Remember I told you about our dog field plans – well, I think we might be on. That fencer Natasha knows has given us a brilliant quote. It's even cheaper than the original quote Maggie got when we first thought of the idea of a dog field and that was years ago.'

'What's the catch?' Sam asked. He had a damp patch on his shirt where he'd sponged something off it. Baby sick, Phoebe thought guiltily, but she was too excited about the dog field to comment.

'It's not really a catch as such. But we're doing a kind of bartering exchange. He's got two Romanian rescue dogs that he can't exercise off the lead so we've done a deal. He'll have free use of the field whenever he wants and the rest of the time it will be used by paid hirers. Maggie's going to be thrilled. This will be an ongoing fundraiser forever and a day. Dog fields are super popular, and the best bit is that he reckons it'll be done in time for us to open at Halloween. That's only a month away.'

'Sounds great.' Sam remembered that she'd mentioned the dog field before. He'd been going to ask her at the time if she was sure there was enough room. The donkeys didn't need all that space, but Ninja was in that field too.

He'd missed his chance. There was no way he could pour cold water on the idea now. Phoebe looked way too excited.

Maybe this was just another sign that he should be thinking of rehoming Ninja. Downsizing his life to accommodate the new regime. Even the word regime sounded hard and unfriendly.

It was too late to mention it now, that was for sure. Sam swallowed against the ache in his throat. It would be OK. Everyone except him was already happily on board with this new chapter in their lives. He would catch up soon. He'd always been a late starter.

8

People might not be able to afford high-end new kitchens but they could definitely still afford vet care for their animals, Phoebe was pleased to see. She'd always kept her prices as competitive as possible, and her New Forest practice was thriving.

She was glad she and Sam were doing a slow handover into their new regime with Lily, and she knew their plans were only possible because of their family's help. Louella and Jan were helping out as much as they could and Maggie and Eddie had begun to do regular babysitting, which meant that Phoebe got to see her grandmother a lot too. And while Lily was obviously a massive draw, Phoebe knew that there was a little part of her grandmother that didn't want to let go of her role at Puddleduck Pets either.

Maggie cared deeply about the animal rescue centre she'd started, and she was in her element keeping an eye on how it was running and being able to see the animals and hand out advice to prospective owners.

True to his word, Eddie had created some posters about the

pitfalls of keeping wildlife as pets, and they were now on the walls of the practice alongside the posters promoting the spaying of domestic pets. They were also prominently displayed around the rescue centre.

He'd also made up some fact sheets about owls, foxes and African pygmy hedgehogs. Marcus and Seth had done most of the research on the hedgehogs, and Phoebe had done her best to memorise as much as she could. She now knew far more about the cute little hedgehogs than she'd ever dreamed she'd need to know.

Tori had promised to do a feature on the dangers of keeping wildlife which would include the little hedgehogs and which would go into the December issue of *New Forest Views*, which they'd decided would be good timing and hopefully would make people think before deciding to buy unsuitable pets as Christmas presents for their unwitting relatives.

Phoebe's first full day back at work fell, rather appropriately, on World Animal Day, which was 4 October. It was a Friday, which she'd decided was a good day to catch up on what had happened during the week.

Although Sam was scheduled to look after Lily, he'd had to go over to Hendrie's to help out because his father had an emergency dentist appointment. Fortunately, Maggie and Eddie had stepped into the breach and had come over to look after Lily.

'Are you sure you don't mind having Roxie as well?' Phoebe asked Maggie for what seemed like the hundredth time, as she got ready to walk round to work. She was in bigger trousers than she'd been pre-pregnancy, she still had some baby weight to lose, but boy, was it good to be out of those feeding bras.

'Of course I don't mind. She'll be company for Tiny and Buster.' Tiny, who was Maggie's not very aptly named enormous Irish wolfhound, was currently lying by the Aga, and he pricked up his ears at the sound of his name. Buster was her ancient black Labrador whose old age was being eked out by careful arthritis medication and the fact that he spent most of his time either asleep or being fed on Sainsbury's Taste the Difference mince.

'Thanks. And you had remembered the fencer is coming to make a start on our new dog field, hadn't you?' Maggie had heartily approved of that plan, as Phoebe had anticipated.

'Of course I'd remembered. Eddie's dealing with him. But I shall take a trip up there later and make sure that everything's going to plan. I am still perfectly capable of basic childcare – and dog care.' She rolled her eyes. 'So stop fretting and get to work.'

'Right. Fine. I will.' Phoebe smiled despite herself. It felt great to have Maggie back here at Puddleduck. She contemplated telling her grandmother that she'd missed her being here a lot but decided the old lady would probably just accuse her of sentimentality if she did that.

'Go on, shoo,' Maggie urged, her eyes bright. 'Someone needs to earn some money. All these hungry mouths to feed.'

When Phoebe got to her practice, it was to find a hive of activity. There were three clients in the waiting room, two with cats and one with a cockerpoo who was wagging her tail so hard she kept bashing it against the shelf of treats and knocking off bags which her owner kept replacing. Marcus was behind reception and Jenna was putting up a poster. 'It's a World Animal Day one that someone brought in,' she informed Phoebe. 'It complements the Voice for Wildlife posters that Eddie did, don't you think?'

Voice for Wildlife was the name they'd given their campaign to educate the general public about the dangers of keeping wildlife as pets.

Jenna was right, Phoebe saw. The World Animal Day poster, which featured a wolf standing in front of a map of the world on a green background, was very similar to Eddie's posters, which were red and green.

'Same colours,' she remarked. 'They look great.'

'They had that celebrity wildlife guy, Malcolm something or other, talking about wolves on the radio today,' said the cockerpoo owner. 'They're thinking of reintroducing them to parts of England and Scotland. What do you vets think?'

'I suppose it depends where they introduce them and how controlled it is,' Phoebe said. 'I can't see farmers being very happy about it.'

'It'd be a nightmare,' one of the cat owners piped up. 'They're predators, aren't they? They'd decimate the local cat population. And they'd kill small dogs.'

'I don't think they're letting any go in the New Forest,' Marcus told her. 'So we should be OK here.'

'They've already done it with wild boar,' said Mrs Cockerpoo. 'One of my friends got gored by a wild boar in the New Forest. She had to wait eighteen hours in A&E and then she had thirteen stitches in her arm. Actually, it might have been the other way round, I'm not sure.'

Phoebe escaped to find Max, who was in the back consulting room, looking at a patient record.

'Oh, hi, Phoebe. How's it going? Good to see you're back.'

'Pleased to be back. Are all those clients waiting to see you?'

'No, the cockerpoo's Jenna's but she's early. In fact, so's my patient. The owner thought it was a tooth problem on the phone. I was just checking to see when he last had a descale. I'm sure we did it when he was under anaesthetic for an ear problem not long ago.'

Back to normality, Phoebe thought happily. At least for a day, and it felt good. Here in her practice with its dust-free surfaces and shiny implements and the faint smell of sterile wipes she felt confident. She felt at home.

'And the other cat?' she asked.

'He's waiting for a prescription. I thought Jenna had done it.'

'She's putting up posters.'

'Ah. Yes, that's right, I said I'd do it. I got distracted.'

'I'll do it,' Phoebe offered. 'What does he need?'

Max told her and she disappeared into reception and sorted it out. While she was there, she saw Max usher the woman with the other cat into his consulting room.

Even though she didn't do any real work that morning – she was more of a glorified prescription dispenser – by the time lunchtime came, Phoebe felt as though she was back into the swing of things. Maybe this was what she'd needed all along. To be in the familiar space of her practice again, feeling that she was a whole person again, and not just a mother.

A wave of guilt washed through her and she dismissed it. She did not need to feel guilty just because she wasn't being a mother twenty-four seven. That was another thing she'd discussed with Tori, who'd felt the same apparently when she'd first had Vanessa-Rose.

What was it with this guilt thing? It seemed to underlie pretty much everything to do with mothering. Maybe that was because she was a new mother – she'd noticed that second-time parents on Mumsnet, which was still her main source of information, were much more laid back. She decided it was something else to put on her list to discuss with the health visitor.

It was a relief when Marcus distracted her by showing her something on the computer. 'I keep meaning to ask you about Mission Owl Rescue,' she said. 'Did anything else happen about that?'

He grinned and tapped his nose. 'It did but if I told you I'd have to kill you.'

'What's this?' Jenna, who was just going out for lunch, paused. 'Are you talking about the owl in the shed?'

'I don't know about any owl in any shed,' Marcus declared with a perfectly straight face. 'But if you should happen to be driving along the Salisbury road at dusk you may catch sight of an owl sitting on a gatepost.' He widened his eyes and looked from one to the other. 'It can quite often be seen hunting at dusk, so I think we could say that it's been repatriated to the wild.' He looked at Phoebe. 'Is that the right word – repatriated? Or do I mean resettled?'

'I think resettled might be more what you mean,' she said lightly. 'That's good news.'

They all smiled, and she felt warmed. There were still a lot of good people around who cared passionately for wildlife and were ready to go the extra mile for them. The vast majority of people were brilliant.

She was just about to go back to the house for lunch and to see how Maggie was getting on with Lily when the glass doors of the reception burst open and a man in jeans and an olive fleece jacket hurtled through them at speed.

Phoebe's heart sank. Only people with emergencies ran into the practice, although he wasn't carrying an animal. He was so out of breath that he couldn't speak. But he was white faced, as if he'd just had a tremendous shock.

'What is it?' Phoebe asked gently, slipping into the calm persona of someone who'd had years of practice with panicking people. 'Do you need our help? Is there an injured animal?'

'I dunno. I think...' He shrugged, and seemed to gather himself a little in the face of such cool professionalism, although he was still panting. 'It's not me, no. Nothing's injured yet, but I think it will be. It's in your field. Stalking a donkey?'

'What's stalking a donkey?' She looked at him, now totally mystified.

Max, tuning instantly into the situation, had pricked up his ears too and had come across to stand by Phoebe's side.

The man put his hand on his chest. 'Something big and grey. I think it might be a wolf.'

'A wolf?'

Phoebe and Max spoke together with varying levels of incredulity.

'In my field?' Phoebe added.

'Yep.' The man blew out a deep breath. 'I thought I was seeing things. There are no wolves in Hampshire, are there? Although I did catch something on the radio this morning about a wolf release. Maybe they've already done it. Or maybe one escaped. Jesus.'

Max was shaking his head. 'I'm pretty sure it wasn't round here.'

'I know what I saw,' the man said stubbornly. 'Bold as brass, it was, loping across the field.' He wiped his sweaty forehead. He'd finally stopped puffing.

'What were you doing in my field anyway?' Phoebe asked, still trying to gather her thoughts.

'I'm doing the fence, aren't I? I arranged it with Natasha.' For the first time, she noticed he had a hammer in his hand.

'We should investigate,' Max said. 'I'll go up there.'

'I'll come,' Marcus said quickly. He looked animated at the prospect of seeing a wolf.

'I'm coming too.' Phoebe looked at Jenna. 'Would you mind holding on here a minute, just while we sort this out?'

'No problem.' Jenna sounded relieved they didn't need her in the posse. 'Be careful, won't you?'

'Wolves aren't dangerous,' Marcus said confidently. 'Not lone wolves anyway. Not if you don't corner it, and I can't see it attacking a donkey. They're way too big for a wolf.'

Phoebe couldn't believe they were standing here in the middle of a Friday lunchtime discussing a wolf running amok in the neddie field. She was about 90 per cent sure the fencer was mistaken, but he did seem very sure of himself. And he'd certainly looked pale when he'd come hurtling in.

A few seconds later, Phoebe, Max, Marcus and the fencer, who'd introduced himself as Dougie, were walking quickly up towards the neddie field. Before they'd got as far as the five-bar gate at the entrance, Phoebe saw they weren't the only ones to have headed this way. Ahead of her, walking along the perimeter fence line, was Maggie, pushing a buggy.

Phoebe felt her heart freeze in her chest. What was Maggie doing out here with her precious daughter? Oh my God, she wouldn't know, couldn't know, about the wolf. Of course she didn't. She opened her mouth to yell and then she spotted Roxie trotting along sedately by the buggy. Buster was there too, sniffing a fencepost. And Tiny was a little way behind. A jolt of realisation rocked through Phoebe's body.

'It's there,' yelled Dougie. 'Sneaking up on the old lady.' He swore.

'Where?' Marcus vaulted over the fence in one movement and Max was close behind him, fired up and ready to go, although not quite so agile.

'That's not a wolf.' Phoebe felt laughter bubbling up in her throat. She caught hold of Dougie's arm and pointed. 'Is that what you mean? That grey dog?'

'Yeah, that's it. That's it. Hang on.' He stared at Phoebe as if he'd only just heard her. 'Did you say dog?'

'That's Tiny. He's not a wolf. He's my grandmother's wolfhound.'

'Whoa. What?' Dougie let out a deep sigh of amazement. 'That's not tiny. It's enormous.'

'No, I mean his name's Tiny. It's an ironic name. Wolfhounds *are* enormous.' Phoebe was laughing openly now. She couldn't seem to stop. Adrenaline mixed with the relief of knowing there was no threat after all to her precious family. 'But they're definitely not dangerous.'

'That one isn't, anyway.' Marcus had started laughing now too. 'He spends most of his time asleep by the Aga.' He turned towards Dougie. 'Wolfhounds are a lot bigger than wolves. Wolves are only about the size of German Shepherd dogs. Just for future reference.'

'How was I to know that?' Dougie's face was now scarlet with embarrassment. 'It looks like a bloody wolf.'

'Well, it's the same colour, I'll give you that,' Max said. He was shaking his head. There was disbelief in his eyes, but Max had always been the diplomat. 'It's an easy mistake to make from a distance. Did you say he was stalking a donkey?'

'Yeah.' Dougie shifted from one foot to the other. 'I might have got that bit wrong. I mean, I was over the other side of the field. The sun was in my eyes.'

Then he started to laugh too. Maggie, who'd clearly been alerted by all the kerfuffle at the gate, had spotted them and was heading over with the buggy, along with her little entourage.

'Lovely day,' she said as she reached them. 'Are you lot all out for a walk?' She raised her eyebrows. 'Catching the rays?'

Maggie knew something was up. Phoebe could see it in her

eyes. They probably all could. But it was Marcus who enlightened her.

'Dougie here mistook Tiny for a wolf,' he said, grinning. 'We're the search and rescue team. Dashing out to save the day.'

Maggie snorted. 'You brave lot.' She paused to adjust Lily's cover. The baby was sound asleep, completely oblivious to the drama that had just unfolded around her. 'I did wonder why he was sprinting across the field earlier.'

'Better safe than sorry,' Phoebe said, deciding it would be best if they didn't take the mickey out of Dougie too much. It would be awful if he decided to down tools and stop doing the fencing.

'Exactly,' Max agreed, throwing Marcus a warning glance.

But Dougie didn't seem that bothered. He obviously had a sense of humour. 'Can I say hello to the, er, wolf?' he asked Maggie. 'Is he – um – friendly?'

'He does like a tickle under the chin,' she told him.

While Dougie petted Tiny and the great shaggy dog closed his eyes and raised his head in blissful appreciation, Phoebe smiled down at Lily, who'd just woken up and seen her mum.

It had been an eventful first morning, but she'd loved every minute – well, almost every minute – and at least she'd have something completely different to talk to Sam about tonight.

9

Phoebe and Sam were still talking about it a couple of weeks later as they walked around the newly fenced dog field.

'It's a good job Dougie saw the funny side,' Sam said. 'But I wish I'd seen Marcus vaulting over the five-bar gate. Did you say he did it in one hit? I bet that was impressive.'

'It was.' Phoebe chuckled, and her eyes lit with amusement at the memory. 'Who knew Marcus was so agile! Apparently he and Natasha have got a gym membership. God knows when they find time to go there.'

'No.' Sam paused to look upwards. 'Dougie's done a great job on the fence.'

He never had said anything to Phoebe about his reservations over the now much smaller area next door. She had been happy again lately. It would have felt selfish to stir things up unnecessarily. Ninja was OK, although he still didn't get ridden as much as Sam would have liked. Unbeknown to Phoebe, he'd been putting out feelers at Brook Stables to see if anyone was looking for a horse on loan. That would feel less final than selling him.

So far no one was. It was the wrong time of year to take on a horse – with all the dark evenings and cold weather ahead. Summer was the best time. Sam hadn't given up though. There must be someone who would want to take on his beloved horse.

'He has done a good job. I'm pleased.' Phoebe's voice jolted Sam back to the present. She was running her hands over the sturdy stock fence that now enclosed just over two acres of what had once been part of the donkey field. It was eight foot high, tall enough to deter even the most determined of escapee dogs. Floodlights were installed at intervals around the fencing so the field could be used on the darker winter mornings and nights that lay ahead. Sam had nailed up poo bag dispensers at regular intervals too with notices, knocked up by Eddie, that said, 'Please clear up after your dog.'

Phoebe and Maggie had had great fun sourcing some dog toys. They'd got balls on ropes, ball throwers and various tuggy toys, some from charity shops in Bridgeford, and Natasha had asked the Puddleduck Pets team of staff and volunteers for donations. These were all in an old wooden trunk that Maggie had found left over from her move, and this was now just inside the gate of the dog field. Eddie had painted on the front: 'Please replace toys when finished for other dogs to enjoy.'

The humans hadn't been left out either. Phoebe had sourced a second-hand shed from Gumtree, which Sam and his father had collected, dismantled and re-erected in one corner of the field. It was wired up to electricity and even had a kettle and selection of teas and coffees and hot chocolates with an honesty box so dog owners could have a cuppa while their dogs played safely in the field.

Alongside the shed they'd put a pub-style picnic table and chairs so there was somewhere to sit, should an owner want to chill out with their drink. There was also a clock, a subtle reminder that the field was hired by the hour and wasn't indefinitely available.

In the end, the creation of the dog field had been a good diversion for both of them, Sam thought. They'd spent less time together than usual, or at least that's how it had seemed to him, because although they had a common aim, one or other of them would usually be looking after Lily. So they passed like ships in the night.

They'd been too busy and too tired to talk about anything else for the last fortnight. Maybe that was a good thing. Sam had a theory about sadness – the less you pandered to it, the smaller it would become. And throwing yourself totally into a project definitely gave you less time to think.

Although just occasionally when he saw Snowball heading out for a night's hunting or coming back from one in the morning, he found himself envying his cat's freedom to come and go as he pleased.

* * *

Phoebe wasn't quite as oblivious as Sam thought she was to his current state of mind, but she had put his quietness down to the huge adjustment they were both making to parenthood. Of course it was hard for new parents. It was the one thing everyone agreed on. The first few months were tough.

If you could get through it without any major upsets you were doing well. And from that point of view they were smashing it. She was pleased that Sam had been so interested in the dog field. He'd always liked being outside and he'd thrown himself into helping with a vigour she hadn't seen since before Lily was born.

She had a feeling he was relieved not to have to be at

Hendrie's so much. She knew that in an ideal world he'd have spent less time in the Post Office and Stores and more time focusing on riding lessons. That wasn't possible at the moment, but he could go back to it when Lily was older. They wouldn't be this busy forever.

Maggie had said the dog field should have a name. So it would have its own branding, separate from Puddleduck Pets and Puddleduck Vets, and after some brainstorming, she, Phoebe and Natasha had come up with The Puddleduck Pooch and Mooch. Eddie had made two signs. One for the shed and one for the access gate on the road.

Visitors hiring the dog field would be able to get in via a gate on the road that bordered Puddleduck Farm, so they didn't have to come with their possibly reactive dogs through Puddleduck Farm itself. This gate would be kept padlocked at night, with a key safe in case anyone was interested in hiring the field during the hours of darkness, when it would otherwise be kept locked.

The most difficult thing to set up had been the website with its automated booking and payment system. Luckily, one of the volunteers was a genius with websites and Phoebe had paid her to create an all-singing, all-dancing website with The Puddleduck Pooch and Mooch logo on it, which was a silhouette of a person and a dog, walking, and it was looking fabulous.

Visitors would be able to book a twenty-five or fifty-five-minute slot, which allowed five minutes for changeovers. They could also do package deals of six slots in advance, and as an incentive they'd get the sixth one free. There was a form that needed to be filled in with the owner's name, address and car registration, as well as all the details of the dogs they were bringing, which had to be signed to say they were up to date with their vaccinations and wormers. There was also a section where visitors had to declare whether they were bringing an XL bully dog and if so that they had it registered.

The whole thing had been done on a very tight budget. It had been a real team effort and the best thing about it, Phoebe thought, was that it had been done at record speed. The dog field was still scheduled to be up and running by Halloween. There were just a few little techie glitches with the website still to sort out.

'It's a pity we're just coming into the winter months,' Phoebe said to Natasha when they were chatting about it one lunchtime a couple of days before Halloween. 'But at least we've got everything sorted now, and it can start earning some money.'

'Dougie and Sarah are thrilled about it,' Natasha told her. 'They're planning to bring Romi and Lunar over four or five times a week. They both love people, but they're not so keen on their own kind and they tend to run if they see another dog, so the secure field's perfect for them. Are you OK with them coming that much? Sarah was asking. She said they didn't want to take the mickey by abusing the fact they're getting their slots for nothing.'

'They can bring them every day as far as I'm concerned, as long as they book out the slot,' Phoebe said happily. 'They'd have to come over an awful lot before we get even close to reaching the proper cost of that fencing. It's great. Thanks so much for suggesting it.'

'Everyone's helped make it a reality,' Natasha said, with her usual understated humility. 'I'm just pleased it will help raise money for our animals and that it can tick along without too much extra work from us.'

Phoebe nodded. There was some work involved, of course. Fields needed maintenance, grass cutting being one of the regular jobs that would be necessary, and the poo dustbin needed to be emptied daily. Also, she knew she couldn't totally rely on dog owners to clear up after their dogs. The field needed to be checked periodically. Fortunately there was a field water supply already in situ that they used for the donkeys, so water was on tap for the dogs too. Also, luckily, the field was on a slight slope which meant it was well drained. They shouldn't have too much of a mud problem even during the wettest times of year.

As the field would be officially open on 31 October, Phoebe, Maggie and Natasha had decided to introduce a Halloween theme for the first week. Maggie and Eddie had got a giant poster of a Halloween scene, a dark forest, complete with a scary-looking gothic castle and evil orange grinning pumpkins and stuck the whole thing on a board, which Eddie then cellophaned over in case it rained. The board was propped up against the shed in view of the picnic table, and, as Maggie said, it would make a great photo opportunity, just in case anyone should want to share photos on their social media. Spider webs made out of black rope were strung up around the entrance of the shed as well as some actual real pumpkins that they'd left in a basket on the picnic table.

Thanks to an advertorial in *New Forest Views*, for which Tori had waived the cost because Puddleduck Pets was a charity, they were booked up solid for the whole of November. But their very first customers and star guests would be Dougie and Sarah with Romi and Lunar. Phoebe had invited them to take the first slot ever which would be at 10 a.m. on 31 October, which fortuitously fell on a Saturday.

Puddleduck Vets was open as it always was on a Saturday, but Phoebe wasn't working and Seth had promised that as long as it was quiet enough, one or two of her staff would pop down at ten. 'We can be rent a crowd. We should make a thing of it.

Will you be needing me to smash any bottles of champagne or cut any ribbons?'

Phoebe had laughed. When she'd opened Puddleduck Vets they'd had an official launch party and it had been Seth who'd cut the ribbon then.

'I wasn't going to do anything that official, but now you come to mention it, I think I've still got a bit of that ribbon.' She met his eyes. 'Much as I'd like you to cut it, I think I'd better ask Natasha. None of this would have happened if she hadn't suggested it.'

Seth nodded. 'I heartily approve of that plan.'

Natasha was thrilled when Phoebe mooted the idea to her. 'I'd love to. I've never been asked to open anything before. I don't have to make a speech though, do I?'

'How about, "I declare The Puddleduck Pooch and Mooch open to the public,"' Phoebe suggested.

'That doesn't sound too difficult.'

'We might have to film it and put it on social media.'

'I'll get my hair done then.' She giggled. 'Actually, I probably won't. But I won't wear anything too old and tatty.'

'I don't mind what you wear.'

Phoebe's parents had said they'd come over for the unofficial opening too. It was trickier for Sam's parents because Hendrie's busiest day was Saturday, but Maggie and Eddie would be there, of course. Tori had said she'd come and take any photos or video footage that needed doing, which was great because Tori was well practised at all of that. The only thing left to do, Phoebe decided, was to pray for sunshine. Her weather app wasn't very optimistic on that front. It was currently forecasting a 72 per cent chance of rain at 10 a.m. on Halloween.

10

Fortunately, the weather app was wrong. When Phoebe woke up on the morning of Halloween it was to the lightest of blue skies. She stood at the window of their bedroom and looked out at the mist rolling in drifts across the surrounding fields. It looked very spooky out there and a pale white, almost round moon with just the tiniest slice missing was still sailing high in the sky. From the look of it there would be a full moon tonight and she imagined the inky black silhouette of a witch on her broomstick flying across it later. And kids turning up for trick or treat. Not that kids often ventured out here on Halloween. It was too far out in the sticks.

Fleetingly, she thought about the two kids next door, Archie and Francesca Holt.

She'd never met Francesca, who'd been born in October last year, so she'd now be one. Where had the last twelve months gone? Oh, yes, she'd been pregnant for a lot of it.

She sighed, fleetingly sad that she hadn't heard from Archie since he'd sent her a brief thank you after his work experience, either. He'd always stayed in touch via WhatsApp messages.

He'd never been one for long spiels of text but he'd always sent her pictures of his animals.

Last year he'd rehomed two dogs from Puddleduck Pets. Chloe and Spot. He hadn't even sent pictures of them lately either. Phoebe guessed he was immersed in his own life. He was growing up fast. Perhaps it was inevitable he wouldn't have kept in touch with her so much, even if she had still been seeing his father. Rufus Holt – Lord Rufus Holt now – seemed like part of another life.

He *was* part of another life. Phoebe gave herself a little shake. Everything moved on. Everything changed. Even the sky had changed since she'd been standing at the window. It was pale blue and pink now with tiny wisps of cloud. She should get going. Sam had got up hours ago. She'd been aware of him rolling over in bed and kissing her. 'Have a lie-in, love. I'll sort out Lily. Big day, today.'

By nine forty-five, there still wasn't a cloud in the sky, and a small crowd had gathered in the yard outside the doors of Puddleduck Pets ready to walk down to the dog field. As well as Sam, Phoebe and Lily, the crowd was made up of Maggie and Eddie, Natasha and Marcus, Phoebe's parents and Tori, Harrison and Vanessa-Rose. Vanessa-Rose's face was painted up with black whiskers and Tori had a spider's web on her cheek.

'I couldn't resist,' she told Phoebe. 'And we're going to a lunchtime party at one of the neighbour's, so it won't be wasted.'

Maggie had entered into the spirit of things too, and she was wearing a black pointy witch's hat and carrying a besom. 'I'd have brought Snowball with me,' she joked to Phoebe, 'but I thought there might be too many dogs around for that cat's liking.'

'There'll definitely be at least two. I can't wait to see Romi and Lunar charging about off the lead. Dougie said they don't come off the lead very often. I'm going to take a video of that for posterity.'

A few minutes later they were all at the gate of the dog field where Dougie, Sarah and their two dogs were waiting for them.

Phoebe saw Maggie bend and offer her hand to one of the black and tan hounds palm side up, and he stretched out his nose for a sniff. They were big dogs and looked a bit like Doberman crosses but leaner. Phoebe smiled at Dougie and Sarah before busying herself tying the blue and yellow ribbon across the gate, ready for cutting, while Tori got out her camera and adjusted the lens.

In view of the fact that everyone had been told Romi and Lunar could be reactive around other dogs, there were no other canine guests at the opening. Phoebe was relieved they'd made that decision. Romi and Lunar both looked a little overwhelmed.

She looked around for Natasha and beckoned her over.

'Right then, are you ready?' She handed Natasha a pair of scissors.

'Yep.' Natasha grinned and stood by the ribbon with her scissors poised while Tori lined up her camera. 'I think we need Dougie and Sarah and the dogs in it too,' she announced, beckoning them across. 'So if you two could just stand here. Great. OK, I'll take a couple of stills first and then I'll do the video.'

Tori snapped away happily, although they had a couple of false starts with the video because both Lily and Vanessa-Rose began to grizzle when they realised their mums had gone out of sight. Then, on the third attempt, Romi decided to cock his leg on the gatepost halfway through Natasha's speech.

'Never work with children or animals,' Tori said, resetting

her video and repositioning everyone yet again. 'Right then. Third time lucky.'

'I now declare The Puddleduck Pooch and Mooch officially open,' Natasha said for the third time when everyone was quiet again, and she snipped the ribbon with a flourish. Everyone clapped and cheered, and they all trooped into the dog field, where Tori and Phoebe took more photos of the dogs by the pumpkins and the Halloween-themed shed.

Then finally, Sarah and Dougie unclipped their dogs' leads in unison. 'You're free, guys,' Sarah said with a slight catch in her voice. 'A whole field of your own to play in whenever you like.'

Lunar, who was the smaller of the two dogs, stared around her, saucer eyed, and then celebrated her new-found freedom by running across to the fence, humping her back and having a poo.

'Typical,' Sarah said as everyone cheered again. 'You can always rely on a dog to let you down, can't you!'

'Too right!' Dougie headed over with a poo bag, wrinkling his nose, and everyone cheered again.

But after her slightly inauspicious start, Lunar pricked her ears, her attention caught by something on the far side of the field, and then scented the air, before putting her head down and racing towards it. Romi followed her, and before long the two hounds were running flat out around the field, zigzagging backwards and forwards on the short yellow grass and doing zoomies around each other while the small crowd standing and sitting at the picnic table watched them.

'Look at them go.' Dougie's voice was overawed. 'I've never seen them run like that before.'

'They're having a wonderful time,' Sarah said. She turned towards Phoebe. 'I've always wanted to see them do that, but we could never risk letting them off the lead Thank you so much for setting all this up, Phoebe. It's just brilliant.'

Phoebe saw she had tears in her eyes and she felt a warmth deep in her heart. She touched her arm. 'No. Thank *you*. We couldn't have done it without your Dougie.'

* * *

It wasn't just Romi and Lunar and their owners who loved the dog field. Everyone else who tried it out in the first few days loved it too. A few of them left five-star reviews on TripAdvisor and some left lovely reviews on The Puddleduck Pooch and Mooch website too.

Most of the people who'd booked slots were people Phoebe already knew. Either because they were clients of Puddleduck Vets or they'd rehomed dogs from Puddleduck Pets. She knew this because several had either phoned or called in personally to tell her.

'I guess the acid test will be when it's people using it who we don't know,' she said to Sam one evening when they'd just finished clearing up supper and were now relaxing in the front room with the wood burner lit. They'd taken to using it more as the weather had cooled.

'There's no reason they shouldn't love it too. Stop fretting.'

'I am, aren't I. Sorry.' She frowned. 'I seem to stress out about things a lot more these days than I did before I had Lily. Do you think giving birth makes you more sensitive about everything?'

'Well, don't ask me. I'm not in a position to comment.' He raised his eyebrows. 'That's another one for Tori, isn't it?'

Their conversation was interrupted by a rapping at the front door, and Roxie, who was very laid back except when it came to visitors, charged out into the hall, barking loudly.

'I'll go,' Sam said, getting up. 'Are we expecting anyone?'

'Not unless it's someone else to tell me how great the field is – or they could be calling to complain, I suppose. I'm pretty sure someone booked it tonight. Oh, gosh. Maybe I forgot to put the floodlights on.' She clapped her hand over her mouth. 'Sorry, there I go again, second-guessing everything.'

Sam shook his head in mock reproof and disappeared in sock-clad feet to answer the door.

A few moments later, Phoebe heard voices in the hall, Sam's low and friendly and then the slightly higher voice of a younger person. It sounded like Archie; surely it couldn't be. Phoebe had just got up to go and see when the door opened and Sam was back with a very excited Roxie.

Behind Sam was someone wearing a dark coat and scarf and woolly hat. It was Archie. But a taller Archie than Phoebe remembered. He'd shot up in the last couple of months. 'Trick or treat,' he yelled, bounding into the room.

'I've already told him that was last week.' Sam was clearly as delighted to see Archie as Roxie and Phoebe were. 'But he insisted on coming in anyway.'

Archie and Phoebe grinned at each other.

'How did you get here?' She stepped forward to greet him. 'Did you walk round?'

'No, Jack's dad dropped me. I stayed over at Jack's for half term. He's getting on great with Casey's Girl.'

'That's good to hear,' Phoebe said, pleased. Casey's Girl was a horse Jack's family had rehomed from the sanctuary last year.

'We've been having dressage lessons with Jack's cousin, Caroline.' Archie flicked a glance at Sam. 'She's not as good a teacher as you. She gets cross when we don't do what she says.'

'Is that right?' Sam laughed.

'Yeah, she can be a right meanie. We wanted you, but Marjorie at Brook said you're not doing lessons any more.'

'I'm having a break,' Sam said evenly. Phoebe thought she saw a flash of disappointment in his eyes, but it was gone almost immediately.

'Please can you let us know when you're starting up again? Jack and I are going to fall out with Caroline soon, I know we are. And Dad says you shouldn't fall out with your family.'

He sounded so grown up, Phoebe thought, and then he spoiled it by saying, 'Jack says he doesn't really mind as he's got loads of cousins. He's lucky. I haven't got any. I wish I had some cousins.'

'But you've got a sister. How's Francesca doing? And how's your dad? Are you stopping for a drink?'

'Chesska's growing up fast. She knows who I am. She always gives me a smile when I go in her room. Thank you for asking... Dad and Emilia are fine too. They send their regards. I'd love a mango and apple J20 if you've got one?' Archie looked at Sam hopefully and he nodded.

'I'll go and see what I can find, young man. And I'll make a pot of tea for us.'

When Sam had disappeared, Phoebe held out her arms. 'Do I get a hug? It's ages since I've seen you.'

Archie gave her a tentative hug, and she thought, *That's probably my last hug. He'll be back to shaking hands again soon. All stiff and formal now he's thirteen. He's growing up, becoming a proper teenager.*

'It's not that long,' Archie said, grinning. 'Although you are a bit thinner than last time I saw you. Congratulations on the birth. I've forgotten...' He clapped his hand over his mouth. 'Was it a girl or a boy?'

'A little girl. We've called her Lily. Please say thanks again to your father for the flowers. They were gorgeous.'

'I will. Cool name.' Archie lost interest in babies and he wandered over to pet Roxie, who wagged her tail and sniffed his hand. 'She can smell my dogs. They send woofs and wags.'

'Come and sit by me.' Phoebe gestured to the sofa, and then sat back by the arm where she'd been sitting, and Archie joined her.

'So did you come round to nag Sam about riding lessons? Or is this a general social visit? Or was there something else I can help with, my darling?'

'It *is* a social visit. And I did want to nag Sam about riding lessons.' Archie's face grew serious. 'But there's something I wanted to ask you about too.' He put his hands behind his head, leaned back on the sofa and let out a sigh. 'We've got a bit of a cat problem.'

11

Phoebe looked at him in surprise. 'A cat problem? I didn't even know you had any cats.'

'Emilia's got two. Or she did have. That's the problem.' He fidgeted. 'They've both disappeared.'

'Oh, my goodness.' Mind you, it must be hard to tell if a cat went missing from Beechbrook because they had a huge estate to play on. 'When you say they've gone missing, do you mean from the garden?'

'I mean from everywhere.' Archie spread his hands wide. 'We thought at first they'd probably just wandered off into the grounds and got lost, but we've had quite a good look and they're not there. And it's been a week,' he said, pre-empting her next question.

'That does sound strange. How old were they?'

'They were kittens. Posh ones. They looked like little tigers. I think they were called Savannahs.'

Phoebe frowned. 'Yes, I remember Maggie talking about Savannahs not that long ago. Weren't they originally bred by crossing an African serval cat with a Siamese?'

'I'm not sure. But I wouldn't be surprised if they were. They were amazing looking.'

'So what happened? Had Emilia had them long?'

'Hardly any time at all. It was about a week after they were allowed out. You know, like, after their first injections. I think she brought them here for those. So you might have seen them.'

He looked hopeful. Phoebe hadn't seen Emilia for months. Not that this meant anything. Max might have done the vaccinations.

'I don't think I did, but I've been on maternity leave. I've only just gone back to work.'

'Oh, yeah.' Archie rested his chin in his hands. 'It's weird about the kittens going missing, though, don't you think? I wanted to check with you if anyone has brought them in, thinking they're lost.'

'I'll check first thing tomorrow. Are they microchipped? We usually scan just in case we have any strays turning up. Especially pedigree strays.'

'I thought you would say that. Emilia did too. Yes, they are microchipped. So you'd have found out they were ours, I guess.'

'I think we would, yes. But have you got any pictures of them on your phone? Could you maybe make a poster that we can put up in the surgery? We could put one up in Puddleduck Pets too.'

Archie nodded. 'That would be good. Thanks. I'll get Emilia to help me. Although it didn't help last time.'

'Last time? Are you saying this has happened before?'

'Yes, the first two kittens Emilia got disappeared as well. Minka and Charly. Dad got her them for her birthday in February. She'd always wanted Savannah cats and she wanted them to grow up around Chesska. So he bought them for her. She was really upset when she let them out and they didn't come back.'

'Oh, my goodness. I bet she was. So she's lost four kittens?' Phoebe felt a jolt of sympathy for Emilia. They'd not got off on a very good footing when they'd first met, but they'd resolved their differences a while ago and Phoebe had grown to respect the younger woman a lot.

'Do you think a fox would kill a kitten, Phoebe? That's what Harrison thought must have happened and he was keen to go and shoot all the foxes on the estate, but Dad wouldn't let him.' He looked worried. 'I was glad. I don't like the idea of foxes getting shot. I know it has to happen sometimes but...'

Wow, he was growing up fast. Although Phoebe seemed to remember that Rufus wasn't keen on foxes being destroyed indiscriminately either. He'd certainly stopped the hunt from crossing his land since his father had died.

'It's possible a fox might take one. But Savannahs are bigger than your average kitten. I am so sorry, Archie.'

'What's this about foxes?' Sam came back with their drinks on a tray. He'd brought biscuits too, and he set the tray on the coffee table and sat on the other sofa facing them.

Phoebe told him what had happened, and like Phoebe, he was shocked. 'Two kittens are possible, but four is very odd. We can definitely get posters up.'

'And I'll check with Natasha tomorrow, just in case,' Phoebe promised.

'Thanks.'

For a while they talked about how things were going up at the big house. Emilia was revelling in motherhood by the sound of it. 'She takes Chesska to Turtle Tots at the pool every Wednesday,' Archie told them cheerfully. 'And they go to mother and baby yoga days twice a week too. She says it's good for development.'

Phoebe hadn't got organised enough to do any of that with

Lily yet, and she felt a twinge of envy. But then again Emilia didn't have anything else to do, and she'd had plenty of practice with babies and children, having been a nanny in her former life.

'She's sleeping through the night too,' Archie went on obliviously. 'Emilia says it's just a matter of getting into a good routine.'

'Of course it is. It's the same with Lily.' Phoebe had no idea why she felt the need to lie to Archie. But she did. 'I expect it helps with getting her figure back too,' she added wistfully.

'I don't know. She seems pretty thin to me.' Archie frowned. 'You do, too, Phoebe.'

'Thank you.' Phoebe flushed, aware that Sam had just shot her a curious look, and, feeling guilty for fishing about how Emilia was getting on – she was regretting that already – she changed the subject.

She told him about the new dog field. 'It's for fundraising for the rescue.'

'Sounds brilliant. Not that Chloe and Spot are ever likely to need a dog field,' Archie said, 'when they've got the run of Beechbrook. But I'll definitely pass the word round to any other dog owners I meet.'

'Thanks, and I'll check with Natasha about lost kittens.'

'I'd better get back,' Archie said.

'I'll drop you,' Sam offered.

* * *

'That was a nice surprise,' Phoebe said when Sam got back again from Beechbrook. 'It does sound odd about those kittens, doesn't it? I wonder if a fox did take them. What do you think?'

'I'd have said yes if it was just one, but not two. And even more unlikely as it's now four. I'm surprised Emilia let the second lot out so soon.'

'Maybe she thought lightning wouldn't strike twice.'

'Yes.' He looked at her thoughtfully. 'You know you shouldn't go comparing yourself with Emilia, honey. They have a completely different life to us.'

'All the money in the world, you mean.'

'And a lot more time,' Sam said gently, and for some reason Phoebe couldn't fathom, a tear ran down her face.

'Hey.' He thumbed it away, before holding her gently by the shoulders. 'What's up? Talk to me.'

'Nothing's up. I'm being stupid. You're right. I *was* comparing myself to Emilia – unfavourably, of course. But like you said, they do have a lot more time than us. They don't have an animal rescue and Emilia doesn't have to work full time.'

'Neither do you. You don't have to go back as quickly as we've planned. I'm fine to carry on at Hendrie's. We'll manage financially. We don't need a lot of money.'

'Thanks, Sam.' She hesitated and fumbled for a tissue from a pack on the table and blew her nose. 'But it's fine, really it is. I want to go back properly. I don't think we're rushing it. And if it turns out that we are, then we can just step back a bit, can't we? Nothing's set in stone.'

'Of course we can. And I can start taking Lily to Turtle Tots if you like when she's old enough. She won't miss out. Although I'm drawing the line at going to yoga.'

They both smiled.

'It's a deal.'

Beyond the window, a flicker of light caught Phoebe's attention and she moved across to look out. In the far distance a shower of coloured stars lit up the night sky. Thankfully, the firework display was too far away to upset any of the animals on

Puddleduck Farm. They were a long way from the nearest organised firework display, and fireworks were prohibited in the New Forest except between certain hours on key days like 5 November and New Year's Eve. It was 6 November today so the legal zone had passed.

Phoebe dropped the curtain. Most people in the forest were very responsible. They were too aware of the dangers to livestock.

* * *

Later, when they were getting ready for bed, Sam's mind flicked back to that conversation. He'd felt a surge of hope when Phoebe had hesitated about going back to work. Just for a moment he'd thought she might have changed her mind about going back full time.

But he'd realised almost immediately that this wasn't the case. And of course it made the most sense that it was Phoebe who was full time because she was the main breadwinner.

He'd been tempted to tell her he missed his horse. He missed giving riding lessons too. Earlier on, he'd dearly wanted to tell Archie that he'd be happy to tutor him again. He'd had a brief fantasy about them doing some lessons in the donkey field. Private lessons were lucrative. He wouldn't even have to pay Brook Riding School now they had their own land. He could make a far bigger contribution by doing that than working at Hendrie's, especially if his pa was now helping out there too.

Not that there was a lot of space left for tutoring now, thanks to the dog field. Sam felt sometimes as if he were floundering about in this strange new world of parenthood looking for an exit sign. But every time he thought he saw it, it disappeared again.

Of course he wasn't looking for an exit sign, he berated himself. He loved Lily and he adored Phoebe. But fatherhood was just so different to what he'd expected. And no matter how hard he tried, he was still occasionally plagued with doubts that he was really up to the job.

12

The next day Phoebe asked Natasha, just in case four Savannah kittens had slipped under the radar, but as she'd expected it was a no.

'Are you sure they didn't get scared by fireworks and go off to hide somewhere? I know it's banned but we've heard a few over the last couple of weeks. There were some last night going off somewhere.'

'Yes, I spotted those, but I wouldn't have thought so. They'd have come back by now.'

'Hmmm, well, if anyone else had asked that question I'd have suspected theft.' Natasha's eyes darkened. 'Savannahs are expensive. But I can't see anyone stealing them from the lord of the manor. It's not like they can just sneak into his garden. He'd spot them. His drive is a quarter of a mile long.'

'Yes, that's true.' Phoebe had a sudden thought. 'Did that lost cat you mentioned a while back ever turn up? That wasn't a Savannah, was it?'

'No, it wasn't. But it was one of the posh breeds. What are those really big ones?'

'A Maine Coon?'

'Yes, it was one of those. And it hadn't been found last time I checked with her. That's why the poster's still up. Although that was a while ago now. I'll give her a ring.'

When Natasha reported back, she was shaking her head. 'Oscar hasn't turned up. She thought I was phoning with good news. It was horrible to say I wasn't. Why did you ask about him anyway?'

Phoebe shrugged. 'I'm not sure. Just some weird hunch I had that someone might be stealing posh cats and then using them to breed from. The cat equivalent to a puppy farm. He was a tom cat, wasn't he?'

'Yes, but the Savannahs were kittens.'

'Female kittens,' Phoebe said. 'And kittens don't have to be very old before they can produce their first litter.'

'Yes, you're right. Blimey. I really hope it's nothing like that. It would be quite tricky to steal from Lord Holt, though, wouldn't it?'

'Yes, it would, and that does put the kybosh on my theory a bit. But ever since Sam showed me how many African pygmy hedgehogs were for sale on Pets4Homes it's been in my head that there are a lot of unscrupulous people out there breeding animals for money without all that much thought for their welfare.'

'Yes, that's very true. We haven't had any more of those cute little hedgehogs in the surgery, have we?'

'No, thank goodness.' Phoebe sighed. 'And the other one did get a home. Ignore me. It's probably just baby brain seeing conspiracies where none exist.'

'All the same, I'll keep an ear out in case any other expensive cats go missing,' Natasha said seriously. 'Did you say Archie was going to pop in with some posters about Emilia's kittens?'

'He said he would.'

'I'll keep an eye out for him too.'

* * *

Archie must have dropped off the posters, although Phoebe didn't see him, because the next time she went into the practice she saw they had put his lost cat poster up.

The four kittens were extremely cute. They all had silver coats and leopard spot markings. She hoped they hadn't been stolen and fallen into the wrong hands, but Natasha was right. It seemed extremely unlikely. It was a mystery though.

As November flew past, she felt as though they were finally getting into a routine with Lily. Louella and Jan were helping out, along with Maggie who was at Puddleduck Farm as much as she could manage, with her two dogs never far from her side. Sam and Phoebe shared Lily's care the rest of the time. A new normality was unfolding, and Phoebe was finally starting to relax.

The dog field was working out well too. They were now booked up for most of December. They even had bookings on Christmas Day and Boxing Day. It was heartwarming that so many people cared enough about their dogs to pay out for regular slots in a field. So far there had been no problems with anyone outstaying their welcome either. Everything was hunky dory. The only slight fly in the ointment was that Phoebe had noticed Sam was looking pretty frazzled.

He never complained though, and every time Phoebe asked him if he was OK he said of course he was. So she concluded that, like her, he was just adjusting to the gorgeous little bundle of chaos that was Lily, and maybe men just took longer to adjust to parenthood than women did.

Much to her relief, no more African pygmy hedgehogs had turned up needing treatment and she was beginning to think Seth might have overreacted about them becoming such a popular pet.

But then halfway through November, when Phoebe was in the surgery for one of her full days, that changed. She was in reception when a young woman, dressed in a pillar-box-red voluminous coat, came in pushing a buggy in which sat a small boy in a blue bobble hat, sucking a dummy. The woman had some difficulty getting through the practice doors, partly because of the buggy and partly because she was rather on the large side. What looked like an Amazon delivery cardboard box was balanced on the rack of her buggy.

'He's got sick,' she said, lifting the box with some difficulty onto the reception counter. 'Dunno if he needs to be put to sleep.'

Phoebe, who'd just been discussing a patient with Jenna, glanced across at her.

'What sort of animal is he?' Marcus was asking.

'African pygmy hedgehog,' the woman said, and Phoebe pricked up her ears.

'Do you want to bring him through?' she called over.

The woman looked at her gratefully. 'Thanks. How much will it cost?' There was something close to panic in her eyes.

'Why don't I have a look at him first?' Phoebe said kindly. 'Then we can go from there.'

The woman, whose name was Lauren Brown, followed Phoebe into one of the two consulting rooms, complete with buggy, toddler and box, and put the box gently on the examining bench.

'What seems to be the problem?' Phoebe asked, opening the box carefully so she could get a look at her patient.

'He's been sick all over himself. I don't think it's anything he's eaten. I haven't changed his food. I know you shouldn't do that. Look, you can see.' She pointed into the box and Phoebe saw that she was right. There was a gummy white substance spread over the hedgehog's dark prickles.

It was difficult to see much more of her patient because he was curled into a tight brown ball. Phoebe pulled on some protective gloves so she could handle him properly.

'How many times has it happened?'

'Dunno exactly but I think it started yesterday. Do you think it's serious? He doesn't look very happy, does he?' She screwed up her face. 'Mind you, I wouldn't be very happy if I'd done that all over myself.'

It was hard to gauge the hedgehog's state of mind, curled up in a prickle ball as he was. Phoebe wasn't sure she'd have been any the wiser if she could have seen his face. She wished she knew more about the species as she lifted the tiny hedgehog out in cupped hands.

'Has he got a name?' she asked, playing for time.

'We call him Olly.'

'And where do you keep Olly?'

'In one of them glass things. We got it from the man who sold him. He seemed nice. He said it was big enough.'

'Is it heated?'

'Course. I know they need keeping warm. They're from Africa, aren't they? It's a bit hotter over there than it is here.' She looked around the small consulting room and shivered slightly. 'It's not that warm in here, is it? That probably won't help.'

'Isn't it?' Phoebe hadn't thought the room was particularly cold. She turned the hedgehog over so she could see his face and underside. She'd agreed to look at him on impulse but if she was honest, she wasn't sure where to start. He looked healthy enough. His eyes were bright and he wrinkled his nose at her. 'I'm just going to put Olly back in the box for a minute and have a word with my colleague. Are you OK to wait?'

The toddler, who'd been quiet up until that point, said, 'I need a wee, Mummy.'

Lauren looked at Phoebe hopefully. 'Is there somewhere I can take him?'

'Of course. I'll show you where it is.'

Phoebe led her out and showed her the staff toilet which wasn't really for customers, but in the circumstances she couldn't really say no, and then she went to find Seth.

'He had to nip out to see a dog that wouldn't get out of the owner's car,' Jenna told her. 'Can I help?'

Phoebe explained about the hedgehog. 'I'm out of my depth. I probably shouldn't have agreed to see him.'

Marcus swivelled round on his chair. 'Did you say he'd been sick but otherwise he seemed perfectly healthy? What did it look like?'

Phoebe told him and he grinned. 'I think that's something called self-anointing. It's a weird thing APHs do when they come across a strong smell. They spread this white sticky substance all over their prickles. It's totally normal but it can freak owners out the first time they see it. Hang on a sec.' He tapped on his phone and brought up some images to show Phoebe. 'Does it look like that?'

'It looks exactly like that.' Phoebe flicked through the pictures and felt a massive wash of relief. She skimmed through the descriptions and then switched to her own mobile so she could look on a vet forum the practice was signed up to. Fortunately, she wasn't the first person who'd asked about it and she came across a detailed account written up by another vet.

Satisfied now that what she was looking at was the same thing, she thanked Marcus profusely.

'Just call me Supervet,' he said, pleased as punch. 'I think there's a mention of it on our fact sheets too. Hang about.' He rummaged in a drawer to the left of the reception desk and pulled out a leaflet. 'Yep, there it is. Bullet point six.'

'That's fantastic. Great job, Marcus.' Phoebe took the leaflet. She got back to the consulting room at about the same time as Lauren and her son and told her the good news.

'So he's not dying then?'

'He's not dying. It's just a weird thing hedgehogs do. Scientists don't really know why but there's a theory they're trying to camouflage themselves against predators.' Phoebe told her everything she'd just learned on her crash course in hedgehog ailments and was grateful when Lauren seemed satisfied.

'How often is he going to do it? Because you have to admit, it does look pretty disgusting.'

'Hopefully not too often. It can be sparked off by a strong smell. Does that ring any bells at all?'

'Oh my God. Maybe it was the paint. We've been doing some decorating and it does smell pretty strong. Could it be that?'

'I think it could be, yes. The main thing is that it's a totally normal behaviour.'

'Right.' Lauren looked relieved.

'We do have a fact sheet that tells you more about these little fellows.' Phoebe handed it over and Lauren scanned it and nodded.

'I think I know all that – apart from the anointing thingy. I also didn't know they couldn't hibernate. But it makes sense. They wouldn't have the fat stores to keep them alive, would they?' She patted her ample tummy and laughed. 'I reckon I could hibernate for a while with absolutely no problem.'

Phoebe was too diplomatic to answer this, but it was good to see her client looking so much happier.

She charged her a nominal fee for the consultation and Lauren Brown registered as a new patient before she left with Olly in his makeshift carrycase.

Phoebe breathed a sigh of relief. Her next patient was a golden retriever called Ellie, who had a nice simple ear infection, and the rest of the morning went smoothly with nothing more challenging than a cat with a torn ear who'd been out fighting.

At lunchtime she caught up with Seth in reception and told him what had happened earlier.

'Marcus saved the day.'

'Supervet at your service,' Marcus quipped.

Phoebe smiled. 'Yes, and thanks again. But I definitely need to know more about those little hedgehogs. Have we got any actually registered with the practice?'

'There are four,' Marcus told her after checking the system, 'including Olly. They've all registered in the last month. None of them have actually come in with anything wrong though. Until today.'

'Should we be registering them as patients?' Phoebe said, sighing. 'Seeing as I know next to nothing about them.' She glanced at Seth. 'What do you think?'

'You might be right.' He glanced over Marcus's shoulder at the computer. 'I think we've only registered them if they've been existing customers who have other animals registered. Dogs and cats and the like. Is that right?'

Marcus nodded. 'I wasn't sure, but it's a tricky one, isn't it? It's hard to say no when they have multiple animals here. I'm guessing we don't want them to take the whole lot away from the practice.'

'Maybe I should be thinking about employing a specialist vet?' Phoebe mused aloud. 'But I'm guessing there wouldn't be enough work for one.'

'Why don't we see how it goes?' Seth suggested. 'I know a little bit about exotics, and maybe Max fancies increasing his skill set too.'

'Sounds like fun,' Max said, coming into reception in time to overhear the end of the conversation. 'What kind of exotic pets are we talking about here? I've always fancied learning a bit more about big cats. Leopards? Tigers? Elephants?' He rubbed his hands together and looked interested.

'Hedgehogs,' Seth said, quirking a bushy eyebrow, and Max's face dropped.

'Um... OK. I suppose hedgehogs are, um, interesting.'

'Prickly characters,' Marcus quipped.

'Definitely on the spiky side,' Seth added. 'You wouldn't get on the wrong side of one!'

They were still bantering when Phoebe went back to the house to see Lily and Sam. She was pleased her staff were happy, and she was relieved this morning had turned out OK. It was teamwork at its very best.

13

It was date night again. Maggie and Eddie were babysitting so Sam and Phoebe had gone to the Brace of Pheasants, a country pub at Godshill about twenty minutes away. It was mostly frequented by locals, being off the beaten track, but it was always busy. It had an inglenook fireplace, a great pie chef and a range of real ales and fine wines.

They were now soaking up the warmth of the wood burner, its bright orange flames flickering behind glass, and breathing in the delicious aromas of food while they waited for their beef and ale pies to arrive.

Phoebe told Sam about Marcus's helpful diagnosis with the pygmy hedgehog that day.

'He used to be so shy, but he's been so much more confident since he's been living with Natasha.'

'Teamwork,' Sam said, taking her hand. 'Two heads are better than one.'

'I know. It's brilliant. And talking of teamwork, Max told me we'd had all the orphan pups back in for their vaccinations too. It sounded like Jade had great homes lined up for them.'

'That's brilliant news too.' Sam cleared his throat. 'I was thinking about Ninja earlier. I've been neglecting him lately and...'

He broke off because their pies had arrived. The delicious scents of meat and pastry hit her nostrils and Phoebe realised she was starving. By the time they'd thanked the waiter and sorted out their cutlery, she'd forgotten Sam had been about to say something.

For a few moments they ate in silence. The pub had filled up. It was a Friday night and there was a buzz of convivial chatter. As she ate, Phoebe glanced around them. There were several people sitting at the bar with suits on who'd presumably come straight from work, and on the table closest to them were a young couple dressed in bright fleeces and jeans sipping their drinks and occasionally touching each other's hands. They definitely didn't have a baby. They looked far too sparkly eyed to have been juggling parenthood with their careers. Fleetingly, Phoebe envied them their freedom.

The group at the bar were in high spirits too. They were laughing and joking with each other and Phoebe caught the word 'birthday' and realised they were out celebrating. For a moment she felt as though she was caught between two worlds. The world of work and the world of parenthood, and that she didn't really fit into either of them. She felt guilty because she wasn't giving her precious daughter her full-time attention and she felt guilty because she wasn't giving her precious partner and her precious business her full-time attention either.

She knew she wasn't the first woman to feel like this. She'd read loads about guilt on Mumsnet but at that moment the fact that other women felt the same as her didn't help one bit.

'Penny for them?' Sam asked.

She couldn't tell him. It would have felt like a slap in the face when she knew he was doing his utmost to give her the best of both worlds.

'I was just thinking how delicious this pie was and how lovely it was not to have to cook,' she improvised, and then felt guilty again for lying.

'Are you saying my cooking's not up to the standard of the Brace's pies?' His voice was jokey.

'Of course I wasn't saying that, Sam.' She lied to him for the second time in five minutes. More guilt. But then she wasn't alone in her deception. Society did it too. There was a section of society that said women could have it all. Motherhood, a great relationship and a dazzling career. All three were possible. You just needed the right attitude and a little organisation. Phoebe was beginning to think that was a massive lie too. It was pretty difficult to juggle everything without dropping a ball now and again.

Sam knew something was wrong though. He didn't finish his pie; unusual for Sam. He put his knife and fork down when he was about three quarters through and asked Phoebe if she'd like another drink.

'I'm driving, so you might as well take advantage, Pheebs.'

'In that case, yes, please. I'll have a red wine.'

'Coming up.' There were no waiting staff in sight so he went up to the bar to order it and Phoebe watched him, feeling nervous.

She knew he hadn't believed her just now and she had a feeling he wasn't going to leave it there either. Sam was one of the most perceptive people she'd ever met.

A few minutes later, he came back with their drinks and put them on the table, and then he began without any more preamble. 'Do you still want us to get married, Phoebe?'

'What?' Blindsided, she looked at him. She hadn't been

expecting that. 'Of course I do. Why on earth would you think I didn't?'

'I guess because we haven't talked about it lately. I can't remember the last time either of us mentioned it.'

It was true, she realised, but he was still speaking.

'Sweetheart, just now when you were looking at that lot at the bar, were you wishing you had a different life?'

'Um...' He was so spookily accurate she didn't know how to answer. She took a gulp of her wine. 'I don't regret us being together and having Lily if that's what you mean.'

'No. I didn't mean that. Oh, God.' He rubbed his fingers across his forehead. 'That came out all wrong. I just mean...' He paused. 'OK, this time last year we were looking forward to getting married. We were really excited about moving in to Puddleduck Farm. Everything felt really great between us. But we haven't even mentioned getting married lately, and quite often I feel as though you're a million miles away. Or is it me? I'm not sure.'

Phoebe took a large gulp of wine. 'I don't feel distant, but I do feel tired, and I'm worried about the practice. Being an older mum's harder, but I adore Lily. It's amazing being a mum, but sometimes I think I'm rubbish at it, but when I'm at work I feel like I'm still the old Phoebe and then I feel guilty for feeling like that.'

He swallowed. She could see his Adam's apple bobbing. 'Oh, Pheebs, I feel like that too. I thought it was just me.'

'It's not, Sam.' She blinked. She felt close to tears.

Sam looked stricken.

'I'm so sorry. I didn't mean to upset you.' He reached across the table for her hand, but she moved just before he could make contact, searching for a tissue.

* * *

Wordlessly, Sam pulled a mini pack of tissues from his back pocket. He'd taken to carrying them around for baby accidents. He handed her the packet and she pulled out several, dropping some on the table in the process, and blew her nose.

'Can we go home, Sam?'

'Of course we can.' He was aware that she was glancing around, as if she was scared other people might have noticed her tears, but no one was looking their way. Everyone else was too wrapped up in their own worlds to be interested in them.

He sought desperately for a way to retrieve the situation. This was supposed to be a happy date night and he'd ruined it somehow. He'd wanted to share his uncertainty about being a new parent but he hadn't wanted to highlight her uncertainty. He hadn't even known she had any. Maybe his parents had a point about not digging around in feelings, but just letting things be.

He tried to catch Phoebe's hand as they headed for the door, but she was walking just ahead of him. What had just happened? All he had done was to try to start an honest conversation, but it had backfired spectacularly.

They'd got to the car park before Sam heard a voice and running footsteps behind them.

'Sir. I think you've forgotten to pay.' A barmaid's breathless voice reached him, and he turned to see her trying to catch up.

'Oh, God, I'm so sorry.' Sam patted his jacket pocket, located his wallet and was pulling it out when Phoebe, who'd also stopped when she heard the barmaid's voice, stepped in front of him. She pulled out a handful of ten-pound notes and passed them to the barmaid.

'That should cover it. Keep the change.' Brushing aside the

girl's thanks, she turned abruptly and continued across the car park, and Sam felt he had no choice except to follow.

But he felt emasculated now too, not to mention slightly sick.

A few seconds later, he let them both into Phoebe's Lexus and got into the driver's seat. He had cocked that up spectacularly. He had meant to make things better, not worse. Now Phoebe clearly thought he was accusing her of being distant, but he hadn't meant it like that. He'd just meant to start an honest conversation.

As he drew through the open five-bar gate onto the hardstanding at the front of Puddleduck Farm, he racked his brains about what to do. Doing any more talking tonight didn't seem like an option. But going to bed with all this hanging between them wasn't an option either.

* * *

'You're home early.' Maggie met them at the kitchen door. 'I wasn't expecting you back for at least another hour. Were you missing your little one? She's been as good as gold.'

'We were, weren't we, Sam?' Phoebe's voice sounded perfectly normal now and she looked at Sam for back-up, her eyes pleading with him not to contradict her.

'Yeah, and we're quite tired.' He yawned as Phoebe bent to pat Roxie, who'd come to greet her.

Tiny and Buster were both asleep by the Aga, a position they'd spent a lot of time in when they'd lived here permanently and took up again every time they came to visit. Even Snowball was in for a change – curled up in a fluffy black ball on a kitchen chair out of range of the dogs and looking perfectly content.

Sam swallowed an ache in his throat and wished he could stop envying his cat.

'Then we shall get off and let you two get to bed.' Maggie didn't seem to have noticed anything amiss. She gathered up Eddie, who'd been sitting at the kitchen table, called to her dogs, and gave Roxie a stroke and Phoebe a hug.

'We'll see you next time.' Then she looked keenly at Sam, and he knew that she had noticed. But she was being diplomatic. That was unusual for Maggie.

He saw them out and then went back into the kitchen.

Phoebe was making up Lily's nighttime bottle and didn't look at him, so he went to stand beside her.

'I know we need to talk some more, but I really am exhausted, Sam. Do you mind if we do it another time?'

'Of course I don't mind.' He put his arms around her from behind and to his relief she relaxed into his hug.

Maybe it wasn't as bad as he thought. He knew they were both tired. There had been so many changes lately. So maybe it had just been his timing that was out. He resolved to try harder. More than anything in the world he wanted to be the supportive partner and caring dad that Phoebe and Lily deserved. Everything else was secondary to that. They were all that mattered to him.

14

'I thought there was something going on when you came back last night.' Maggie's eyes were serious as she met Phoebe's.

It was the following morning and Phoebe was at Maggie's bungalow where she had just called by unannounced. She was supposed to be at work. Sam had Lily, but she'd just dropped off some medication to a cow with an udder infection and Maggie's bungalow was on the way back. Or at least it wasn't much out of the way, and it was lunchtime and her next appointment wasn't until two thirty.

It had started raining as she'd got out of her car and she'd made a dash for Maggie's blue front door. Flaming November. It had rained a lot this last week and one or two people who'd booked out the dog field hadn't turned up for their session. Phoebe didn't blame them.

She was now pacing around her grandmother's big terracotta and pale green kitchen. The colour scheme was echoed by the pots of herbs on the windowsills, and the delicious scents of coffee and cinnamon scones filled the air. Maggie had always been good at baking but she'd done even more since she'd moved here.

'We had a misunderstanding in the pub,' Phoebe said.

'But, my darling, if this is about you and Sam you should really be having this discussion with him, not me.'

'Yes, I know, but I wanted to talk to you first. Did you find it hard when you had Mum and you still had to work on the farm? I mean, did it get difficult with Farmer Pete or was it just all hands on deck as usual?'

'Of course I found it difficult. Everyone does, but my darling, things were very different in those days. Our roles were more defined, for one thing. Your grandfather milked the cows and I did the childcare. We got an extra dairy man in for a while. I couldn't really pack up baby Louella and take her out on the farm, even if I'd wanted to.'

'No, I don't suppose you could.' Phoebe smiled despite herself as she tried to picture her grandmother milking a cow with a baby in a papoose. It was impossible.

'Why don't we sit down a minute, darling.' Maggie drew out two chairs at the kitchen table and beckoned her across.

Phoebe put her elbows on the wooden table, which was a small version of the one Maggie had left behind at Puddle-duck. She felt suddenly close to tears again and she swallowed.

'You're right. It is different today because I'm the major breadwinner, and I know Sam sometimes finds that tricky. He's still old-fashioned in a lot of ways. And I love that he is. But it means, like you say, our roles aren't so clear cut. Sam's really hands-on with Lily and he's doing less at Hendrie's now his dad's sold the business. I don't think that's doing much for his self-esteem.'

'No.' Maggie chuckled gently. 'But it's what you agreed, isn't it? And it will all settle down, I'm sure. It's still early days...' She hesitated. 'Is there anything else bothering you?'

'I nearly got caught out at work yesterday.' She told Maggie about the hedgehog.

'Luckily Marcus was on the case.'

'That could have happened to Seth or Max, I'm sure.'

'Hmm, maybe. I don't think either Seth or Max would have dived in and offered to treat an animal when they knew they didn't have the requisite experience. They'd have referred the consultation or turned it down. She wasn't even a client of ours. I just acted on impulse. I wouldn't normally do that, Gran. I'd usually be a lot more rational.' She dipped her head as she felt a tear run down her face and then another.

For once, Maggie didn't pick her up for saying 'Gran'. Phoebe heard the chair legs scrape on the floor as she shifted her chair a little nearer and then she felt Maggie's touch on her arm.

'It's possible that you're trying to go back to work too early. Has anything else happened that you may have reflected on later as being not quite rational?'

'Not at work. Although a couple of weeks ago I did come up with this crazy theory about a kitten-farming operation that might be going on locally.'

She told Maggie about Archie's visit and the Savannah kittens going missing and the Maine Coon that had disappeared a few months earlier.

'That doesn't sound too off the wall.' Maggie shook her head. 'People are very strapped for cash at the moment. Which makes it a prime time for scammers to operate. Where there's a scam there's a scammer.'

'I know, but that's where my theory fell down. You wouldn't just happen to be passing Beechbrook House and see the kittens. You'd have had to know they were there. Twice, not just once...'

'Yes. OK. We'll keep that one on the back burner then. Is anything else bothering you?'

'This is going to sound really unhinged.'

'Go on...'

Phoebe's voice felt so raw that it was difficult to get the words out. 'I sometimes catch myself thinking about the baby we lost – he'd have been a little boy and... and...' She broke off into a sob.

'Oh, love. That's not unhinged. That's grief. That's natural. And it's not at all surprising. You didn't have time to grieve properly for him. You were pregnant again so quickly. Of course you would think about him. Your little fig. Come here.'

She shifted her chair even closer and for a few moments Phoebe sobbed in the soft warm circle of her grandmother's arms. It was all true. Although she hadn't thought of it quite like that, what Maggie was saying made perfect sense. She had got pregnant again quickly and the excitement of that had distracted her from the pain of losing her first baby. She had been pleased, back then, that the grief could be put behind them, but she'd never really considered that the grief wasn't done. Because the sadness after her miscarriage had seemed endless and black and all-encompassing and getting pregnant again had lifted it. Getting pregnant had been a brilliant distraction.

'I hadn't thought about it like that,' she said eventually. 'But it's true. Poor Sam must have felt it too. We never spoke about it but I think we were probably both terrified it might happen again. I didn't go near any stairs for the whole time I was pregnant with Lily. I was terrified I'd fall down some again, even if I wasn't rushing.'

'I'm not surprised,' Maggie said. 'Have you told Sam all this?'

She frowned and shook her head. 'No. Do you think I should have done?'

'I'm not sure. I know it's important to make peace with the past, but I do think you need to look to the future too. You and Sam have an amazing, beautiful daughter and it's all going to get easier, week by week, trust me, darling, it really will. I think you and Sam should enjoy these precious times with Lily. Focus on what's good, focus on what's happening now.'

Maggie got up stiffly. 'Have you got to get back? Or shall I make us another pot of coffee?'

Phoebe glanced at the clock. 'I think I should probably get back. But thanks. It has helped talking to you. It always does.'

'Any time, darling, but...'

'I'll talk to Sam. Don't worry...' Phoebe pre-empted her. 'And I'll stop trying so hard to be the perfect mother, and vet.'

'And the perfect girlfriend, and the perfect rescue centre owner.' Maggie winked. 'And did I mention the perfect amateur sleuth?'

Phoebe was laughing as she got back into her Lexus. Maggie was amazing. However sad she felt, however cross or frustrated she was when she arrived feeling in pieces, she always felt 100 per cent better when she left.

She knew she needed to talk to Sam. But anything felt possible now. The rain had stopped and the sun had come out over Maggie's red-roofed bungalow and was now glinting off the wet roof tiles and making them sparkle. The blue front door looked cheery and bright.

It would be OK. She pressed the starter button on the Lexus. Her world was in perspective, once more.

* * *

Sam's morning had been tricky. Lily was crying a lot and he couldn't seem to soothe her. He knew she was probably picking up on his tension; he still felt uneasy about what had happened last night. He'd been hoping Phoebe would come in for lunch but she hadn't yet.

'It's OK, sweetheart. It's OK.' He rocked Lily in his arms. 'Mummy will be back soon.'

He looked at the kitchen clock. He was surprised she hadn't come in already. She always came in for lunch. She must have been held up with a client. Maybe he should take Lily out for a stroll. Maybe that would help soothe her. He glanced out of the window. It looked like the rain had finally stopped.

Roxie could come too. She'd appreciate a walk. They'd been in all morning. Even Snowball had been hanging around inside. His big black cat wasn't a fan of the rain.

He strapped Lily into her buggy and went to get his coat from the front door. It was only when he was unhooking it that he saw that Phoebe's car wasn't outside. So she'd gone out to a client then. He was surprised, and a little hurt that she hadn't even messaged to let him know.

Maybe she had and he hadn't heard it. On his way back to the kitchen, he grabbed his mobile from the side.

There were two messages, but neither of them was from Phoebe. One was from Turtle Tots who he'd contacted just after Archie had told them about it, saying there was a space for him and Lily if he wanted it.

Sam scrolled down. The other was from someone Sam had never expected to hear from again. Judy Barker.

He did a double take, certain for a split second that he must have misread it. But no, it was Judy. She was an ex – in fact, she was a double ex. They'd split up and got together twice before he and Phoebe had been an item. There had been a lot of passion and fire with Judy – she was that sort of woman. Moody, dramatic, super sexy and super high maintenance.

Her parents had never approved of him. They'd both been stockbrokers and richer than Croesus, but that hadn't bothered Judy and Sam at the time. A great deal of their relationship had been spent in bed. The chemistry had always been mind-blowing.

Jesus, Sam, what are you thinking? He caught himself. *You're practically married and you're a father.* Lily's cries had subsided to whimpers when he'd strapped her in her buggy. 'Oh, sweetheart.' He knelt beside her on the flagstone kitchen floor. 'I'm sorry Daddy's been grumpy. Shall we go out and see if we can find Mummy?'

Lily waved a fist at him.

Sam felt his heart turn over with love for her, and he felt a flash of guilt – that message on his phone felt like a bomb waiting to go off. That was crazy. It wasn't his fault that Judy Barker had messaged him. He slid his mobile into his pocket. Out of sight, out of mind. He would find out what she wanted later.

15

Phoebe was about to go up and see Sam and Lily when she spotted them in the yard heading her way. She went to meet them. 'Sam, I'm sorry. I got waylaid on a call. But I should have let you know.'

'It's fine. Don't worry. I guessed it was something like that.'

To her relief he didn't sound too put out. 'How's our beautiful baby?' She leaned over the buggy and touched Lily's hair. 'Have you got a smile for your mummy?'

Lily gurgled and Phoebe's heart swelled with love.

'And how's our Roxie?' she added, bending to stroke the dalmatian, who was waiting patiently for her attention.

Roxie wagged her tail and Sam raised his eyebrows. 'Roxie's got a confession to make, although I can tell you about that later if you're in a rush.'

'I'm not in a rush. What's she been doing?'

'She's been stealing cat food again. You know how we always put the bowl up on the big windowsill in the front room so Snowball can reach it and she can't?'

Phoebe glanced at him curiously. 'She can't get up there, can she?'

'Apparently she can if she puts one paw on the back of the sofa and leans across. I caught her today, the little monkey.'

'Oh my God, the clever little madam.' Phoebe laughed. 'I bet Snowball loved that.'

'I think he actually came to tell me. I was in the hall and he came out of the front room yowling and when I went in there I caught her in the act.'

'So our dog's a thief and our cat's a grass. I guess we'll have to find a new place for his bowl.' They both laughed now. 'I popped in and saw Maggie when I was out,' Phoebe added. 'She helped me get some things into perspective. We can have a proper chat later.'

'Great.' His face closed down a little and she realised it probably hadn't been the most diplomatic time to tell him that bit. 'I'd, er, better get back in to work. Are you going for a walk?'

'We are. Just around here in case it starts raining again.' He touched her arm. 'I love you.'

'Love you too, Sam.'

A few minutes later, feeling much lighter and with a pleased Roxie beside him, Sam pushed the buggy with a peaceful Lily down towards the neddies.

Ninja, accompanied by one of the donkeys, came ambling across the damp paddock to greet them. Sam pulled the buggy up to the fence but not too close and handed out carrot slices to soft, eager mouths.

Lily, who already loved the donkeys, shouted out something that sounded like 'donk'.

It would be donkey, not daddy, that was her first word, Sam thought ruefully.

He glanced over towards the dog field. There was someone with two German Shepherds in there. Both dogs were tracking round the perimeter fence. Their black and tan coats and low waving tails were distinctive against the short green grass. Then their owner blew two sharp bursts on a whistle and one of the dogs ran back towards him. The other one ignored the call and continued sniffing. Sam watched them for a moment. One responsive dog and one with no recall by the look of it. No wonder they needed a secure dog field.

He was pleased their new venture was going so well. Even if it had meant there was no room left for him to do any riding lessons. It was a brilliant source of income for the charity. He was also relieved Phoebe hadn't been bottling things up after last night but had talked to Maggie. They'd always been twin souls.

He sometimes wished he had a close friend – someone he could sound off to about things without worrying he'd be judged. But Phoebe had always been his best friend. It was a double-edged sword, sometimes, having a soulmate who was also your best friend.

'Get over yourself, Sam,' he said aloud as he crossed behind the dog field and walked up towards the perimeter fence line of the Puddleduck Farm land. This was the furthest point of their land and where it came closest to the Beechbrook estate. He looked up at the belt of woodland that shielded Beechbrook House.

A bright rainbow curved across the sky above the trees, a shimmering arch of red, yellow and green. One end of it disappeared behind the woodland coming down in the place where Sam judged the manor house to be. That was appropriate. Wasn't there supposed to be a pot of gold to be found at the foot of a rainbow? Rufus had plenty of gold.

On the other hand, there was more than one type of gold in

life, Sam thought, counting his blessings. He had a partner he adored, he had a beautiful baby and he lived in this amazing place in the countryside. It was a dream life by anyone's standards, and the insecurities that plagued him occasionally about not being a good enough father, not being up to the job, were temporary. He was sure they were.

He looked back at Lily. She'd fallen asleep, her dark eyelashes resting against her pale rose cheeks. She was so perfect, so precious. He had so much to be grateful for. Then, almost on autopilot, he took his mobile out of his pocket and read Judy Barker's message.

* * *

Phoebe's afternoon flew by, as they always did when she was working. It had been good to listen to Maggie's quiet wisdom at lunchtime.

She hadn't realised how sad she'd still been feeling about the baby they'd lost. She wondered if Sam felt it too. They hadn't been communicating so well lately. They'd both been so tired. But now she had spoken to Maggie about it, she felt as though she had let go of a little bit more of her grief around it. Her head felt a lot more ordered and serene. Although Maggie was right. She needed to talk to Sam about it too.

It was a relief to finish her appointments, and she didn't hang around chatting to her staff for too long at the end of the day. She and Sam needed a proper heart-to-heart. It would be good to get home and talk everything through with him. Sam had always been so calm and steady. He would get it, she knew he would. Then everything would be well again with their world.

* * *

Sam had taken advantage of Lily settling down for much of the afternoon in her play gym to cook a spag bol for their dinner. It had felt good to cook a proper meal. He hadn't done much cooking lately, and even a simple bolognese was a big step up from the rushed mix of cheese on toast and ready meals they'd been living on lately.

He was keen to talk to Phoebe. Maybe to tell her something of how he'd been feeling lately. He'd thought he was being supportive by not telling her, but maybe he'd just made things worse.

They had loads to look forward to. Christmas was approaching fast. Lily's first Christmas. And they needed to talk about having a christening for Lily, not to mention getting their wedding back on track. His spirits lifted.

* * *

'Something smells nice.' Phoebe wrinkled her nose in appreciation as she came into the kitchen with Roxie at her heels. 'Oh, Sam, you've been cooking. That's really sweet.' She crossed to the Aga where the pan was bubbling on the simmer plate. 'It's ages since we've had one of these.'

'I was going to do some garlic bread to go with it but I just checked the freezer and we don't have any.'

'Yes, that would have been nice. Do you want me to go and get some?'

'Don't worry. I'll go. I think our daughter needs changing.' He picked up his car keys and jangled them. 'You can do that bit. I'll nip up to the Co-op.'

'That seems like a very fair trade to me. Can you get some more nappies while you're there? I think we're a bit low.'

He'd been gone about twenty minutes when Phoebe heard the ringtone of a mobile. Not hers, which was still on silent from being at work. Sam must have left his behind. She spotted it on the table and went across.

The name flashing up on the screen was Judy Barker. Why did she recognise that name? Phoebe felt a jolt of unease – God, yes, it was Sam's ex. They'd talked about her once at length. Things hadn't worked out between them because Judy's posh parents didn't approve of Sam, but he'd been in love with her enough to have tried to make the relationship work a second time and they'd got back together for a while. Phoebe could remember him telling her about it. Why on earth was Judy calling him now?

She was tempted to answer it but she hesitated too long and the ringing stopped. Then for a moment she stood in the kitchen feeling uneasy. What if Judy was trying to reconnect with Sam again? Third time lucky. Maybe she didn't know Sam was a father now and settled with Phoebe.

The ping of an answerphone message being left sent a chill through Phoebe. The last thing they needed was an ex turning up, footloose and fancy free. Sam might be tempted. He might welcome the idea of an afternoon away from nappy changing and domestic chores.

Well, he wouldn't if he didn't see the message. Neither of them had passwords on their phones. They'd never seen the need. They often joked that trust was a good password. Phoebe snatched up his phone and, with her heart beating fast because she thought she'd just heard the slam of a car door outside, she deleted the answerphone message.

She was sure there was a way of deleting the record of the

call too. Yes, there was. A quick sideways swipe and she'd deleted Judy Barker out of existence. What if she'd texted too? She was about to look and see when she heard the front door bang and with her face flaming, she put Sam's phone down and went quickly over to Lily.

She was chatting to their daughter happily when Sam came back into the kitchen.

'One garlic bread with cheese. And I got a spare for the freezer.'

He'd bought flowers too, Phoebe saw with a stab of guilt, a bunch of red and yellow roses in cellophane wrapping. And he was getting out her favourite New York cheesecake.

'Dah dah!' He put it on the table.

She wished she could turn back the clock by five minutes. She was already regretting her crazy impulse to delete that message. She was also regretting not listening to it. It had probably been totally harmless, and now she'd never know. Cheeks flushing, she blew him a kiss.

'Thank you. I've got a bottle of red out and the kettle's boiled ready for the spaghetti so if we put that in the Aga now everything will be ready at the same time.'

'Sounds great.' He came across the room and put an arm round her and smiled down at Lily. 'Shall I finish the dinner, Pheebs, while you feed Lily and put her to bed?'

'It's a deal.'

16

For once, Phoebe found herself hoping Lily wouldn't settle down straightaway so she'd have a bit more time before she had to face Sam. But ironically, because she didn't want her to, Lily settled down almost immediately.

'I am a terrible mother,' Phoebe said softly as she bent over to kiss her forehead. 'Well, I'm a terrible partner anyway.'

Her mind spun with the ramifications of deleting Sam's message. What on earth had she been thinking? What if Judy phoned again and said she'd already called once and left a message? Hopefully she wouldn't. But Phoebe still felt horrendously guilty. She'd have hated it if Sam had done the same thing to her. Not that she ever had exes calling her.

She took so long in the bedroom that eventually, Sam came up. He stood in the doorway and called softly, 'It's ready, Pheebs. Has she gone down OK?'

'She has. She's fine. I'm just coming.'

'And are you OK?' he asked as she came to the door.

His voice was so concerned and gentle that she felt guiltier than ever about that message. 'I'm good.' She paused. Maybe she should just tell him now – fess up to making a stupid decision. But that might cause another upset and lead to them not talking properly yet again and she was desperate to sort things out properly between them. No, on balance, it would be best to keep that quiet for now.

Half an hour later they had finished their bolognese and they'd each had a slice of the creamy cheesecake and Sam had cleared up. Roxie had been treated to a few strands of meat-sauce-soaked spaghetti, which she loved, and Snowball had deigned to lick his strands of spaghetti clean. He liked the sauce, but he clearly wasn't going to make himself look undignified by trying to eat the spaghetti. Roxie waited politely until he'd left his bowl and then helped him out by wolfing it down herself.

Sam topped up their wine glasses. 'Shall we take these into the front room? I've lit the fire in there.'

'That sounds brilliant.'

The animals followed them in. Snowball jumped up onto the big windowsill as though he was looking for his bowl, but Sam had already moved it. There was a chunky green vase in its place. Snowball sniffed it disdainfully before settling down, paws outstretched, for a snooze.

Roxie glanced up hopefully too, and she looked disappointed when she realised there was no cat bowl. She lay down on the carpet beneath the windowsill with a humph.

'That's scuppered her little game,' Phoebe murmured, glancing across.

'I know. Mean, aren't I?'

'You're not, Sam, she was definitely getting chubby. I did wonder why. We don't overfeed her.'

'No, we don't. But at least Snowball hasn't been wasting away. He's quite capable of catching a mouse if he's hungry.'

There was a little pause and Phoebe wondered if he was

trying to think of a way back into the conversation they'd begun last night.

It felt lovely sitting in the cosy room by the fire with their animals snoozing peacefully and their daughter asleep upstairs. It seemed a shame to shift the mood. On the windowsill, Snowball was snoring. Every so often he stretched out his paws or swished his tail in his sleep. He was perilously close to that vase, Phoebe thought, wondering if she should get up and move it.

Sam cleared his throat. 'I'm sorry about last night,' he began. 'I didn't mean to upset you, Phoebe, with what I said about the wedding. Truly. I've just been worried lately, and maybe I've projected that on to you.'

'I'm sorry too. I shouldn't have reacted like I did. And tonight's been really lovely. Let's start again.'

He nodded. 'Do you want to go first?'

'OK.' She took a deep breath and told him what she had told Maggie earlier about the grief she'd felt lately for the baby they'd lost. 'I thought I was over it when we got pregnant with Lily, but I couldn't have been. I think I'd just pushed it all down inside. And then I pushed it even deeper because I was really scared at the beginning that it would happen again. Even though logically there was no reason why it should.'

'Oh, sweetheart, I should have guessed. I was scared too.'

'You never said?'

'I know. I was terrified of tempting fate.'

'I think we both were.' She met his gaze. 'I don't know if it was the same for you, Sam, but for me it faded as we got closer to the birth. I guess it was the hormones and the excitement. But it never totally left and lately I've felt awfully sad about it again. I don't suppose the exhaustion has helped. Or the crazy hormones.' She paused, feeling tears clogging her throat suddenly. 'I feel like I should have worked it out earlier. But grief isn't like a switch, is it? It doesn't just disappear in one hit. It ebbs and flows and sometimes when you think it's done with, it isn't and it comes back up again.'

'I know, and I don't think we should beat ourselves up. This is all new territory for both of us. And there isn't a right way of dealing with grief. Or parenthood, come to that.'

For a moment they were quiet, both lost in their own thoughts, and then just as Phoebe was about to say something else, there was a thud and a yelp and both of them jumped as Roxie shot across the room away from the windowsill.

Phoebe stood up to see what had happened. The vase was now lying on its side on the carpet. 'Oh, my goodness, Sam, I think that vase just fell on her head. Snowball must have knocked it off with his paws. Roxie, love, are you OK?'

Roxie came warily back across the room, looking around for her unknown assailant, and Phoebe checked her over, but fortunately there didn't appear to be any damage. On the windowsill Snowball opened his yellow eyes briefly, and then shut them again, and stretched out his paws, as if blissfully unaware of the drama he'd just caused.

'If I didn't know better, I'd say he did that on purpose,' Sam said. 'Revenge for all the dinners she's stolen.'

Phoebe shook her head. 'He couldn't have done, surely.'

'I wouldn't put it past him. He's usually very careful where he puts his paws.'

'Well, he certainly gave her a fright, poor lamb. I don't think she'll be going near that windowsill again in a hurry.'

She was right. Roxie climbed up on the sofa beside Sam instead and he stroked her ears. 'Did that wicked cat throw a vase at you?'

Roxie turned accusing brown eyes towards the windowsill

and thumped her tail. 'I swear she knows exactly what I just said,' Sam murmured.

'I'm sure she does too. Animals are amazing, aren't they? Much better at communicating than we are. Maggie always says that. I guess we just need to keep talking,' she added, 'and stop trying to mind read and second guess each other.'

'I'm up for that.' He put an arm around her shoulders. 'Any time you want to talk, or even just to cry, I will always be here. You do know that, don't you?'

'Right back at ya, Sam.'

She felt a rush of love for him. She should have known he would understand. He had always understood. She wished once again that she hadn't deleted Judy's message. Because now would have been the perfect time to ask him about it.

But she didn't want to end the evening on a negative note. Hopefully he would never find out. She decided to sit on it for now.

* * *

Sam wondered if he should tell her about the time when he'd run out of Hendrie's and stood on the bridge with all those crazy thoughts of wanting to run away flooding through his brain. He'd been going to tell her about his sadness that he'd made a decision to give up Ninja because they were never going to compete again. That he thought he might have found a home for him. That's what Judy Barker's message had been about. She had been speaking to Marjorie Taylor at Brook about finding a horse for a friend of hers.

Although she hadn't phoned back as she'd promised, to put them in touch, so maybe it wouldn't pan out after all.

But after everything they'd just shared, he didn't want to

spin Phoebe back into insecurity and the feeling he wasn't totally committed, so he amended what he'd been going to say.

'I do miss our old life sometimes. I guess that's normal, but that doesn't mean I don't want the life we have now. I love you and Lily more than anything in the world.'

'And you're still OK with me going back to work full time after Christmas?'

'Of course I am. If you're OK with it?'

'I am, and I can't wait to marry you, Sam. But we don't need to rush into it. I want to enjoy the planning. I want to get excited about it all.'

'And saving up's pretty key too.'

'Christmas first.' Her eyes sparkled and he took her hand in his. 'It's going to be amazing.'

And for the first time in a while, Sam felt that she was right. It really was.

17

Max had agreed to take on the challenge of learning some more about African pygmy hedgehogs once they'd had a proper discussion about it. Phoebe would have liked to have done the course herself too, but maybe she could do that at a later date when Lily was a bit bigger. Organising the Voice for Wildlife campaign was enough for her to do for now.

Besides, it didn't matter if Phoebe wasn't a specialist. Seth wasn't either but he could pick up the slack. He already knew more than she did so there should always be someone around who could treat the little hogs should the need arise.

Tori had got in touch with the owner of the hedgehog sanctuary that had taken Bumble and asked if she could interview her, and she'd agreed happily.

'I'll run it by you before it gets printed,' she promised Phoebe. 'It's high time we had a catch-up anyway.'

Tori brought the feature round to show her on the penultimate day of November.

She brought Vanessa-Rose too and although there was quite a big age gap between their daughters – Lily was barely four months old and Vanessa-Rose was a month away from being two – it was really exciting seeing them both together.

When they'd arranged the afternoon meet-up, Phoebe had envisaged the two babies engaging with each other. She'd had a rose-tinted fantasy of how the time would play out, but the reality wasn't quite the same. Vanessa-Rose had just started walking and she was very active. Every time Tori put her down, she was off across the flagstone floor of the kitchen, and she was much more interested in Roxie, the dalmatian, than she was in Lily.

'Spotty dog,' she yelled excitedly as soon as she saw her. 'Spotty dog.'

'She's met Roxie before,' Phoebe said curiously. 'Why is she so fascinated now?'

'I think that might be Harrison's fault. There's a really ancient children's programme called *Wooden Tops*. He came across it when he was browsing YouTube and there's a spotty dog in it. Vanessa-Rose loves it. I should have realised she'd be excited to see a real life spotty dog.'

Roxie, clearly alarmed at the toddler's determined attempts to stroke her, kept moving out of the way. 'I'll put her in the other room,' Phoebe said. 'I can't guarantee she won't snap.'

As soon as Roxie was removed from the room, Vanessa-Rose began to yell. 'Want spotty dog. Want spotty dog!'

Tori finally managed to distract her with the production of Mr Ted, a blue bear, and promises she could see spotty dog again later if she was quiet and good.

But as soon as Vanessa-Rose calmed down, Lily started yelling.

'I'm really sorry,' Tori murmured. 'It was probably Vanessa-Rose setting her off.'

'It's all right, she just needs changing.' Phoebe grinned as she sniffed her daughter and fetched a nappy. 'The joy of motherhood.'

'Blissful,' Tori said with a wink.

Finally, both of their daughters were quiet. Vanessa-Rose was absorbed with her teddy, and Lily was semi-dozing. Their mothers exchanged glances. 'It won't always be like this,' Tori said, her green eyes full of relief. 'When they're a bit older I reckon they'll be the best of friends. The age gap won't seem like anything at all then. While they're quiet I'll show you the article.'

She opened her laptop on the kitchen table and clicked a few buttons so Phoebe could see she'd done a double-page spread. 'I hope it's what you wanted.'

The piece was headed up 'A Voice for Wildlife' to tie in with their campaign name. Tori's feature had several illustrating photos. There was a tawny red fox, crossing a field, a pale coloured ghostly barn owl in flight, and a wild grey rabbit sitting up on its haunches washing an ear. But the biggest – and by far the cutest – photo in the centre of the page was of a tiny white hedgehog. It was being held in the palm of someone's hand and had the cutest little pink face that peeped out from a mass of prickles. Two brown eyes, a tiny brown snout and little brown ears. To emphasise the size of the hoglet, it had been photographed beside a box of paracetamol, and despite the fact it was in the forefront of the shot, it didn't look much bigger than the box.

'Oh my God, that's so cute,' Phoebe murmured. 'Is that Bumble?'

'No, it's a younger one. I took it myself.' Tori beamed as Phoebe scanned through the text.

It was written in Tori's usual concise style, warning of the dangers of making wild creatures into pets. It was exactly what she'd hoped for – Tori had spelled out the pitfalls of keeping wildlife in captivity loud and clear.

She read the accompanying text aloud. 'The African pygmy hedgehog, also known as the four-toed hedgehog, is not native to England and will die if it's kept in the wrong conditions. The RSPCA don't recommend them as pets.'

'It's fab,' Phoebe said. 'I'm sure that will help. When does it go to print?'

'Tomorrow.'

'Great timing too. Thank you so much.'

Vanessa-Rose had stuffed Mr Ted into a gap between a kitchen cupboard and the fridge and was now fussing because she couldn't get him out. Tori went to rescue him for her and discovered she needed changing too. Lily started crying for attention and Phoebe picked her up for a cuddle.

By the time Phoebe and Tori had sorted out their daughters, the subject of hedgehogs and other wildlife was no longer uppermost in Phoebe's mind. 'What are you doing for Christmas?' she asked her friend.

'We're spending it at home. It's easier than being in someone else's house with a little one. My family are popping over on Christmas Day to bring presents. Harrison's are coming Boxing Day. We're not even attempting to all eat together. We discovered last year that it's just too much. Short bursts of family are enough. I'm looking forward to Vanessa-Rose knowing more about what's going on this year though. That'll be fun.' She bounced her daughter on her knee. 'Who comes down the chimney at Christmas time, Vanessa-Rose?'

'Santa Claus, Santa Claus,' Vanessa-Rose chanted. 'Santa Claus with lots of presents.'

'Yes, lots of presents for good girls. Are you a good girl?'

Vanessa-Rose nodded vehemently.

'And what do you want Santa to bring you for Christmas?'

'Spotty dog,' Vanessa-Rose said instantly.

'Oh my God. That'll teach me to ask her. We're definitely not getting a dalmatian.'

'Why not?' Phoebe asked, widening her eyes as innocently as she could.

'Because getting the magazine out every month and looking after madam here is quite enough. The last thing we need is a dog.' She shook her head. 'I don't know how you and Sam manage with a whole rescue centre full of them. Not to mention a vet practice.'

'Natasha does a lot of the work and I'm not back at work full time yet,' Phoebe said promptly. 'Ask me again when I am.'

'Are you still planning that for January?'

'Yes, I think so.'

'Crazy girl.' Tori looked at her keenly. 'So what are you and Sam doing for Christmas? Is it open house again, like last year?'

'Yes. The whole family are coming over. I can't believe we've been here a year.' Her eyes misted slightly. 'This time last year I didn't even know I was pregnant, and here we are with Lily coming up to her first Christmas. It's unbelievable.'

'It really is.' Tori's eyes were soft too. 'I'm so glad you and Sam are happy together. And I'm so glad you've got Lily now.'

There was a poignant pause and Phoebe wondered if they were both remembering the miscarriage. She hadn't told Tori about her recent sadness about the baby she'd lost. Since she'd spoken to Maggie and Sam it had faded again, and she was reluctant to stir it up once more.

She and Sam were OK again too. She never had mentioned Judy Barker's call and neither had he, so presumably it had just been a one-off. She wasn't about to tell Tori about that either. She still felt guilty about deleting it.

'It does get easier,' Tori was saying now. 'Being new parents, I mean. Having a baby is a massive upheaval. Your hormones are all over the place for one thing. You're not sleeping properly – there's an adjustment period. I was exactly the same.'

'Were you really? I don't remember you finding it that tough.'

'That's probably because I just put a brave face on it. It's crazy. Everyone pretends they're coping wonderfully even if they're not. It's a shame we're not all more honest about our feelings.'

Phoebe blinked away an unexpected tear. 'Thanks. Thanks for saying that.'

'It's true, honey. You're doing great. And while we're on the subject of Christmas, do you and Sam and Lily fancy coming to see the lights at Blenheim Palace with us? We took Vanessa-Rose last year and it was wonderful. They have this light trail with music which takes about an hour and a half to go round. There's a Christmas market there and you can see Father Christmas on the trail. Everyone says it's one of the best light shows in the south and it's only about an hour and a half from us. It's just north of Oxford.'

'It sounds brilliant. I'll ask Sam.'

'Ask me what?' Sam came into the kitchen at that moment, with Roxie at his heels. 'Hi, ladies. Had you shut Roxie out on purpose or was it an accident?'

Phoebe started to tell him but her words were drowned out by Vanessa-Rose yelling, 'Spotty dog. Spotty dog,' and wriggling to be put down.

Roxie did a swift about turn, clearly deciding discretion was the better part of valour, and legged it back the way she'd come. They all laughed.

'Ah, I see,' said Sam. 'Good to see you, Tori. And definitely yes to Blenheim Palace. One of my customers mentioned that the other day. I'm just making hot chocolate. Anyone else want one?' He headed for the Aga.

'No, thanks, it's time we got going. It's nearly her teatime.' Tori got to her feet and started gathering possessions while Vanessa-Rose toddled determinedly in Sam's direction.

Sam turned to greet her. 'Hello, sweetheart. She's walking well.'

'They grow up faster than you think,' Tori remarked. 'If that's any consolation?'

'If you're telling me that they don't keep you up all night forever, then yes, it is. So thank you.'

They all laughed. There was a huge warmth in the room and it wasn't just the heat of the Aga.

'I'll check out the slots for Blenheim Palace,' Tori went on, 'and message you the details. They've started already and they go through to 3 January, I think, but it's nicest to go in December.'

'Sounds great to me,' Phoebe said.

'We can maybe do cards and presents then as well.'

'Oh, Jeez. Christmas shopping. I haven't even thought about doing any of that.'

Tori grinned. 'You've got twenty-four whole days left if you start tomorrow.' She blew Phoebe a kiss from the doorway. 'No one will care what they get for Christmas this year. They'll all be far too busy fussing over Lily. You wait and see. That's what my family were like on our first year. Make the most of it and accept every bit of help you can get. That's my advice.'

'That sounds very sensible,' Sam said. 'And we will, won't we, Phoebe?'

'Yes, we will.' Phoebe blew a kiss back to her friend. 'That's a promise.'

18

As it turned out, this wasn't a hard promise to keep. It was the busiest beginning to December Phoebe could remember. Sam got carried away with advent calendars. He bought one for Phoebe with chocolates inside. And he bought one for Lily, which showed festive pictures of fir trees, reindeers and puppies and said Baby's First Christmas. It was beautiful to look at and Lily loved it, but it was also a keepsake because alongside each date it had spaces for parents to write in little things that had happened that would become memories for the future.

'It's gorgeous, Sam,' Phoebe said, running her fingers over the colourful pictures. 'Thank you so much.'

He'd also got advent calendars for their animals. Snowball's had catnip toys and Roxie's had dog treats. 'No one should be on a diet in December,' he joked as he put the calendars up in the kitchen, close to the back door. Luckily they had plenty of wall space.

Phoebe was now back at work Mondays, Tuesday and Fridays when either Sam or Maggie or Louella or Jan had Lily, depending on whether Sam was doing a shift at Hendrie's. Lily seemed to thrive on seeing so many people. She was a happy little baby and not clingy at all.

Puddleduck Vets were rushed off their feet. Everyone on their books, it seemed, wanted to get any niggling problems with their animals sorted out before the Christmas break.

That was before you factored in the prankster calls from people who wanted them to go out to see a reindeer who had a very shiny nose. Or a poorly partridge, stuck in a pear tree. Or two French hens.

Jenna nearly fell for the French hens call. Phoebe overheard her asking the client questions on the phone.

'You say you've got two hens that seem off colour? What kind of hens are they? French ones, mmmm. I'm not sure what those are…'

A few seconds later she paused, disconnected the call and cursed under her breath. 'Honestly, if I get one more person who thinks it's funny to phone up and wind me up and then sing me lines out of "The Twelve Days of Christmas" I'm going to thump them.'

'It'll be tricky to thump them over the phone,' Marcus said, who'd just come in to take over from her. 'Although I do get what you mean. They're total timewasters.'

Jenna shook her head in exasperation. 'Most of them are kids who think they're being terribly funny. They've probably been dared by their mates.'

'Yes, but they're still wasting our time. We could be talking to people who really need our help and they're blocking the line. If anyone pulls that stunt on me, they'll get more than they bargained for.'

This almost backfired on him because later that same day a man who said he was a local farmer phoned up to ask them about five geese they had who'd been laying but had suddenly stopped.

'Are you sure it wasn't six geese you had?' Marcus quizzed them. 'Six geese a-laying. If you think I'm falling for that old chestnut, you've got another think coming. The joke's getting old, mate. Try another vet.'

He disconnected with a smirk of satisfaction. 'They'll have to try harder than that to fool me.'

Probably no one would have been any the wiser, but five minutes later the same man phoned Phoebe because he happened to have her mobile.

'I think your receptionist has been on the Christmas sherry,' he said crossly. 'Either that or he's lost the plot. I just phoned about a suspected case of bird flu and he told me to find another vet. Did you know about this?'

'I'm so sorry.' A mortified Phoebe explained why Marcus had been so curt, and luckily by the end of their conversation the farmer had calmed down a bit and saw the funny side.

Seth went out to see the geese and was relieved to report that it wasn't bird flu either, but coccidiosis, which was a parasite that was easily treated.

After that, Marcus was mercilessly ribbed by Jenna and Max and Seth humming 'The Twelve Days of Christmas' every time they saw him. But they were also all more careful to interrogate prospective clients before jumping to conclusions.

Tori and Phoebe arranged the Blenheim Palace lights trip for mid-December and it was definitely one of their festive highlights.

They'd booked tickets for four thirty which was one of the earliest slots available. It would be dark enough to see the lights but wouldn't make too late a bedtime for the little ones.

Harrison drove them up in his 4x4, which was the only

vehicle they had big enough for them all to fit into as it had six seats. There was a very festive atmosphere in the car as Phoebe, Sam and Tori sang Christmas songs for the little ones, and even the somewhat sombre Harrison had a grin on his face a lot of the way.

The atmosphere at Blenheim Palace was incredibly festive too, they discovered as they walked through the huge ornate gates of the venue and into the Christmas market. It reminded Phoebe of a German street market where dozens of wooden huts, themselves festooned with Christmas lights, were lined up in the courtyard of Blenheim Palace, a few hundred feet away from the imposing house itself.

Street food of all descriptions was on sale, from Asian dishes to kebabs to fish and chips. There was even a noodle bar, and the cool December air was full of the delicious scents of chilli and cinnamon and spice.

Sam and Harrison queued up for food and mulled wine, while Tori and Vanessa looked after the little ones. Lily and Vanessa-Rose were both wide-eyed before they got anywhere near the light trail.

'This is wonderful,' Tori said as they pushed their buggies around stalls that were selling all sorts of things, from handmade wooden tree decorations to sparkly jewellery to boxes of Christmas biscuits to gingerbread men. 'Really Christmassy. I've always fancied going to a real German market. We should go one year when the girls are older.'

'It's amazing.' Phoebe glanced around them. There was a sensory feast for the eyes and ears everywhere you looked. Classical music bounced across the air and the palace itself was lit by dozens of lasers that flickered beams across it, sending a light show of glittering colours across its stately façade.

The lights were even more amazing, they discovered once

they'd all eaten their impromptu supper and gone through into the formal gardens. The areas on either side of the path were ablaze with colour as they travelled through a winter wonderland of music and light show magic. Music swelled out from hidden speakers so each section was a feast for the senses, and each section was worth lingering over. One of the first sections of path overlooked a lake and the entire surface of the water was lit with silver and gold lights that rippled and glittered like waves on an ocean in time with an orchestral version of 'Jingle Bells'.

'Wow!' Even Harrison looked impressed as they all paused to watch and take photos, even though Phoebe knew no photo would do justice to this display.

Because everyone had a time slot, the venue wasn't overcrowded either so they could walk in comfort without any jostling. There were no crowds.

A little further on they passed a giant tree with a skyscraper of a trunk over which a river of moving lights changed through streams of green, purple, blue, silver and gold in an ever-changing myriad of colour to the accompaniment of a rousing version of 'My Favourite Things'.

'That's got to be one of the tallest trees I've ever seen,' Tori said, craning her neck.

'It's a cedar, I think,' Harrison told them. 'I'm sure David Attenborough featured it on one of his programmes. They've got the Harry Potter tree here, too, somewhere.'

'We should come in the day some time,' Sam said. 'I bet it's just as spectacular then.'

Towards the end of the trail, they went through a twelve-foot-long archway of glittering silver lights.

'It's like something out of a fairy tale,' Phoebe said to Tori as they paused at the entrance and took more photos of each other and the girls while Sam and Harrison discussed the practicalities of powering so many lights at once.

'LEDs or ordinary?' Harrison pondered.

'They'd need a whole power station for this lot,' Sam replied.

'I'll go with magic,' Tori said in Phoebe's ear as the two little girls stared around them, wide-eyed. 'This is a magical place.'

The highlight as far as the little ones were concerned was a hologram of a scarlet-cloaked Father Christmas, sitting in his silver and gold sleigh, drawn by eight dancing reindeers, racing across the dark sky and then a backdrop of fir trees. Vanessa-Rose was totally transfixed as Tori held her up to look and Lily shouted and waved her fists.

Phoebe and Tori only managed to persuade the little ones to leave the Father Christmas loop at all with the promise that they could meet the real Father Christmas, who was just up ahead of them, if they did.

Vanessa-Rose cried when the big man standing outside his grotto said, 'Ho, ho, ho, happy Christmas,' but Lily was more than happy to go for a cuddle and have her picture taken with him.

'She's amazing,' Phoebe said, slipping her hand into Sam's. 'She's not scared at all, is she?'

'She's used to meeting lots of people at Puddleduck Farm, though, isn't she? She's going to grow into a proper social butterfly.'

They finished the trail with mugs of fragrant hot chocolate and the chance to toast a marshmallow on a long stick over a barbecue of flaming hot coals.

'They might be the most expensive marshmallows I've ever bought,' Sam murmured as he came back with a handful of them on sticks.

'Yes, I said that last year.' Harrison frowned. 'We were going to bring a bag, weren't we, Tori?'

'Yes. I forgot. And we could have afforded a sack at these prices,' she said, laughing. 'But thanks, Sam.'

'Thank *you* for suggesting we come,' he told Tori. 'It's been amazing.'

'A proper bit of Christmas magic,' Tori said happily. 'Before we get back into all the mayhem and madness of the final December countdown.'

'The calm before the storm,' Harrison said, 'unless you're one of those organised people who does all your Christmas shopping in the January sales.'

'Which we're definitely not.' Phoebe wiped the stickiness of marshmallow from Lily's face. 'You enjoyed that, didn't you, sweetheart?'

'Worth every penny, then,' Sam said, crouching down beside her in the buggy.

'She's loved every minute of it,' Phoebe said. 'So have I.'

As they walked back through the vast dark car park to find Harrison's 4x4, it was like coming back to the real world again, but they all agreed that it had been a fantastic evening. A proper start to Christmas. An oasis of calm before the festive madness and mayhem hotted up into the frantic countdown towards the big day.

19

One afternoon, a few days after they'd seen the lights at Blenheim Palace, Phoebe was in reception at Puddleduck Vets when a man dressed in jeans and a ski jacket called in to ask if they had any kittens needing a home.

Phoebe was instantly on the alert. Maggie had always been wary of rehoming animals too close to Christmas. 'The last thing we want is for them to become unwanted presents,' she'd said to Phoebe and Natasha plenty of times. 'So we need to be extra thorough with home checks if we're anywhere near the festive season. Make sure people are rehoming them for the right reasons. Also that they're planning on keeping the animal themselves and not giving it to someone else.'

'You're not actually in the right place,' Phoebe told the prospective kitten re-homer. 'We're Puddleduck Vets. You need Puddleduck Pets. You need to go back across the yard and you'll see a sign on the barn door. You should find someone in there. Ask for Natasha.'

'Cheers, love.'

As soon as he'd left, Phoebe phoned Natasha's mobile and

told her about Mr Ski Jacket. 'He seemed OK, but there was something just a little bit off about him. I can't really put my finger on it, but I wanted to warn you.'

'Thanks. Forewarned is forearmed. I'll keep an eye out.'

Phoebe disconnected the call but then she started second-guessing herself. Perhaps she was being oversensitive. She was quite tired. The man was probably very nice.

She got on with afternoon surgery and put him out of her mind. It was great being back at work three days a week. It was enough time for her to feel she knew what was going on in her practice but it meant she could spend a lot of time with Lily too.

At the end of that day, they'd finished tidying up and Phoebe was about to lock up when Natasha appeared on the other side of the glass door. She opened it and peered round. 'Hi, Phoebe, I was hoping I'd catch you.'

Her face was grim.

'Is everything OK?' Phoebe was instantly on full alert. As were Marcus and Jenna, both of whom had been about to leave.

'Well, yes, it is, but I just wanted to give you an update on that bloke you sent across earlier.'

'The one who wanted a kitten?' Phoebe had almost forgotten him.

'Kittens, plural,' Natasha informed them. 'That's what alerted me that there was something fishy going on. He said his daughter had recently lost two cats to old age and he was keen to replace them for her. He said he was quite happy to take more if we had more because she loved cats so much and she'd got plenty of room because she has a farm. That's when alarm bells started ringing. Not many people want to rehome more than two kittens. And I didn't buy the daughter story. Most farms have cats already – they often have ferals, and they're certainly not looking for more.'

'We have three tabby kittens, don't we?' Phoebe pricked up her ears.

'Yeah, we do,' Marcus confirmed. 'There were four in the litter but one's already reserved.'

'He must have already been nosing around in the cattery and seen them,' Natasha continued. 'Anyway, like I said, I didn't buy the daughter story. It didn't ring true, so I told him we didn't have any. Then he started arguing and saying he thought I was mistaken. He'd definitely seen some very pretty kittens that he was sure his daughter would love. I let him take me down there to point them out, and then I said I thought they were already reserved but I'd check if he could let me have his contact details. He gave me a mobile number and went.'

Marcus looked at her in concern. 'What happened next?'

'I thought I'd do a spot of research so I looked at cats for sale online and would you believe he had an advert running for three Savannah kittens for sale. Same mobile number as he'd given me. There were photos and everything, and get this...' Natasha bristled with indignation. 'The photos were of our kittens. It looked from the photos like he'd even got them out of the pen. I don't know how he managed that. It couldn't have been today. I've been here all day. I'd have seen him hanging around.'

'Maybe it wasn't him who took the photos,' Phoebe said. 'We've had a few people interested in those kittens because they're so pretty with that silvery fur. On Saturday one of the volunteers got them out to show to a woman who's rehomed from us before. I think she was taking photos. She might have put them on her social media. Who knows? She probably thought she was helping.'

Marcus swore under his breath and then apologised.

'Don't apologise.' Phoebe bit her lip. 'I'd like to wring that bloke's neck. How dare he? And they're not Savannah kittens anyway, they're tabby.'

Jenna intervened. 'Savannahs are bigger but the colour isn't that different. You could get your tabbies and your Savannahs mixed up if you didn't know the difference. Tabbies are more stripy and Savannahs are spotty but they can be similar, especially when they're that silvery colour that ours are. They can look the same to the uninitiated. Although the price tag's not. How much was he trying to sell them for?'

'Five hundred pounds each,' Natasha said. 'Look, I'll show you.' She got out her phone and scrolled through it. A couple of minutes later she shook her head. 'The advert's gone. He must have known I was onto him.'

'Thank goodness you were.' There was a sour taste in Phoebe's mouth. 'I wonder if there's anything we can do. I'm not sure it's a police matter, is it? Has he actually broken any laws?'

'Passing off ordinary kittens as a specialist breed might be fraud,' Marcus said. 'But I can't see the police being in a hurry to rush out and arrest him. Besides which, we don't even have any evidence, do we? If the advert's gone. Did you screenshot it?'

'No, unfortunately, I didn't. I was too cross, babe.' Natasha's dark eyes flashed with annoyance. 'I wish I'd looked as soon as he'd gone but I didn't have time. It's been mad busy today. I don't think he even gave me his real name, annoyingly. When I asked him he said Jukes, or it may have been Dukes. I asked him to repeat it but he said no need, he'd be answering the phone anyway.'

'Don't beat yourself up,' Marcus said. 'It's brilliant that you thought something was off.'

'I might not have done if Phoebe hadn't been suspicious.' Natasha sighed.

'Teamwork,' Phoebe said. 'I'm with Marcus. Don't beat yourself up. I'm not sure there is anything we can do. But I'll have a word with Maggie and see if she's come across anything like this before. I'll also give Jade at Duck Pond Rescue a ring. It's definitely worth getting the word out to other sanctuaries in the area.'

She bit her lip. The day had taken on a darker tone. The fact that someone had come into the rescue pretending they wanted to rehome kittens, when their plan was to sell them off online, made her feel sick. She and Natasha and Maggie and everyone else who worked at Puddleduck Pets did everything they could to ensure their animals went to really good homes.

Selling animals online, especially just before Christmas, was the opposite of that.

Sam was equally horrified when she told him about it.

'As soon as Lily's in bed, I'm going to phone round the local rescues,' she told him.

'I'll help you. I'll have a word with Ma and Pa tomorrow. We can put the word out with customers too.'

Phoebe didn't manage to get hold of Jade that night, but she left a message, and the following afternoon, Jade phoned her back.

She was as horrified as Phoebe had been.

'Although we shouldn't be that surprised, should we? There are scammers everywhere these days. Especially at this time of year.'

'I know. I'm hoping he was a one-off, although we have had some kittens going missing in this area too. Which could be a coincidence, I suppose. Have you heard of anything like that?'

'Not directly, no, but you're right. Maybe there is a link. No smoke without fire. If I hear of anything suspicious around here, I'll let you know.'

'Thanks. We've been trying to work out if he was actually

doing anything illegal. I don't mean by pretending the kittens were something they weren't, I mean by pretending he was rehoming animals, but then selling them on.'

'Well, that I can help you with. Have you heard of Lucy's Law? It was brought in around Covid time. It bans the third-party sale of puppies and kittens, which makes it illegal to sell them before a certain age unless you're the breeder. So he'd definitely have been breaking that.'

'Thanks, yes, that does ring a bell.'

'But at least he didn't get away with it. And nasty though it is, it does sound like he was just someone who saw the opportunity for a scam and went for it. He can't have been that bright either. Because one of his potential buyers might have spotted they weren't buying a Savannah and reported him to the police.'

'By which time he'd have been long gone.'

'Yes, that's true. Well, hopefully it's a one-off. Thanks for letting me know anyway. I'll pass it on to everyone I speak to.' Jade paused. 'How's motherhood going?'

'Brilliant, fantastic. Tiring.'

'Every new mother says that, I reckon,' Jade said happily.

Phoebe could hear the smile in her voice. 'Did the lurcher puppies get good homes?' she asked, glad they were back on the positive.

'Oh, yes. They got the best. Ben's got one of them. He's Finn's little boy. Finn's dad has one, and Dawn, my right-hand woman, has the other one. So they're all very close to home and I shall see them all regularly too which is brilliant. Two of them have been named after artists, Banksy and Monet. Ben named them. Although he's called his little girl Chocko, which does actually really suit her.'

'That's fantastic news. If ever you're anywhere near this way, I'd love to see one or any of them.'

'If ever we're over that way, we will be sure to pop by.'

It was great to end the conversation on a high, and Phoebe was relieved that Jade, like her, had thought that Mr Smarmy Ski Jacket was just an opportunist scammer, rather than anything more sinister.

She updated Natasha and her staff at the practice, and she was keen to compare notes with Sam. But he was working at Hendrie's. They could catch up when he came in.

Phoebe took Lily back to the house, where they played a game of peekaboo. Lily was getting brighter and more vocal by the day. And although Phoebe knew she wasn't going to start saying proper words for a few more months yet, she'd bought a game to get her off on the right footing.

The game involved flashcards with pictures of animals and people on them, and Lily loved it. She mostly shouted out Doh, or Moh, or Bo at the different cards but she was quite consistent.

Sam had said he was sure Lily's first word would be 'donkey', but Phoebe was determined to make sure Lily's first word was 'Daddy', and she'd decided it was never too soon to practise.

By the time they'd finished the game, it was gone six and Sam still wasn't back from work. That was unusual. He was rarely late, and if he planned to be he usually messaged or called her. Maybe he'd had to run an errand for his parents which had taken longer than expected. Phoebe decided she wouldn't start worrying just yet.

Sam would probably walk in full of apologies any minute.

20

Sam wasn't running an errand for his parents, but he was holding the fort because Ma was taking Pa for another dentist appointment. Pa had been having trouble with a tooth for a while and he wanted it sorted before Christmas.

'I don't want to be in pain while I'm trying to eat my Christmas dinner,' he'd grumbled. 'So I've decided to have the bugger out.'

The Hendries didn't usually have big Christmas dinners – they tended to boycott tradition and get fish and chips – but because it was Lily's first Christmas they'd been invited to Puddleduck Farm with the rest of the clan.

Because of this, Sam felt a bit responsible, so when his father had managed to get a cancellation, a 4.30 p.m. appointment, for the extraction and his mother had offered to take him – in case he felt giddy afterwards; Ian Hendrie hated dentists – Sam had said he'd cover the last part of the day.

'We'll probably be back in time to shut up shop,' Jan had said. 'But if we're not just close up as normal, Sam.'

It was nearly five-thirty, closing time, and they weren't back yet and Sam had served a steady stream of customers.

He'd just weighed out some apples into a paper bag for a regular and then cashed up her other purchases and packed them into her shopping bag for her when the bell on the door tinged and he realised another customer had come into the shop.

'We're just closing,' he called out. 'But I can serve you if it's a quickie.'

'A quickie sounds great to me, Sam.'

He glanced up in shock. Not that he needed to look to confirm her identity. He'd have recognised that laughing, sultry voice anywhere.

'Judy! What are you doing here?'

'Charming. You might sound a little more pleased to see me, Sam. I come in peace. And I have glad tidings of great joy. Well, I have glad tidings anyway.'

She sashayed across to him, her immaculate blonde bob bouncing around her shoulders and flashing red Father Christmas earrings swinging from her ears.

He stared at her open-mouthed. She was the very last person he'd expected to see, and she looked spectacular.

Not that he'd ever seen her look much less than spectacular. Even when she was dressed for riding in her Barbour and old jodhpurs, she looked great, but today, clearly dressed as she was for a party, she looked stunning. She was wearing a short skin-tight gold dress made of some shimmery material and a jacket with a fur-lined collar.

'It's great to see you.' He gathered his scattered wits. 'What can I do for you? I take it you haven't come in for any shopping?'

'You are correct. I was in the area so I thought I'd pop by and see why you haven't responded to my message.'

'I did respond to your message. The last time we spoke you said you'd heard of a possible home for Ninja and that you were going to look into it and let me know if they wanted to come and see him.'

'And they did. And I phoned you. And I left a message, which you never answered.'

'No, you didn't.'

'Yes, I did.' She smiled at him, whipped out an expensive-looking mobile from her miniscule sequinned handbag and showed him the record of a call she'd made. It was dated a month ago. 'I didn't chase you up because they weren't in a massive hurry, and I'd sensed that you might not really want to sell your darling horse so I thought I'd leave it. But then they happened to phone again yesterday to see if the horse was still available and I happened to be in the area today. So I thought I'd call by in person and check you out. Figuratively speaking.'

Sam frowned and picked up his own mobile, which was on the shop counter beside the scales.

He scrolled through his received calls, which didn't take long. They were mostly between him and Phoebe. 'Look. See?' He held out the phone to Judy.

She took it, tapped a few buttons and said, 'It's been deleted, Sam. There. I've just called up the deleted list. My voicemail message has been deleted too.'

'That's ridiculous. I wouldn't have deleted it…'

'Have you got a jealous girlfriend?' Judy widened her eyes. 'Maybe *she* deleted it. No matter. I'm here now.' She put both hands on the counter and leaned forward provocatively, revealing even more of her cleavage, which Sam was determined not to be distracted by.

'And my question is – would you like to take me for a latte in The Crown so we can discuss it?'

Taking her for a latte was the last thing Sam wanted to do. His head was spinning, and it wasn't just her giddying presence. Surely Phoebe wouldn't have deleted one of his messages without telling him. It didn't make sense.

'I'm expected home,' he began, just as the shop doorbell tinged again. For goodness' sake, surely not another last-minute customer. But to Sam's chagrin it wasn't a customer. It was worse. It was his parents.

'Sorry, son. That took longer than we expected.' Ma's voice chimed across the shop. 'Shall I turn the door sign round?'

'Yes, please.'

His pa came across to him, holding his mouth with one hand. He gave Judy a brief, interested glance, before gesturing that he was going on up to the flat. He looked slightly dazed, or maybe that was the aftereffects of the anaesthetic.

His ma wasn't so circumspect. Her eyes were popping out on stalks as she took in Judy's party clothes and flirty demeanour.

'I think this customer has finished, haven't you, madam.' Sam silently begged Judy not to give him away. And the laughter in her eyes told him she wouldn't.

'I'll see you in The Crown in five,' she said in a voice only loud enough for Sam to hear.

He nodded. 'That's great. Thank you very much.'

'By-ee. Have a great Christmas.' Judy sashayed across the shop past his ma, who looked as if she was trying to remember where she'd seen her before.

'I was about to cash up,' Sam said in an effort to distract her.

'I'll do that,' Jan offered. 'You get home, lad. And thanks for covering.'

Sam thanked her and escaped. He knew his face was flaming. It was a relief to get outside into the cold December darkness.

Every instinct he had told him that meeting Judy in The Crown was a bad idea. He knew dozens of people in Bridgeford. What if someone saw him and told Phoebe? But that was ridiculous too. He wasn't doing anything he shouldn't. On the contrary. And if Phoebe hadn't deleted that message he doubted Judy would have come by at all. Had she really deleted that message? He definitely needed to get to the bottom of that.

His mind flicked back through the weeks. He couldn't remember what he'd been doing last week, let alone a month ago. They might have more help with Lily now and they might have been in much more of a routine, but it was still very hard work fitting everything in. The days flew by in a haze of work and babies.

If he didn't go to The Crown, Judy might turn up again. Besides, he did want to know about the people who wanted Ninja. They might not be suitable but if they were it would be a relief. Judy was right – he wasn't in a hurry to let go of his horse – but that didn't mean it didn't have to happen.

A few minutes later, he pushed open the front door of the pub and went into the dimness of the lounge bar. A giant Christmas tree, festooned in red and gold baubles with its top scraping the ceiling, lit up one side of the room, and Judy, in her shimmering gold dress and flashing earrings, lit up the other.

She was sitting in a booth – The Crown was divided up into private booths – and attracting admiring glances from a group of men propping up the bar.

When she saw him, she waved a hand and he walked over to meet her. There was a large glass of white wine on the table in front of her.

'I changed my mind about a latte but I figured you might be driving so I've ordered one for you. They're bringing it over.'

'Thanks.'

'Don't thank me, you're paying. I set up a tab. Sit.'

'Bossy as ever,' Sam remarked, but he sat on the padded bench seat opposite her anyway. 'Tell me about the people who want Ninja.'

'Straight to the point as ever,' she countered with a grin. 'So how are you, Sam? I heard on the grapevine you'd got yourself tied down with a sprog. Is that true?'

'Settled down, not tied down.'

'Whatever.' She waved a careless hand. 'So who is she, this message-deleting female of yours? Anyone I know?'

Sam had no doubt at all that if she knew he had a baby he knew who her mother was, but on the other hand they didn't move in the same circles so maybe she didn't.

'Her name's Phoebe and we don't know that she deleted that message.'

'No, of course we don't.' She took a large sip of wine and winked at him. 'Is that your childhood sweetheart, Phoebe? The one who's a vet. When did you two get married?'

'We're not married. But yes, it's the same Phoebe.' He didn't like her tone, but he was here now, and Judy had always been something of a wind-up merchant. He refused to get ruffled.

'Happy news. That's if you planned the baby, did you?' She looked at him keenly. 'And she didn't just trap you into it.'

'Of course we planned her,' Sam lied. 'She's beautiful. Do you want to see a photo?'

'I assume it's the same baby whose picture is on your screensaver. You used to have Ninja on there.'

She'd seen his phone. That's how she knew. She hadn't heard it on the grapevine at all. She was just fishing.

Before he could respond, Judy held out her left hand and waggled her fingers so he couldn't fail to spot the enormous rock on her engagement finger.

'I'm getting married too. But we thought we'd do things in the right order. Wedding first, babies second. Actually, I think you two have met. His name's Claude. He was at my cousin's wedding. He was on our table, I think.'

Sam felt a wash of humiliation as the memory of her cousin's wedding reception flashed into his head. That had been an awful occasion. It had been when he'd realised that Judy's parents would never in a million years accept him as a suitable partner for their daughter. They'd deliberately invited him to a society wedding so they could get him to see he'd never fit in, not to mention humiliating him as publicly as possible in the process.

'The hooray Henry with the hedge fund,' Sam said dryly. 'I remember it well.'

'No, darling, that was Tarquin. Claude's the one whose father owns the island in the Bahamas. We're going to have our wedding there.'

'I see. Well, I wish you every happiness.'

'We're not married yet. It's a couple of years off. Lots to plan. And all my friends have to save up so they can join the celebration.' She leaned over the table and touched his hand. 'Anyway, seeing as neither of us are actually married yet... I was wondering if you fancied a get-together. For old times' sake.' She licked her lips suggestively. 'We were always so good in the bedroom department.'

He reacted instinctively, snatching his hand from hers.

'No.' Suddenly he felt sick. What had he ever seen in this woman? What was he even doing sitting here while she flirted unashamedly? What on earth had he been thinking?

He pushed back his chair and got out his wallet in the same movement. 'I'm going,' he said, putting a twenty-pound note down on the table in front of her. 'That should cover the drinks.'

He was vaguely aware of her staring at him, open-mouthed in shock. Judy had never dealt well with rejection. Then he turned and strode back towards the exit, narrowly missing the barmaid carrying a tray with his latte to their table.

Outside once more, Sam took a lungful of the cool December air and tried to contain his anger. He should have listened to his instincts. He felt slightly dirty now, and it didn't matter that he hadn't done anything he couldn't justify. He'd have given a lot to wipe the last twenty minutes of his life from his memory.

He didn't care who it was who wanted Ninja, the horse wasn't going to them. He wouldn't sell him to any friends of Judy's. Not after that little performance. It would have felt like selling his soul. He walked briskly back along the High Street towards Hendrie's. The yellow and blue Christmas lights strung across the roads usually cheered him, but tonight they looked garish, and the sparsely branched Christmas tree lit up with blue bulbs, with its gold star on top, looked suddenly cheap.

Sam was out of breath as he reached Hendrie's, and he headed down the back alleyway to the parking space where he'd left his Subaru.

It wasn't the tree and the lights that looked cheap tonight, he realised with a gasp of insight as he unlocked his car. It was the way he felt that was colouring everything. He felt cheap and somehow vaguely tainted. And he was desperate to get home and see Phoebe and Lily.

21

Phoebe had run through a dozen scenarios for Sam's lateness before she'd finally given up being patient and rational and she'd tried phoning him. The call had gone straight to voicemail, which meant he was probably driving. So she'd left it another half an hour – that was plenty of time for him to have got home – and then she'd texted him.

The ping of the text alert going off threw her, as she saw him coming through the kitchen door.

'Oh, Sam. I was starting to worry. That text is from me.'

'I'm sorry. I got held up. Dad had a dentist appointment. I should have let you know.' He came into the kitchen. He looked stern. Stern was an expression Sam didn't do very often and Phoebe felt a flicker of unease.

'Is everything OK?' She glanced at his face, and he nodded briefly, before going across the kitchen to Lily, who was in her play gym.

'Hello, sweetheart.' He tickled her tummy and she gurgled in delight. 'How's my darling girl?'

Roxie had got up to greet him, and had gone across wagging

her tail so hard that her whole spotty bottom wriggled, and Sam was now tickling her under the chin. But he didn't hurry towards Phoebe. He stayed kneeling on the flagstones for a few seconds longer, communing with his daughter.

Snowball had just strolled in too, his tail held high as he purred a welcome. Was Sam going to greet him before her too? Phoebe felt a flicker of irritation.

'Do I need to be a baby or a dog to get a hello tonight?' she asked, and he glanced up.

'No, of course not.' Now he did get up and he came across to where she sat at the kitchen table and pulled out a chair opposite. But he didn't kiss her like he normally would. 'How was your day?'

'My day was fine.' She looked at him keenly. There was definitely something up. 'How was yours?'

'I had a visitor actually.' His voice was mild, but his eyes were more serious. 'Judy Barker dropped by the shop.'

'Oh!' Phoebe hated the twang of jealousy she felt, which was followed almost immediately by a jolt of guilt. It had been ages since she'd deleted that voicemail. She'd managed to put it out of her mind but she had a feeling it was about to come back and bite her. 'What did she want?' She couldn't meet his eyes.

'She wanted to know why I hadn't answered a message she'd left me about a month ago.'

Phoebe stayed silent. This was excruciating. He couldn't know she'd deleted that message. If he did, surely he'd have asked her about it before.

'So what was the message?' she said, before finally meeting his eyes and feeling her face flame. This was awful. She should have just told him. Confessed to a moment of insanity. Maybe it wasn't too late... But before she could say anything, Sam went on quietly.

'She wanted to talk to me about Ninja. I've been thinking of putting him on loan and she knew someone who might be interested...' He broke off and looked pained. 'Pheebs, I've got to ask you this. The voicemail Judy left me was deleted. Did you delete it?'

She nodded slowly. 'Yes. Yes, I did. I shouldn't have. And I'm sorry.' God, this was mortifying. But by far the worst thing about it was the shock in his eyes as he looked at her. And then the hurt, and then the bemusement.

'But why?' He spread his hands in bewilderment. 'Don't you trust me?'

'Of course I do.'

'Clearly you don't.'

'I do, Sam. It was a moment of madness. Call it baby brain. I saw her name flash up when you were out. And I felt jealous and then when she left you a message I felt threatened. So I just deleted it. I regretted doing it the second I'd done it. Truly.'

'Then why on earth didn't you say something? We've had weeks.'

'I know.'

He was angry. Sam was hardly ever angry, but Phoebe could feel it bristling from him. So could Roxie. She had just slunk across the room to her basket alongside the Aga. Snowball had done a swift about turn too. Animals were always attuned to anger and they feared it.

Lily was the only one who seemed oblivious to the tension. She'd been in a sunny mood all day. She waved her arms and gurgled again, unaware of her parents' change of mood.

Then, with one swift movement, Sam pushed back his chair and stood up. 'I need to get my head around this. I'm going out.'

'Sam, please. Don't go out. We can talk about it now.' Phoebe could hear her own voice rising in angst. She saw him hesitate at the back door which he'd so recently entered, and lean one hand against the old cob wall. His knuckles were white with tension.

For a moment she thought he would come back into the kitchen. In all the time she'd known him, he'd never walked away from her in anger. But he didn't hesitate for long. He didn't even look back at her. He opened the back door, closed it quietly behind him and was gone.

It felt much worse and much more final than if he'd slammed it behind him.

Phoebe burst into tears. In another life – in a life before Lily – she'd have gone after him. But she couldn't go anywhere fast with Lily – packing up her daughter and all of the baby paraphernalia they needed for even the shortest trip was a lengthy process. So she stayed where she was at the kitchen table, which was strewn with coloured paper chains. Green, yellow and pink that were destined to be strung up around the oak beams in the old kitchen.

She and Maggie had made them for Lily earlier in the day but she'd been going to ask Sam if he fancied helping put them up. Not because she couldn't put them up herself, but because she wanted him to be involved in this Christmas, which felt like one of the most important they would ever share. Their first Christmas with their daughter in their dream house. They had everything they'd ever wanted. Each other, a beautiful baby, their loving family, this amazing house.

Not that it felt very amazing right now. Phoebe shook her head to clear it. She'd thought they'd got the communication thing all sorted, so why on earth had Sam decided to sell his beloved horse without even telling her?

* * *

Sam hadn't got very far despite the fact he'd left the house in such a hurry. He'd realised as soon as he'd got into the car that the fuel gauge showed almost empty. So going for a long forest drive to clear his head wasn't an option.

By the time he'd refuelled and had pulled off the garage forecourt, he was thinking more clearly. Maybe he had overreacted by storming off. The truth was he'd been shocked by Phoebe's confession. A part of him had been convinced there would be a less damning explanation. Some kind of technical reason for Judy's phone message going missing.

Finding out there wasn't had shaken him. He'd never have scrolled through Phoebe's private messages. Sam realised his hands were locked with tension around the steering wheel and that he was breaking the 40 mph speed limit. Mindful of the danger to the forest animals, he slowed back down to 38.

He shouldn't be driving round the New Forest second-guessing it all. Phoebe was right. He should have stayed and talked to her. They weren't going to resolve anything unless they discussed all this stuff properly. He had to go home.

* * *

Phoebe had given Lily her bath and put her to bed by the time she heard the sound of Sam's car pulling up outside.

She had also washed the tears from her face and given herself a good talking to. She was now sitting in their front room with the log burner on full blast, feeling a great deal clearer headed than she had earlier.

She also felt a little ashamed of herself. Sam must think he'd shacked up with a raving lunatic. He had never been anything else but wonderfully kind and supportive; he had turned his whole world inside out to facilitate hers, while she had been jumping at shadows.

In her mind's eye she could hear Maggie's voice berating her – even though she hadn't shared any of tonight's drama with Maggie. She didn't need to – she knew perfectly well what Maggie would have said. It was about time she stepped up to the plate and supported Sam like he'd supported her.

The fact he had been arranging to get Ninja a new home without even telling her had been a shock. Had their communication really got that bad? She realised suddenly that it had been pretty one-way. She had shared most of what she was feeling with Sam lately, but he didn't share much with her. He mostly said he was fine and everyone knew what F.I.N.E. stood for. Fed up. Insecure. Neurotic and Emotional.

'I'm in here,' she called, getting up to greet him as the front door banged behind him.

'Hey.' He stood in the doorway of the back room. 'I'm sorry I stormed off.'

'I'm sorry I put you in that position.'

He acknowledged this with a slight dip of his head. 'Did Lily go down all right?'

'Touch wood. We need to talk, Sam.'

'We do.'

For a moment they stood a small distance apart and then they were in each other's arms. She wasn't sure who made the first move. It didn't matter. If they could still hug each other they had a chance of sorting all of this out. They could rebuild the trust.

'Shall I make us a hot chocolate?' Sam asked. 'Or would you prefer wine?'

'Hot chocolate, I think.'

She felt like a child when, a few minutes later, they carried two mugs of sweet-smelling, steaming hot chocolate with miniature marshmallows floating on the surface into the front room once more, before sinking down onto the comfy sofas while Roxie stretched out full-length by the wood burner.

'I haven't got any excuse for deleting that message, Sam. It's not because I didn't trust you.' She met his steady gaze. 'I can't even really work out for myself what was going on in my head. Apart from maybe what we talked about before. I'd been feeling that old grief again for the baby we lost. And mixed up with that I was feeling insecure and frumpy and I thought maybe Judy wanted you back and you might be tempted to go and this is starting to sound like a crazy rambling. I'm not trying to make excuses. I'm just trying to explain.'

He nodded. 'Do you still feel insecure now?'

'No.' She lowered her eyes. 'Frumpy, maybe...'

'You're not frumpy. You're beautiful. And Judy would never be a threat to you. She could never hold a candle to you.'

She could hear the truth of that in his voice and see it in his eyes, and she felt another little wash of shame. 'Having Lily has been the most wonderful thing but also the most massive thing I've ever done. It's been such a huge adjustment.'

'I'll second that.' His eyes were tender.

'But why didn't you tell me you were planning to find a new home for Ninja?' she went on gently. 'That's a massive thing too, Sam...'

22

It was the morning after the night before. Not that Sam had a hangover. At least not a physical one. He'd always been sceptical of the label 'emotional hangover'. How could emotions give you a hangover? But now he thought he knew. He'd felt a throbbing ache across his temples before he'd even opened his eyes.

When Phoebe had asked him about Ninja last night, it had opened the floodgates. For the first time since Lily had been born he had opened up to her about how much he was missing parts of his old life.

Now, as he lay in bed with his head still aching, in that half state between sleep and wakefulness, his mind flicked back to last night's conversation.

'I'm planning to find another home for Ninja because it isn't fair on him,' he had told Phoebe. 'He's too young to be kicking his heels in a field and only going out a couple of times a week. The truth is, I haven't got the time for him any more. And there's no way around that. There are only twenty-four hours in a day.'

She had looked at him aghast.

'Phoebe, it's not that I don't love being a family – please don't think that. It's just that we have so much more on and all the bits that used to make it seem worthwhile have gone.'

'The horse bits?'

'Yeah, the horse bits.' He'd run a hand through his hair and looked at her. 'It's not just riding and competing on Ninja. I knew that would have to go. It's being a riding instructor too. I miss teaching far more than I thought I would. It was always more of a vocation than a job. But I don't think I fully realised that until I stopped.'

'I should have realised it though.'

'Why should you? You're not telepathic.'

'Because I know you. You've always loved horses. You adore Ninja. You love teaching, and competing has been a big part of your life for years. Sam, you've always been part horse, haven't you? I've been able to go back to work doing what I love and you haven't. I've been selfish.'

'No, you haven't.'

'But there should be a balance, Sam. It can't all be hard work.'

'Horses are time consuming though. And competing even more so. And I'm pretty sure I'm not going to be able to fit tutoring pupils around everything else.'

'Maybe you could if you cut down your hours at Hendrie's. Isn't that why your dad packed up the kitchen fitting, so he could help more?'

'Yes, but Ma wants to cut her hours too.'

'And that's so she and my mum can help out with Lily. They want to be grandmas, Sam, and we should let them. We should set up a proper rota instead of this ad hoc stuff we do now. My mum's going to have a lot more time after Christmas when she's properly retired. You could launch yourself as a riding instructor working from Puddleduck. Isn't tutoring pretty lucrative?'

Sam hadn't seen her so animated for ages. This was the Phoebe he remembered. The Phoebe he loved.

Setting up his own riding instructor business from Puddleduck wouldn't be as simple as all that. But it was possible. Anything was possible. And possibilities made the world a much sunnier and more joyful place.

He'd told her about going to the pub with Judy and how he'd regretted it as soon as he'd agreed to it. They had both cried a little too. Such honesty was an emotional rollercoaster. But what he did know was that their lovemaking last night had been amazing. Better than it had been before Lily had been born. The bed still smelled of them. Sam smiled, still in his half-awake, half-asleep place.

Then he rolled over in bed and realised that Phoebe wasn't in it. He hadn't heard her get up. He opened his eyes and checked his watch. It was still early. Half an hour before normal getting up time. And it was Sunday, so not a work day for either of them. He swung his legs over the side of the bed and pulled on his joggers. Lily wasn't in her crib either.

He found them downstairs in the kitchen. Phoebe, still in her robe, was making toast and she'd clearly just fed Roxie, who was picking out the meat from the biscuits and leaving a trail of mess across the floor. Lily, still in her nighttime romper suit, was in her play gym. She had rolled onto her stomach, something she'd just learned to do, and she could hold her head up for short periods. He and Phoebe greeted every new milestone with glee. It wasn't all hard work. There were moments of absolute joy too.

'You're up early.' Sam went yawning across the kitchen. 'Is everything OK?'

'Everything's fine, honey. I actually had the best night's sleep ever. I think it was because we had that brilliant chat last night. I feel so much better now I know how it really is with you as well.'

'You do? And there was me thinking you'd feel better if you didn't know I was struggling.' He shook his head at the irony. Phoebe had no sign of an emotional hangover at all. She looked bright eyed and bouncy.

'You do know it's Sunday, don't you, Pheebs? When we normally have a lie-in.' He raised his eyebrows suggestively.

'I do. But I figured...' She shot him a glance. '...that as we made up in bed so spectacularly last night, you might be tired. You were snoring pretty loudly.'

'Hmmm. Not so romantic.' He grinned. 'Fair comment. I hope I didn't wake you up with that.'

'You didn't. I've actually just been looking at the calendar. Mum texted me this morning to remind me we need to chat about Christmas when I have time. She wants to know what we want her to bring so she can get it organised. She also reminded me that she's currently got the whole of January free for babysitting duties so she was asking which days we'd like her to do.'

'That's very organised of her.'

'You know my mum. She said she was going to liaise with yours too, so they could coordinate days.'

'At this rate we won't have anything to do,' Sam murmured, grabbing a slice of toast off the table, which it looked like Phoebe had already buttered, and taking a bite.

'Oh, I think we will.' She came across to join him. 'You can start setting up your riding instructor business.'

'I might not get too many takers in January. The ground's a bit hard.'

'But you'll need to set things up, won't you? You're going to need to advertise it, and won't you need another horse? Or were you thinking of using Ninja for your students?'

'Wow, you have been thinking this through. But I don't think I'd need a horse. Most students will bring their own.'

'Ideally we'd have an indoor school,' Phoebe went on happily. 'Then it wouldn't matter about the weather.'

'Yes, that's true, but they cost a fortune. And I don't just mean to build, I mean the rates that have to be paid on them.'

'Business loan?' Phoebe grabbed a piece of toast too and ate it while she made up a bottle for Lily.

'Um. Wow. I guess it's worth finding out about.' Sam felt dazed. This, he thought, was the reason Phoebe was a high-flyer and he had always travelled through life at a much more sedate pace. 'Have we got room for an indoor school now we've got the dog field?'

'I think so. Yes. We should do a recce. We could do it today. Lily loves going down to see the neddies, and Roxie's always up for a walk. Maybe you could go riding too.'

'O... kaaay.' He drew the word out. 'I'm sure we can fit some of that in.'

'And later on this afternoon,' Phoebe continued happily, 'I thought we could take Lily to see Father Christmas and his elves in the grotto.'

'That sounds brilliant. Where's that?'

'The closest one's at Lymington. Apparently it's a half-hour experience. There are professional actors and musicians. And I know Lily's a bit young but it'll still be fun, won't it?'

'It would be fun. I'm totally up for that.'

They decided to go for their walk just before lunch. Phoebe had insisted Sam go riding first and he knew she was still feeling guilty about deleting Judy's voicemail, and was trying to make it up to him.

But it was one of the best rides he'd had for ages. It was a crisply cold December day, and there had been a hard frost overnight which had only just melted by the time he'd tacked up Ninja and rode him out into the New Forest.

Sam felt a lightness as he trotted along the sandier forest paths and slowed to a walk where the ground was too hard to risk spraining his horse's legs. He knew that some of his buoyant mood was down to the fact they'd agreed he wouldn't sell Ninja, although he'd said he wasn't going to rule out putting him out on loan, should the right home come along.

'The way I see it,' Phoebe had said, 'is that we need a short-term solution, not a long-term one. Have you considered that someone else could help with Ninja's exercise for a while? I'm sure we must know someone who'd jump at the chance. Maybe Archie would know someone, or even one of the volunteers. That way you'd be able to keep him relatively fit and you'd still ride him too. And then once we get a bit more of a proper work-life balance after Christmas you could start riding more again, and in the spring maybe do the odd competition.'

He hadn't considered it. But he'd agreed with Phoebe that it was worth a try. He had nothing to lose. And if it didn't work out they could think again.

* * *

The Father Christmas grotto exceeded both Sam and Phoebe's expectations. It had been set up in a huge marquee on the edge of the forest, which had been decked out to look like a cave and was full of twinkling lights. There were dozens of Christmas trees festooned with glittering silver baubles and a full-size piano where a male elf dressed in red and green and wearing a bobble hat with a jingling bell was playing Christmas songs.

Father Christmas himself was sitting on a white and brown fur-covered throne in one corner surrounded by presents and strumming a guitar. Another elf close by shook a tambourine. All of them were incredibly cheery and clearly having a whale of a time, encouraging the small crowd of children and their parents to sing along with them.

The atmosphere was gorgeous. Phoebe had thought Lily might find it all a bit overwhelming but she was wide-eyed and as happy as she'd been when she'd met her last Father Christmas.

When it was their turn to go and collect a present, Lily wasn't at all fazed about sitting on the big man's lap for a photo, as long as she could see her parents on either side of her.

By the time they came out of the grotto into the swiftly gathering dusk they were all in high spirits.

'This is what it's all about, Sam,' Phoebe murmured as he strapped Lily back into her buggy. 'Magic and sparkle and joy. We're always going to remember this day.'

Lily waved her arms in agreement and Sam bent to kiss them both.

'I know,' he said. 'And I think I've just spotted a hot chestnut stall over there. Do you fancy some?'

'Yes, please. It's ages since I've had hot chestnuts.'

While Sam queued up to get some, Phoebe took Lily to see the glittering lit-up model of a full-size reindeer and sleigh that stood near the entrance, just outside the marquee. She'd been relieved to discover there were no real reindeers at the grotto when she'd booked it. She'd always felt that a patch of muddy England was no place for a reindeer, however well it might be looked after.

Lily was just as enchanted with the lit-up version. She

stretched out her hands towards it. 'Donk,' she exclaimed in delight.

'Reindeer, darling,' Phoebe told her. 'It's a bit like a donk.'

'Donk. Dahdonk. Donkeeeee.'

So much for her saying 'Daddy' then. Sam had been right.

She'd be saying more words soon. Phoebe couldn't believe how fast she was growing up. She wanted to treasure every single precious moment. She waved as she saw Sam coming back towards them with two steaming paper cups of hot chestnuts. Maybe she wouldn't tell him what Lily had just said. Some fibs were kind ones. She looked at her daughter and mouthed the word 'Dad-deee. Say, Dad-deee.'

'Donkeeee,' Lily yelled excitedly, just as Sam reached them.

He laughed. 'I told you that would be her first word.'

'I know you did, darling. It was the reindeer that set her off.' Phoebe pointed. 'I'm sure she'll say "Daddy" next though.'

'As long as she's talking and as long as she's happy, she can say whatever she likes. I don't mind.'

He blew Lily a kiss. Then they ate the hot chestnuts as they strolled back towards the car beneath a now starry darkening sky with the faint sounds of the Christmas songs following them. Phoebe couldn't remember ever feeling so happy.

23

Phoebe, Sam, Maggie, and the mothers had a family confab about January childcare arrangements. This had been revised from their original plans. Phoebe would still go back to work full time as they'd agreed and Sam would have Lily on Mondays, Tuesdays and Fridays. That meant he could work at Hendrie's on Wednesdays and Thursdays. The plan was for him to pick up his tutoring commitments at Brook on a Saturday once more while they looked into the practicalities of him teaching from Puddleduck.

Maggie and Eddie would have Lily on Wednesdays and Jan and Louella would share Thursdays and Saturdays.

'We'll trial it,' Phoebe said. 'If it doesn't work we'll change it.'

Everyone was happy with that.

But first there was Christmas to organise.

Sam and Phoebe went to town putting up decorations at Puddleduck Farm. They had two Christmas trees, which they collected from a nearby farm. Both of them were rooted and in pots so they could be planted outside afterwards. One was in the kitchen and one in the front room and they spent a happy couple of hours decorating them both with Lily, who loved the sparkly silver tinsel and the shiny red and gold baubles.

The paper chains they'd made were strung up around the kitchen and the hall, and bunches of mistletoe adorned several doorways. A snow globe Phoebe had owned since she was tiny had pride of place on the front room mantlepiece and there were so many Christmas cards they ran out of places to put them. To Phoebe's disappointment there was no actual snow, nor was there any forecast. It wasn't likely to be a white Christmas. It rarely was in the New Forest, although they sometimes had a sprinkling in February or March.

Puddleduck Vets looked pretty festive too, although they'd decided not to have a tree this year, in case of injury to any animal patients that might want to sniff it. Also, putting trees inside and expecting dogs to stop doing what dogs usually did on trees was just unrealistic and impractical.

Phoebe took her staff out for their Christmas meal on the Saturday before Christmas. She'd booked the Italian in Bridgeford and everyone had brought their partners.

The Italian was jampacked. Several Christmas parties were clearly being held there and the atmosphere was very festive. Red and green streamers hung from the ceiling, matching the red, green and white décor of the restaurant, and there were silver crackers and party poppers on every table, all of which were being put to good use.

The gorgeous scents of basil and garlic and cinnamon hung in the air, mingling with the smells of wine and beer and customer colognes. Everyone was dressed to the nines. Marcus and Natasha had let their hair down for once and had both had a glass of wine before the main course had even arrived.

Seth and Myra, who never drank much, had said they'd be

happy to be taxi drivers after the meal, and Phoebe, who didn't drink much either, had also offered to drive people home.

Maggie and Eddie were babysitting Lily so Sam was able to go along too. Max, who'd recently started dating a vet he'd met while he'd been doing the course on APHs, had brought her along. Her name was India, and Seth, who'd met her before, had told Phoebe she was 'a proper character'.

It turned out he was right. India was a very pretty dark-haired and diminutive woman who was a specialist in exotics, and she regaled them with stories about tarantulas, red-eyed tree frogs and snakes.

'Once I got called out to a python that the client said was lethargic. When I got there, Monty' – she rolled her eyes – 'had escaped because the client hadn't closed the vivarium properly – obviously not that lethargic then.' She gave a throaty chuckle.

'What did you do?' Myra asked her, agog.

'The client asked me if I'd stay ten minutes while he looked for him – he didn't think he'd have got far – so I sat on the sofa with my feet up. Just in case Monty made a sudden reappearance.'

'I'd have done the same,' Seth said with a shudder. 'I'm not a fan of snakes.'

'Did he make a sudden reappearance?' Marcus wanted to know.

'Yes, he did. There was I, happily sitting with my feet up looking the other way, and then Monty slithered along the back of the sofa and tongue flicked my ear.'

'Oh my God.'

'He never did.'

'Blimey O'Reilly.'

There was a chorus of deliciously horrified exclamations from everyone around the table.

'Did he really do that?' Natasha asked, wide-eyed.

'He did. I don't think I've ever moved so fast in my life. And I'm not even that scared of snakes.'

'I am,' Seth said. 'I'd have had a heart attack.'

'He would,' Myra confirmed. 'So what happened next?'

'The client was very apologetic and he caught him, and we both agreed that Monty seemed to have recovered from his lethargy and didn't need any further investigation. He was the biggest python I'd ever seen though. At least ten feet.'

'I didn't think pythons even got that long,' Marcus gasped.

'They don't,' Seth said, and India threw her head back and laughed.

'No, I may have exaggerated slightly about that bit.'

Max put his arm around her and she winked at him. He was clearly besotted with her. Phoebe was pleased.

Lots of women made it clear they'd have loved to date Max, the practice heartthrob, but she'd never known him be interested in any of them. She could see why he liked India. She was gorgeous, uber smart and clearly didn't take herself too seriously either.

At the end of the evening, Phoebe slipped away to the bar to pay the bill. Myra spotted her on her way back from the ladies' and the older woman came across to speak to her.

'Thank you for inviting me along. It's been really, really lovely. Seth and I don't get invited to too many parties these days.'

'You are so welcome.' Phoebe remembered they didn't have much in the way of family. Before she'd had Lily, she and Myra had once had a heart-to-heart about trying and failing to have a baby. It hadn't been long after Phoebe had had her miscarriage and Myra had confided she'd had several miscarriages herself, which was why she and Seth didn't have any children.

'Seth has shown me photos of your gorgeous Lily.' Myra's eyes misted and Phoebe touched her arm.

'You should come and meet her some time. I'd have asked you before, but I wasn't sure how you were... around... babies...' She broke off, aware that she sounded crass.

But she was relieved to see Myra was smiling. 'Oh, my dear, that's very sensitive and thoughtful of you, but I'm fine. I love little ones. Even though we didn't manage to have any of our own.'

'I haven't forgotten the one we lost either,' Phoebe blurted. 'I think of him often.'

Myra nodded. 'I don't think we ever really do forget them but we do move on. We have to move on.' She was still smiling but her eyes were a little more serious now.

'Come over after all this madness is over.' Phoebe gestured around them at the party that was going full swing in every corner of the Italian. 'You'd always be very welcome.'

'Thank you, my dear. I'd really like that. I will.'

* * *

Phoebe had loved Christmas since she was a little girl. And for as long as she could remember, most of her Christmases had been spent at Puddleduck Farm.

Even when she and her brother Frazier had been very small, she had fond memories of them being packed up along with boxes of food and drink and bags of presents and transported over to what had in those days been a dairy farm.

Cows couldn't be left so Maggie and Farmer Pete just had open house from 23 December, where everyone mucked in with the Christmas preparations and cooking and it was all pretty casual. Phoebe had loved being in the big old farmhouse kitchen, which was always full of dogs and cats and sometimes other animals Maggie was looking after. The only rules were that children didn't go into any of the fields where cows were grazing, and they were careful around hot things.

In those days, the Aga had been powered by wood like the fires, and someone was always running in and out with armfuls of wood and kindling to stoke them up. Maggie hadn't had it converted until the nineties.

Part of the routine of childhood Christmases was that Frazier and Phoebe wrote out a note to Father Christmas to tell him they would be at Puddleduck Farm rather than Five Oaks Drive that year and could he kindly use chimney number two when he came calling and they'd make sure they didn't have a fire in it that night. It was so exciting. On Christmas Eve, she and her brother would be packed off to bed early while the grown-ups sat around drinking sherry and eating mince pies.

Not very much had changed in the last couple of decades either. They'd lost Farmer Pete, of course, but everyone was really pleased that Maggie had found love again with Eddie, who'd been a loyal farmhand for years. Apart from the occasional exception, everyone still gathered at Puddleduck Farm for Christmas Day at the very least. Frazier and Alexa brought their children most years.

Last year things had been a bit different because Maggie and Eddie had moved into a bungalow and had handed the reins of both Puddleduck Pets, the sanctuary, and the Puddleduck farmhouse itself over to Phoebe and Sam. But the family had still come for the main event.

This year things were different again, because Lily was here, and it had been raised by Maggie that Phoebe and Sam might not want hordes of people descending on them, but they'd said that they did. They definitely did.

'We couldn't imagine not spending Christmas with you all, could we, Sam?' Phoebe had said, and Sam agreed with her wholeheartedly. In between the hectic run-up to Christmas, he'd been sorting through some of the practicalities of setting up his own business.

Not everyone was staying over at Christmas. Although Puddleduck Farm had four bedrooms, it would have been a squash with their ever-increasing family. Alexa and Frazier were bringing their three little ones over on Christmas Eve so they could wake up and open their presents together. They'd already changed their address on their letters to Father Christmas.

But Maggie and Eddie wanted to sleep in their own bed so they were coming over on Christmas Day morning so they could watch the kids open their presents and Louella and James had decided to do the same thing.

'I'm not sure whether to bring the dogs or not,' Maggie said. 'Tiny's fine but Buster's getting decidedly crotchety these days. I think he's feeling his age. He might not be too happy around a bunch of overexcited kids.'

'It's up to you, but I know Roxie would love to see them. I'd be quite happy if you and Eddie wanted to hole up in the back room with the dogs when it gets too much. It could be your own personal escape room.'

Maggie laughed. 'Eddie just turns his hearing aid off when he wants to escape, love. But that does sound like a tempting proposition. OK, we will bring them then. We'll be able to stay longer if we do. I must admit I don't like leaving Buster on his own for too long these days. I think he has a touch of dementia.'

Jan and Ian Hendrie were also coming over first thing on Christmas Day and were staying for lunch too.

Everyone was helping with food. Louella and Jan were

organising that side of things and had set up a WhatsApp group to do it called Christmas Family Food.

* * *

Seth had offered to do emergency cover on Christmas Day because he and Myra were having a quiet one this year. Max had said he'd do Boxing Day. The three vets were taking it in turns for the rest of the period and Phoebe lived on the premises anyway. If anyone actually turned up with an animal she could be at the practice inside five minutes.

On Christmas Eve, it was so quiet that they closed the practice doors at lunchtime. Phoebe packed everyone off with a bottle of their favourite tipple and an M&S gift voucher. She felt extra indebted to her staff this year. They'd all stepped up to the plate while she'd been on maternity leave. She knew she could never have kept the practice going without them.

And that went for Natasha too. Natasha was also going home early. Phoebe had persuaded her to leave at lunchtime and she was just walking across the yard to make sure Natasha had gone when she saw her walking up to meet her.

She looked worried.

Phoebe frowned. 'Hiya. I thought you'd have gone by now. What are you still doing here?'

'I was just about to go when someone brought a cat in. They said they found him in the forest, but he's not in very good condition. I don't think it's anything serious. He's got a few cuts and bruises, but I'm not certain.'

'Oh, I'll have a look.'

'Are you sure? It's Christmas Eve.'

'Of course I'm sure. I'm on call. Where is he?'

'I put him in a crate in the barn where we used to keep

Saddam. I didn't want to put him in the cattery in case he has anything contagious.'

Phoebe nodded as they both headed for the barn, which was used to store hay as well as being a place where animals could go if they needed to be in quarantine for any reason.

Natasha pushed open the door to admit them and it was a few moments before Phoebe's eyes adjusted to the gloom. The air was full of the sweet fragrance of hay.

'Do you remember that time when the Meow Master came to cure Saddam of his vicious tendencies?' Phoebe said. 'I can never come in here without thinking about that.'

'When his toupee ended up on a haybale. How could I forget?' Natasha smiled. 'I don't think I've ever laughed so much in my life. I thought I was going to explode. The poor chap. I've never seen anyone leg it so quickly. Although we do owe him one, I've often thought.'

'Do we? What for?'

'It was because of him that Marcus set off on his quest to become a behaviourist. If the Meow Master hadn't been so utterly hopeless, Marcus wouldn't have been so motivated.'

'No, that's true.'

They'd reached the crate and Phoebe saw the outline of one of the biggest cats she'd seen in a while. He was a pale silver-grey colour and had clearly once been a handsome boy, but his fur was matted now and in places bits were missing altogether.

'Jeez, I see what you mean. He's been through the wars, hasn't he?'

'You can't tell because of the fur but he's pretty thin too.'

Phoebe crouched down for a closer look. The cat's green eyes were half closed with what looked like an infection. 'Hello, sweetie.' The cat shrank away from her and she frowned. 'He doesn't look much like he's used to humans either, does he? He's a Maine Coon, isn't he?'

'I thought that too. Oh my God...' Natasha gasped and they looked at each other. They'd clearly just had the same thought.

'Wasn't it a Maine Coon that woman lost?' Phoebe asked. 'We had a poster up for a while, didn't we? What colour was that?'

'I think it was a silver-grey male. Same as this one.' They both looked back into the crate.

'Do you know if she ever found hers?' Phoebe asked.

'I don't think she did. She never asked us to take the poster down. So it could be this one. But if it is him, where on earth has he been all this time? Shall I go and give her a ring? It could be a Christmas miracle him turning up like this.'

'Let me have a proper look at him first,' Phoebe cautioned. 'A Christmas miracle would be wonderful. But I want to make sure he's all right first. I wouldn't like to present her with a Christmas nightmare.'

24

A few minutes later, both Natasha and Phoebe were in one of the consulting rooms with the cat, still in his crate.

'Be careful, he tried to bite me when I put him in there,' Natasha warned. 'Shall I hold him for you while you examine him?'

'Thanks, that would be great.' Phoebe's fallback method of examining animals who might be a bit prickly either physically or metaphorically was a towel. Seth had taught her this when she'd first started working for him. It was great for avoiding bites, scratches or even APH prickles as he'd reminded her recently.

The Maine Coon hissed and spat at her as she gently wrapped him in the towel and lifted him out.

'If you can try to keep all four paws out of harm's way that would be great,' she said to Natasha, but the big cat wasn't having any of it. He fought and wriggled and hissed and spat.

'I think it might be kinder if I sedate him,' Phoebe said after a few seconds. 'He's not having it, is he?'

'No, you're right. Bless him. He's not a fan of humans, that's for sure.'

'Yes, it's odd. Most Maine Coons are quite docile. They're known as gentle giants. We've seen a few in the practice.'

While they waited for the sedation to take effect, they chatted about Christmas. Natasha and Marcus were staying at home.

'We've got too many animals to go anywhere, but to be honest, we'd rather have a quiet one. It's all such a big fuss for one day. And don't get me started on the cost. We've agreed to buy each other one not-too-expensive thing each and spend some money on the cottage. We could do with a kitchen makeover.'

'Sounds ideal.' Phoebe had fond memories of the little kitchen at Woodcutter's, which was just about big enough to get in a small table and chairs. The kitchen had been getting a touch shabby when she and Sam had lived there, she seemed to remember.

'We've got the animals presents, of course. Saddam's got a Christmas stocking.'

Phoebe smiled at the thought of the half-feral cat, former terroriser of small dogs, opening his own Christmas stocking.

'Right then, I think this sedation's taken effect, but if you could still hold him for me, I'd be grateful.'

A few minutes later, having completed her examination and also scanned for a microchip – there was one – Phoebe frowned. 'OK, you're right, the cuts and bruises aren't too serious, but there's something else too. I'll need the results of this swab to be sure, but I think he's got feline herpesvirus.'

'Is that the same as the human herpes virus?'

'It's along those lines, but it's specific to cats. It can only be transmitted cat to cat and you'd usually find it where there are lots of cats. So it doesn't look like this fellow here has been living on his own. I'd say he'd been kept with other cats. That doesn't explain why he's underweight though. Or the minor injuries.'

When she'd weighed him he'd been about 15 per cent underweight.

'Could he have been with feral cats?' Natasha asked.

'I suppose so, but where? And why would he have been wandering around the forest? Where did you say the woman found him?'

'She said he was actually in a ditch. It was her dog that found him. He was tangled up in some barbed wire, hence the cuts to his paws. Luckily her dog's used to cats and just barked at him. But he was on his own. No other cats and there weren't any houses around that she could see. Which is why she brought him here.'

'Very odd. Well, as we saw, he's got a microchip. So in a minute we'll have a look on the system. That should shed some light on it. We'd better have him in here in the quarantine crate overnight, I think. Feline herpesvirus is very contagious.'

'Is it curable?'

'It's manageable, but it's not something you can ever get rid of entirely. It tends to flare up periodically. Although there's a lot we can do about that, these days. There are some great new antivirals.'

'So he's got a chance. Bless him.'

'We'll get him on some special food too, so we can start upping his weight. That'll help.'

They settled the cat in the quarantine kennel, and then Natasha helped Phoebe give the examining room another deep clean before they both did the same with themselves, washed their hands and went into reception to check out the microchip on the system.

The record showed that the cat – a Maine Coon as they'd suspected – was called Oscar and belonged to a Mrs Denise Wyatt.

'That's her,' Natasha said with a smile. 'That's the woman who reported him missing. Well, this is going to make her day. It's a pity he's got something wrong with him, but it's good news that it's treatable.'

'Do you want to do the honours?' Phoebe handed her the Puddleduck Vets landline and Natasha took it eagerly.

Phoebe watched Natasha smiling as she listened to the reaction on the other end of the phone, before putting her hand over the receiver. 'She wants to come and see him straightaway. Is that OK? I can wait if you've got to get home for Lily. She said she can be here in about twenty minutes.'

'It's fine. I'll wait too. I'll just nip in and tell Sam what I'm doing.'

* * *

Mrs Denise Wyatt was overjoyed to be reacquainted with Oscar when it finally happened about forty minutes later.

The big cat was clearly just as overjoyed to be reacquainted with her too. He made little kitten-like mewling noises as he rubbed his head against her hand and purred and purred. Even without the microchip evidence it was obvious that these two were the best of friends.

Phoebe swallowed a lump in her throat as she watched the joyful reunion. She could see Natasha was blinking back tears too.

Then finally Denise turned back towards them. 'This is the best Christmas present I could possibly have. Thank you so much. I can't believe it's him. I know you said it was him because of the microchip. But I still needed to see it with my own eyes.'

She had tears running down her face but she didn't seem to care. 'Oh, my goodness. It's a miracle. It really is. I never thought I'd see him again. Can I take him home? Can what he has be treated there? Or does he need to stay here? How serious is it?'

'He doesn't need to stay here, no, but he is infectious. Do you have any other cats?'

Denise nodded. 'We do. My husband just got me a kitten. We picked her up yesterday, as it happens, so we could settle her in for Christmas. I know you shouldn't get an animal just before Christmas but the breeder seemed really nice. And we explained that we'd had one before – we weren't just impulse buyers or anything. She's another Maine Coon. She's a similar colour to Oscar. That's why Ken bought her for me. We've called her Freda. We weren't trying to replace Oscar – that would be impossible, but I truly never thought I'd ever see him again.'

She turned towards Oscar again. 'Oh, my sweetie. You're going to love your new friend. I can't believe you needed to sedate him for treatment.' Denise turned to Phoebe with tears in her eyes. 'He's usually so friendly.'

Phoebe believed her and she didn't want to spoil the moment by saying she was pretty sure Oscar had been kept by someone who wasn't such a cat lover as Denise, so she didn't voice this.

Instead she said, 'Kittens are very vulnerable to this infection, so Oscar would need to be kept separate from Freda. Otherwise you'll have two of them with it. There are medications that Freda can have as a preventative for the future. Do you have her registered with a vet? I'm assuming she's already been microchipped and had her first vaccination?'

'She's not had her first vaccination yet.' Denise flushed.

'We've got that booked in for the New Year. It was our fault, not the breeder's. She wasn't quite old enough and we wanted to take her home before Christmas.'

'I see.' Phoebe felt warning bells ringing. No reputable breeder she knew of would dream of letting a kitten go before its first vaccination at Christmas or any other time of year.

'How old is she, exactly?'

'Five and half weeks. She's fully weaned so it's only a little bit early, and the breeder said their vet couldn't do the jab until January, due to the Christmas rush. But Ken did make it very clear we'd get it done.'

'Do you mind me asking where you got her from?'

'I must admit I don't know all the details because Ken bought her, not me. She's a Christmas present, as I said. But I think he saw an advert online. He said he'd seen the kittens with their mother, as you should do. And we did get some paperwork. We're not completely naïve.'

'I'm sure you're not.' Phoebe hoped she sounded more reassured than she felt.

Denise changed the subject. 'I'm so grateful you found Oscar. How much do I owe you?'

Phoebe told her, and as they went out into reception to settle up, Phoebe reiterated what she'd said about it being especially important to keep the cats separate.

'There's no reason for Oscar to stay here, you can do the medication yourself at home, but I'd hate your kitten to fall ill. She might not survive. Kittens don't have the same immunity as adult cats.'

'I understand. And I will make sure that Oscar's kept well away from Freda. We've got a big utility room. He'll have plenty of space in there. And Freda will have the run of the conservatory until she's housetrained. Also...' She hesitated. 'Would you mind if we registered both Freda and Oscar as patients here? I can cancel the other vet.'

'Of course not. I'll put them into the system now.'

As she typed in the details, Phoebe said as casually as she could, 'I'd be quite interested in the details of that breeder if you could maybe ask Ken. Or even the details of the advert would be good. I can give you my mobile number so you could maybe text them through.'

'OK. I'll ask him and I'll text them through to you later,' Denise said. 'They won't get into trouble, will they? The guy was really nice.'

'No, no.' Phoebe smiled reassuringly. The breeder might be guilty of some pretty sharp practice, but she doubted they'd done anything criminal.

* * *

By the time Denise had put Oscar gently into a cat basket into the back of a brand-new Land Rover and they'd driven off, it was nearly three thirty.

'Thanks for helping out,' Phoebe told Natasha. 'Marcus will be wondering where you are, won't he? Sam just texted me to see how much longer I'll be too.'

'At least we can tell them you've been performing Christmas miracles and not having to deal with some sad emergency.'

'Hmm, yes, although I'm not so sure about the Christmas miracle side of things. I mean, don't get me wrong. I'm thrilled we were able to reunite Oscar with his owner, but I wasn't so thrilled to hear about that kitten.'

'No, that was definitely off. I can't imagine a breeder letting one of a litter go without a first vaccination. That was very odd. Hopefully she'll let you know about the breeder.'

'Yes, fingers crossed,' Phoebe said as she locked up her practice for the second time that Christmas Eve. 'I will definitely keep you posted on that one.' She hesitated. 'This is a bit of a long shot, but I don't suppose you've still got the number of that guy who tried to rehome our kittens and pass them off as Savannahs, have you?'

'I do. Why? Do you think there's a connection?'

'It's possible, isn't it? Definitely worth checking anyway.'

'I'll forward you the number.' Natasha whipped out her phone. 'There you go. Done.'

'Thanks. Have a brilliant Christmas, won't you?'

'You too. See you in a couple of days. Let me know if you need any help with anything at Puddleduck Pets.'

'We'll be fine. We've got it covered. Sam and I will be on the case tomorrow. Maggie and Eddie will help. It's a good excuse not to do any cooking.'

'Who's doing that?'

'My mum and Jan and Alexa. They're all much better cooks than me or Sam anyway. We're doing animals and childminding duties. The kids adore the animals. Lily's the same.'

'Have fun,' Natasha called.

'We will.' Phoebe walked back up to the house. The events of the last couple of hours had unsettled her. There was definitely something odd going on. But in the meantime there was Christmas, Lily's first Christmas, and she felt a flutter of excitement in her heart at the prospect of having her whole family over to Puddleduck Farm.

25

To Phoebe's disappointment, Denise didn't text her the number of the breeder. Maybe she'd had second thoughts. Or maybe she was busy with Christmas, or maybe her husband had decided it was a bad idea to report the breeder to a vet. It was frustrating.

Phoebe wasn't even entirely sure why she wanted the number, but she just had a hunch that it might be useful. She decided to put it out of her mind for now. She remembered what Maggie had said about her being an amateur sleuth. That had been a reference to her wanting to find out about the man who'd tried to rehome the kittens. This was unlikely to be connected to that. Besides, Christmas wasn't the time to be focusing on anything other than family.

So that's what she did. Alexa and Frazier arrived with Bertie, Flo and baby Jake at just after four as planned and because she hadn't seen her brother and sister-in-law and nieces and nephews for what felt like ages, although they'd all come over to meet Lily when she was a newborn, there was a lot of catching up to do.

It was chaos, having four little ones under five to look after, and it was exhausting, but it was fun too.

'I've no idea how you manage three of them,' Phoebe said to Alexa in admiration as she, Alexa and Frazier got the kids ready for bed later. 'Just one's enough for me.'

'I'm used to it,' Alexa told her with a serene smile. 'And this probably sounds nuts but it helps that Flo and Bertie are twins. They entertain each other a fair bit.'

'You mean they wind each other up,' Frazier said. 'Or more to the point, Flo winds Bertie up. She's a little madam.'

Flo poked her tongue out at her father. 'I'm a good little madam, aren't I, Daddy?'

'Sometimes,' he acknowledged, trying to look stern but failing. It was obvious that his daughter was the apple of his eye.

'What's the chances of the twins staying in bed?' Sam murmured, after baths and bedtime stories and goodnight kisses had been done and everyone had looked at the Santa tracker app one last time.

'They're under strict instructions that if they're not good, Father Christmas won't stop by,' Frazier told him.

And actually they did stay in bed while the adults had supper at the kitchen table and chatted downstairs and Alexa complimented Phoebe and Sam on the homemade paper chains and the six-foot potted dark green tree which was on its third set of lights, and the posh party nibbles they were having for supper.

'They're all shop bought,' Phoebe told her. 'We got them out of the freezer from the farm shop. We haven't had time to cook.'

'I'm not surprised.' Alexa glanced across at her. 'You've got a baby, you're both working, and you've got an animal sanctuary to oversee. Just the thought of all that makes me tired.'

'I was going to suggest we play a game,' Phoebe said when

supper was finally cleared away. 'A board game? Or maybe Charades as it's Christmas.'

Sam groaned. 'Can we leave that for tomorrow? You know how much Maggie loves it.'

'She does not,' Phoebe said before realising he was joking. 'Although Eddie was good at that last year. And Dad's quite good.'

'He hams it up for the kids.'

'I'll get some more drinks,' Sam said, getting up from the table. 'Same again, everyone?'

They nodded and when he came back he was carrying Phoebe's phone. 'That's pinged a couple of times. I thought I'd better tell you in case it was urgent.'

Phoebe opened the messages and realised they were both from Denise. Not only had she sent over the breeder's number, she'd sent over a screenshot of the advert too.

Phoebe sent a message back to thank her and then because everyone was looking at her expectantly, she told them what had happened earlier and why she had wanted the number of the breeder in the first place.

'You think he may be connected to the man who tried to get your kittens and sell them on?' Frazier asked.

'Exactly that.'

'And is it the same number?'

Phoebe checked back against the number Natasha had sent her. 'No, it's not,' she said, feeling disappointed. 'That's a shame. I thought I might be on to something there.'

'You could find out what other ads he has running if you do a reverse image search,' Frazier suggested. 'Here. I'll show you.'

A few minutes later he'd found three more online adverts for kittens that had the same photos as the one Denise had sent over, although two of them had different numbers.

'Look,' Frazier said triumphantly. 'That one matches your number. Looks like they use a few. They might not want anyone to be able to pin them down if they're up to no good.'

'Are they up to no good?' Alexa's girl-next-door innocence was clear. 'It's not a crime to sell kittens, is it?'

'No, it's not, as long as you actually breed them yourself, and don't get them from somewhere else.' Phoebe filled her in about Lucy's Law.

'What about Emilia's kittens?' Sam said, his face thoughtful. 'Could they possibly have been stolen to order? Can kittens be stolen to order?'

'I imagine anything can be stolen to order,' Phoebe said. 'Wasn't there something on the news recently about a load of cheese that was stolen to order?'

'Twenty-two tonnes of cheese from a UK dairy,' Frazier said promptly. He'd always had a near photographic memory for trivial facts, which made him a very good person to have on a quiz team.

His forehead creased into a frown. 'And I seem to recall that one December not so long ago, thieves stole a van load of gourmet pies made by a Michelin-starred chef.'

'Wow.' Alexa looked shocked. 'You're right. I remember that, although I've never heard about it happening with animals.'

'It would be interesting to hear Maggie's take on that,' Sam said. 'We can ask her tomorrow.'

'Great plan.' Phoebe raised her eyebrows. 'If it diverts Eddie from Charades, I'm sure she'll be absolutely delighted.'

'Right then, who's up for helping me with the Christmas stockings?'

'Let's all do it,' Alexa said. 'It's one of my favourite bits.'

'I'll get the stocking presents from the car,' Frazier said. 'But we'd better not put them in until the kids are definitely asleep. Or they'll be up and opening them long before tomorrow.'

It was great fun, packing the stockings even though they had to wait until past midnight before putting them back into the bedrooms.

Phoebe and Sam had done their best not to overindulge Lily, knowing she'd be spoiled rotten by the grandparents too, and they'd agreed on just one big present for each other, but stockings were different. Stockings were full of tiny surprises, and they'd had the best fun shopping for their baby daughter's first Christmas.

* * *

To Phoebe's surprise, none of the kids, not even Bertie and Flo, woke up before six the next day. Or if they did, they didn't get up until they heard the adults moving around. Phoebe was up first. But once they were up, there was a stocking-opening fest in the kitchen. The tree presents – which took up half of the front room and a good part of the hall – would be opened before lunch, which would happen sometime around two, but there was a lot to do before then.

There were animals to feed and clean, all of which took a lot longer when you were accompanied by children, Sam and Phoebe were discovering. And the rest of the Dashwoods, the Hendries, and Maggie and Eddie and their animals turned up at various intervals.

The excitement in the air at Puddleduck Farm was intense and the children were hyperactive. The levels dropped off a little bit once they had opened their presents, but were rejigged again when Maggie and Eddie suggested everyone go for a walk around Puddleduck Farm and they'd give a prize to whoever spotted the first robin.

'We'll be back in time for lunch,' she told Phoebe with a wink.

And they were. Even though lunch didn't actually get to the table until just after three in the end.

A roast turkey and a nut wellington were served up with at least eight different vegetables, two types of gravy and various sauces. Jan and Alexa had gone to town on the culinary side. Frazier and Eddie were the only ones who could manage Christmas pudding and Christmas-pudding-flavoured ice cream straight after the main course. Everyone else said they'd save it for the evening.

It was as they sat around at various points in the kitchen, with even Snowball and the dogs too full to move far, having had their own Christmas dinners, that Phoebe remembered to ask Maggie whether she had ever heard of kittens being stolen to order.

'I have as it happens. Expensive breeds are worth stealing to order. They tend to be young because the thieves like to get them before they're neutered, so they can be sold on to puppy and kitten mills and used as breeding animals. It's an absolute tragedy.' Her face hardened as she spoke. 'Why do you ask, love? Has one of your clients lost a kitten?'

Phoebe told her about Emilia's kittens disappearing. 'Although Archie did say they'd ruled out thieves the first time, because it's not the kind of place where an opportunist thief would just turn up.'

'You're right there. They'd have to know where they were, but maybe someone did. Then I imagine it would be quite easy. The Holts will have tradespeople going in and out fairly often, I'd have thought.'

'Yes, they would.' Phoebe felt a little chill go through her. 'That's a horrible thought but I think you might be right.' She explained about Emilia having two lots of kittens stolen a few months apart. And then about the Maine Coon that had gone missing back in September, but had been found in the forest the previous day.

'He could have been dumped there,' Maggie said. 'Or he might have escaped from a kitten mill and been living rough for a while. That could explain why he was so thin. Did you say he was a tom cat?'

'I did. Yes.'

'And did you say the couple who owned him had just bought another similar-looking Maine Coon kitten?'

Phoebe suddenly realised where she was going with this. And so did the rest of the room. They'd all been going silent one by one as they'd tuned into the conversation.

'You're thinking the kitten they bought might actually have been sired by Oscar,' she asked Maggie.

'It's possible.' Maggie cleared her throat. 'How old's the kitten? Do the dates match up? Feline gestation's about sixty-odd days, isn't it?'

'Yes, it is. So yes, it could be. Oh, my goodness, I hadn't even thought of that.'

Maggie clicked her tongue. 'Well, the good news is that Denise and her husband are in the perfect position to find out. They've got them both. A simple DNA test would prove it one way or the other.'

'I'd have to clear it with them. But yes, it would certainly give us a good idea. And then we'd have some evidence that their cat had been stolen and used to sire kittens that would be sold on for profit.'

'I'm not sure how you'd prove who he belonged to in the first place.'

'His microchip was never changed. It still has their name and address on the database.'

'So it's unlikely whoever had Oscar released him then. If they didn't bother changing the chip, which of course, technically they couldn't, they were assuming he'd never be found. What about Emilia's kittens? Were they microchipped?'

'Very probably. I could check.'

'Realistically the chances of finding them are slim.' Maggie's eyes were sad. 'They're probably hidden away in some barn somewhere producing litters; what kind of cats were they?'

'Savannahs,' Sam supplied. 'Another valuable breed.'

'But if we could track them down, we'd have plenty of evidence for the police,' Phoebe finished.

'Something to do in your spare time then?' Maggie said, with heavy irony in her voice.

Phoebe sighed. 'You're right. I don't have any spare time. And it would be like looking for a needle in a haystack. Unless of course we knew exactly where Oscar the Maine Coon turned up. Which I could probably find out. He was trapped in a ditch not far from Rufus's place apparently. So if he escaped, then wherever he came from has got to be reasonably local.'

'And Eddie and I do loads of forest walks. We could start with the ditch and work back and see what houses have gardens that back up onto the forest. Then we could do a recce. Couldn't we, love?'

Maggie raised her voice to speak to her husband, but he was already following this conversation and was now shaking his head impatiently.

'There's no need to go messing around in ditches and clambering over fences,' Eddie said.

'Isn't there?' Disappointment flashed across Maggie's face.

Phoebe suppressed a smile. Her grandmother might be in her mid-seventies, but she was definitely still up for an illicit adventure.

'Nah. We just follow the money. We pretend we're customers and go to the front door. The bloke's got enough adverts. We'll find out where he lives that way. We can soon sniff out a rat, I reckon.'

Phoebe looked at them both with a hesitant smile. 'You will be careful, won't you?' She felt a flash of déjà vu. Who else had she said those words to lately?

Oh yes, the owl rescue team.

And that had turned out better than she'd hoped.

26

Phoebe and Sam had never been huge fans of New Year's Eve, so they had a quiet one, just the two of them, and stayed home at Puddleduck. Their main concession to the date was staying up late enough to listen to the chimes of Big Ben on TV and watching the crowds of London revellers before they headed off to bed.

They discussed their New Year resolutions in bed.

'Mine's planning our wedding and getting my new business off the ground,' Sam said. 'What are yours?'

'Helping you plan our wedding,' Phoebe told him happily. 'And helping Maggie to track down that kitten-milling chappie and bringing him to justice.'

* * *

January got off to a busy start. Puddleduck Vets was busy with people catching up after the holidays. It didn't seem to matter how much information there was about dogs and cats not making good Christmas presents, people still got them. The responsible ones registered them and booked them in for vaccinations.

Their vaccination clinics for January were already full to bursting.

Puddleduck Pets had their usual post-Christmas influx of animals that had been unwanted Christmas presents. To Phoebe's dismay, two of these were African pygmy hedgehogs.

'The woman who brought them in said her husband had got them after seeing a piece about them in *New Forest Views*,' Natasha said, flicking back her brown ponytail and widening her eyes in annoyance. 'Wasn't that the piece Tori wrote trying to put people *off* buying them?'

'Yes, it was. But the photos she used were very cute. So I guess it's raised their profile a bit.'

'Obviously for people who look at pictures but can't actually read,' Natasha said in irritation. 'Do we still have that vivarium that was out the back? Can I plug it in in the haybarn?'

'Yes, and yes, but is it worth contacting the hedgehog rescue place again? She's more set up for them than we are here. And she's probably got more chance of rehoming them too.'

'OK, I'll just put them in there temporarily again and then I'll get on to it.'

* * *

Denise had been shocked when Phoebe had mooted Maggie's theory about the possibility of Oscar being stolen for use as a stud cat in a kitten mill.

'Oh, good heavens, that's awful. My poor baby. Do you think that might be how he got that nasty infection?'

'I honestly don't know, but it's possible. He's clearly been with other cats somewhere.'

Phoebe had let this sink in before she mentioned Maggie's suggestion that Oscar might also have actually fathered the kitten that her husband had bought from the 'very nice' breeder.

'We have nothing to base this on apart from the fact that they're very similar looking and the timings would work. But of course it could all just be a coincidence. The breeder your husband got Freda from might be perfectly legitimate.'

'But he might not be.' Denise caught on quickly. 'Can you do DNA tests on cats to check parentage?'

'Yes, you can. It's a simple mouth swab. To be absolutely accurate we would need to test the mother cat too, but that isn't going to be so easy necessarily. Did you say your husband saw the mother cat when he picked up the kittens?'

'Yes, he did, but not in real life. I've already asked him that. It turns out that he saw a video of them all together. When he went to pick up Freda, the man just brought her out to the door to see him. There were two actually. Freda and another kitten that was similar looking but a boy. The man had them both in a box. He said the mother was very shy. Oh, my goodness, that all sounds terribly suspicious when I say it like that. But Ken wasn't suspicious. Looking back now in the cold light of day he definitely shouldn't have bought Freda, should he?'

Phoebe felt her heart sink. Partly because Denise looked so sad and guilty about the whole situation, but also because the breeder had clearly covered his tracks really well.

'It's not your fault. These people are very clever. They're doing this all the time, don't forget, and they know every trick in the book.' She paused. 'I think it's still worth doing the DNA test anyway. If you don't mind. That will give us an idea of parentage. Which could be vital if you were ever thinking of breeding from Freda yourself.' She raised her eyebrows. 'For obvious reasons.'

'Goodness me. Of course. That would never do.' Denise looked horrified.

Phoebe went on gently, 'It would also be really useful if I could have the breeder's address. The place where Ken went to get Freda.'

'Of course. I'll text that over to you. And if it does turn out that it was actually him that stole Oscar, then we could go to the police, couldn't we? Get him arrested and closed down.'

'That's also a possibility. I really hope we could do that, yes.'

'Hmmm. It's more than a possibility. It's a certainty. If the police don't want to deal with it we'd bring a private prosecution.' Denise's eyes flashed with anger. 'I don't think I've told you what Ken does for a living, have I?'

Phoebe shook her head, mystified.

'He's a barrister. He specialises in criminal law.'

'I see. Wow.' Phoebe didn't know whether to be amazed or delighted. The fact that a clearly intelligent and well-educated man had been naïve enough to buy a kitten under such dubious circumstances astounded her. But on the other hand, why would he have known there was a correct protocol for buying a kitten or a puppy if he hadn't done it before? Why would anyone know how to do anything they hadn't done before? It came back to the same thing as the little African pygmy hedgehogs. It was down to education and spreading the word. That's what they'd wanted to do with the Voice for Wildlife campaign but they still hadn't really got that off the ground. Maybe she should make it another New Year resolution to do more about that. Although it seemed that double-page spreads in *New Forest Views* weren't the answer.

'Could we get you to be our expert witness?' Denise asked. 'As our veterinary professional. Would you do that?'

'Yes, of course I would if the need arises, but don't forget this is all supposition at the moment. All we know for sure is that we're dealing with an irresponsible breeder.'

Denise nodded vehemently. 'Let's arrange for the DNA tests to be done. That'll be a good start.'

Her demeanour had changed completely now she had something to focus on. The guilt had vanished now she had someone to blame.

'And don't forget to text me that address,' Phoebe reminded her.

* * *

'That's a stroke of luck,' Sam said when Phoebe told him what had happened. 'So you don't need to worry too much about the police not taking it seriously. Sounds like they won't need to if Ken's on the case. What's his surname?'

'Wyatt. Why?'

'I just wondered if Frazier and your dad know him. The legal world's quite small.'

'I'll message Frazier and ask.' She tapped out a message to her brother and she got a voice note reply back almost immediately.

'If you mean Ken Thomas Wyatt, then yep, Dad and I know him. His nickname's the Rottweiler. There's a standing joke in the industry. What's the difference between Ken Thomas and a Rottweiler? Answer: A Rottweiler eventually lets go.'

Phoebe and Sam grinned at each other. 'It sounds like our

dodgy cat breeder may have messed with the wrong person this time,' Phoebe said gleefully.

'Fingers crossed, eh!'

Phoebe rang Maggie to give her the update and discovered her grandmother hadn't been idle since their sleuthing chat.

'It just so happens that Eddie and I are looking for a kitten, and Eddie's been doing the tippy tappy onliner dance on the world wide webby thingie and we were just watching a video of some pretty little things that are available in the New Forest. In fact, we've been watching several videos. That's quite a common thing that people do on their tippy tappy onliner adverts.'

Phoebe smiled at the reminder of her grandmother's rather quirky language for all things online.

'Is that so?'

'It is so, and Eddie's just done the Google Woogle business and we've found a house that backs right up close to where Oscar the stud cat was found.'

'You don't know where that was though, do you?'

'I do because Natasha told me. She sent a safety pin of the location.'

'A safety pin? Do you mean a pincode?'

'Pincode. Safety pin, nappy pin, whatever. We've nailed it down – or would that be pinned it down.' She gave a delighted chuckle. 'It doesn't matter. There's a kitten seller very close by. And it just happens to be the one we're going to see. That can't be a coincidence.'

'No, it can't. When are you planning on going to go and see them?'

'Tomorrow morning. I've just arranged it. Would you like us to get you a swab of mummy cat for your DNA test?'

'That would be amazing, although I'm not sure how you're

going to do it.' She explained that Ken hadn't actually seen the mother cat outside of a video.

'Thanks for the heads up. OK. Leave it with us. If the mother cat's there, we'll get you a swab. I'll pop by the surgery and pick one up on the way. That dodgy breeder isn't all that far from you.'

Phoebe heard the ping of a text coming through in her ear. 'Hang on a sec. That might be my client with the address of the place where they got their kitten.'

It was, and to Phoebe's delight it was the same address Maggie had. She told her and got a snort of triumph.

'Have I ever told you you're wonderful?' Phoebe added.

'You don't tell me often enough,' Maggie replied without a trace of irony.

Phoebe went to tell Sam the good news. He'd just finished giving Lily her bedtime feed and was now winding her expertly.

'So the net's closing in on that breeder one way or the other. Do you think she'll be able to get a swab?'

'If anyone can, it will be Maggie. She can be pretty devious if it's in a good cause.'

'And a good cause is an animal in need. Are you coming up for bedtime?'

'I'll be up in two ticks,' she said. 'I'm just going to check at the practice that we've got another DNA test in stock. I think Max said we bought a batch.'

Sam nodded. It was good to see Phoebe so fired up. She was on a mission to find out what had happened to Oscar. Phoebe had always loved a challenge that involved animals. Sam remembered how she had been when she was on the trail of the irresponsible lop-eared rabbit breeder, Belinda Bates. Like Maggie, Phoebe was a passionate crusader for animal welfare. It was probably in the genes. They'd both move mountains to help an animal in need.

For him, it had taken a bit longer to get back into the routine after Christmas. This was partly because he'd been researching indoor schools and setting up your own business. There was a lot involved.

He hadn't yet had the chance to go and see Marjorie Taylor at Brook Riding School about doing some more lessons again, but he would get to it soon.

* * *

Phoebe didn't see Maggie when she called by to get the swab the next day because she was busy doing her morning appointments.

But she had just said goodbye to her last client at lunchtime and apart from Marcus, the practice was empty when Maggie called back again.

'No go, I'm afraid,' Maggie said, coming into reception and shaking her head. 'We couldn't get past the front door. But not for want of trying.'

'What happened?' Marcus asked. The whole practice knew about the Oscar and Freda scenario, although Phoebe had asked them not to discuss it in front of clients, or anyone else. After all, it might all still be a storm in a teacup. Everything they knew so far was possibly just supposition or, at best, circumstantial.

'A man came to the door with this skinny little kitten in a box,' Maggie said with a hint of disgust in her voice. 'I told him I needed to see the mother and father, but he refused point blank. He gave me this cock and bull story about his wife having Covid and them being anxious not to pass it on to anyone else. He said they especially didn't want to pass it on to anyone of our age, the cheeky beggar.'

'But they did still have the kitten, at least.'

'They had *a* kitten. Who knows if it was the other one that your woman saw? It was the right colour, but probably too young, bearing in mind when they got theirs. For all we know they have a whole pile of kittens in that house and they just bring one out in a box. Poor little mite. It broke my heart having to leave it there with that scoundrel.' She bit her lip. 'I tried to push him on it. I said we'd had our vaccinations and weren't too worried about catching Covid, but he wouldn't budge.'

'Do you think the mother cat was even there?' Marcus asked.

'Who knows! I was pretty persistent. In the end the bloke said that he had someone else who wanted the kitten so if we didn't really want it, it didn't matter, and then he near enough closed the door in our faces. Didn't he, Ed?'

Eddie, who'd been standing beside her throughout the conversation, nodded.

'It was a no go,' he confirmed.

'Thank you for trying,' Phoebe said, swallowing her disappointment.

Marcus tapped his fingers on the reception desk. 'It's frustrating. So near and yet so far.'

'I got a picture,' Eddie added, and they all looked at him in surprise.

'I didn't see you take a picture,' Maggie said, astonishment in her voice. 'When did you manage that?'

'When he got the kitten out. I had a clear shot when he was distracted with you arguing about seeing the mother cat.'

'You got a photo of the kitten, let's see it,' Phoebe said eagerly.

'No. Not of the kitten. I didn't think we'd need one of the kitten.' Eddie shot her a look. 'I took a photo of 'im…'

It was Phoebe's turn to look at him in astonishment. 'Blimey, Eddie, that's genius.'

The old man tapped his nose. 'Not just a pretty face, huh.' He got out his phone and tapped a few buttons before turning it round to show them a picture.

Maggie, Marcus and Phoebe all leaned in for a closer look.

Phoebe gasped. 'Oh my God. I recognise that guy.'

27

'Well, don't keep us in suspenders,' Maggie said. 'Who is it?'

'It's Mr Smarmy Ski Jacket. The guy who pretended he wanted to rehome our kittens just before Christmas. I knew there was a connection.'

'Are you sure it's him?'

'Pretty sure. Same thin fair hair and beaky nose. Natasha met him too though, and she saw him for longer. She could probably confirm.'

Marcus was already reaching for his phone. 'We're meeting for lunch, but I'll get her to pop up here first.'

A few minutes later, Natasha hurried into reception and Eddie showed her the photo.

Marcus brought her up to date with developments, and she nodded slowly. 'Yes, that's definitely him. Bingo. So we finally have some evidence that he's up to no good.'

'We know he's selling kittens under fairly dubious circumstances,' Phoebe pointed out. 'We don't know for sure he's running a kitten mill. And we still don't know if he stole Oscar.' She frowned. 'And I'm not sure if there's any way of finding out.'

'We're going to have to resort to Plan B,' Maggie said cheerily.

'What's that?' Phoebe asked her with a thread of trepidation.

'Climb over the back fence and scout around in the garden. They've got a big shed out there.'

'Really, did you see that from the front?'

'No, but you can see it from the back. I told you! Eddie and I did a recce.'

'I don't think it's a good idea to go clambering over people's fences,' Phoebe said hastily.

'Don't you dare say at my age.'

'I wouldn't dream of it.'

'Besides, we don't need to go clambering over any fences. I was winding you up about that. There's a back gate.'

'And what if it's locked?'

'Eddie's got bolt cutters.'

Phoebe decided not to ask her why Eddie had bolt cutters. 'I don't think that's a good idea either. Breaking into people's back gardens is illegal.'

'Only if they catch us. Which they won't. Because we plan to set up a diversion tactic. Natasha's going to help us.'

Natasha looked guilty, and Phoebe put her hands over her ears. 'I'm not even listening to this. There is no way anyone associated with this practice is doing anything remotely illegal.'

'OK, OK.' Maggie gave a deep sigh. 'We won't break in. We'll find another way of luring them out into the open. I'm talking metaphorically,' she added quickly, 'so don't look at me like that.'

Phoebe held her gaze. 'Promise me, Maggie. That you won't do anything illegal, or risky or dangerous. We don't know who we're dealing with.'

'OK, I promise we won't do anything remotely criminal. I

was joking about the bolt cutters,' she added, a touch huffily. 'I'm not completely irresponsible.'

'She was definitely joking,' Eddie assured Phoebe, his eyes serious. 'I may have had some bolt cutters once for farming work, but they'd be too rusty to be much use for anything these days.'

Phoebe had to be content with that. While she wouldn't have put it past Maggie to bend the rules if she thought she could justify it, she was pretty sure Eddie was as straight as a die.

She went back to the house to tell Sam about the latest developments. When she walked into the warmth of the farmhouse kitchen, Sam had Lily on his lap and they were playing peekaboo.

It was such a tender little scene that for a moment her heart turned over and she paused in the doorway to watch.

'Hey, guys, how are you doing?'

'We're doing fine. Here's your mummy.' Sam smiled at her. 'Have you come in to hear how Turtle Tots went?' He still had damp hair.

'Absolutely, I have.' Phoebe crossed the kitchen and held out her arms. 'Hello, my darling. Do I get a cuddle?'

Lily gurgled at her, and Phoebe picked her up. 'You're getting bigger by the day. And heavier too,' she added as she cuddled her. 'So how was Turtle Tots?'

'Tiring. For me, not for her. She loves it. How's your day going?'

Phoebe told Sam about the latest developments with Mr Smarmy Ski Jacket.

'I knew there was something off about him the first time I saw him,' she finished. 'He's definitely up to his neck in something dodgy. I just wish there was a way of proving it.'

'Have you thought about showing that photo Eddie took to

Archie?' Sam asked. 'I know it's a long shot but what if he was involved with taking their kittens? It's worth asking him, isn't it?'

'You're a genius. Yes, of course it's worth it. We could go up there this afternoon, couldn't we? We could take Lily. I'm sure Rufus and Emilia would love to see her.'

'Is it OK to just call by on spec to see a lord? We won't need to make an appointment or anything?'

'Um, no, I don't think so. Although I suppose they might not be in. I'll text Archie and ask him.'

* * *

Sam watched her tap out a message. She'd obviously forgotten he'd earmarked this afternoon for going over to Brook Riding School to see Marjorie about the possibility of resuming some teaching for her.

She was so excited about going to see Archie that he didn't like to remind her. Besides, Saturday afternoon was probably a bad time to visit Marjorie. Weekends were super busy over there. He'd be better going to see her one morning in the week.

'What happened about the little hedgehogs?' he asked while they waited for Archie to respond. 'Did they get rehomed OK?'

'Yes, I think so. Natasha took them over to the hedgehog rescue place. They're in a better position to home them than we are.'

Her phone pinged and she snatched it up. 'He's replied already. Yay, and it's good news. Archie's out riding, but he said he won't be long and Rufus and Emilia are in after three so that's perfect timing, isn't it. You're a genius, Sam. Thank you for suggesting we see Archie. It's a brilliant excuse to see him. By the time we've eaten a sandwich for lunch we'll be about right, won't we?'

'Perfect.' Sam glanced out of the window. 'Hey, look. I think it's snowing.'

Phoebe dashed over to the window and saw he was right. Huge soft flakes were falling out of the white sky. 'Wow. It is. How brilliant. We can show Lily her first snow. We can build a snowman.'

'We'd better see if it settles first,' he said, loving her enthusiasm. 'Besides, I thought we were going to see the Holts.'

'We can do both.'

'Of course we can.'

Sam was looking forward to seeing Archie too. Lord Rufus Holt, not so much. He'd always felt a little uneasy around the man. Possibly because he and Phoebe had been an item once. Sam still felt amazed sometimes that Phoebe had chosen him over a land-owning lord of the manor. He gave himself a little shake.

Behave, Sam. Rufus wasn't a threat. Of course he wasn't. Sam was painfully aware that his own less than buoyant self-esteem was one of the reasons the man still bothered him.

Rufus was married now with a toddler. Briefly Sam wondered if Rufus was as much of a hands-on dad as he himself was with Lily. He guessed they might find out this afternoon.

He looked back out of the window. It was still snowing. If anything it was coming down faster and there was a white sprinkling across the ground. Phoebe was now holding Lily up to look too, and the baby was wide-eyed. 'Oh, Sam, our first snow at Puddleduck Farm. It's settling too. Isn't it pretty.'

'It's gorgeous.'

By the time they'd had their sandwich, there was enough snow on the ground to take a very well wrapped-up Lily out to show her. Sam and Phoebe made a mini snowman, which she adored, and Roxie, who hadn't seen snow before either, danced around trying to catch snowflakes in her mouth, making them all laugh.

At just after three when they left for Beechbrook, there were a couple of inches of snow on the ground, and it was still falling. The Holts were their next-door neighbours and if they'd been walking, they could have crossed the Puddleduck fields in less time than it took to load up the car. Archie had always taken the shortcut and still did, but it would have been impractical to push Lily's buggy across the fields in the snow. If it came down much faster they might not even get to the Holts in the car, Sam thought, looking up at the sky.

But the snow was stopping as they left and at just after three, Sam drove beneath the life-size bronze stag – complete with a thin cloak of snow – that straddled the gateway that led into Beechbrook House. Lily was happy in her car seat and Phoebe was sitting beside him, her face reflective. The Holts' land lay on both sides of the quarter-mile drive. Rufus had grown lavender commercially for the last few years, and in the summer the fields were a vibrant mauve. Today the skeletal bushes stretched out on either side of them looked magical, every twig now decorated with a sparkling coverlet of white that glittered in the afternoon sun.

Sam parked Phoebe's Lexus on the wide frontage alongside Rufus's Mercedes with its heavily tinted windows. The car had a good couple of inches of snow on the roof already. It would have been nice to have so much land, but Sam didn't envy Rufus the imposing manor house, with its dozen or more paned windows and several chimneys, that loomed over them now, however impressive it looked. There must be endless repairs and maintenance looking after that lot. Neither did he envy him the heavy responsibility of being a peer of the realm. A responsibility little Archie would one day inherit too. Bless his little cotton socks.

He wondered how Archie was getting on with his riding. There was plenty of land here to set up an indoor school. In fact, he was surprised Rufus didn't have one for Archie to use.

'You look miles away,' Phoebe said. 'What are you thinking?'

Sam realised he'd switched off the engine but was still sitting motionless in his seat. 'Sorry. I was just thinking about Archie and wondering if Rufus has ever thought of setting up an indoor school.'

'He probably thinks Archie's away at school too much to get enough use out of it. Hey, maybe we should encourage him to get one. You could hire it. It would save us a fortune.'

So he wasn't the only one who'd been looking up costs then. He smiled at her. 'They are pretty pricey, that's for sure.'

'Oh, my goodness, I've just remembered you were going to see Marjorie today, weren't you?'

'I was, but don't worry. We didn't have any arrangement. I was just going over on spec and Saturday probably isn't the best day. Especially in view of how the weather's turned out. I might have had trouble getting back.'

She looked relieved as she got out of the car and began to unbuckle Lily from her car seat, while Sam grabbed the carrycot and the rucksack that accompanied their daughter everywhere.

'Right then,' Phoebe said. 'Let's go and see if we can shed any more light on the kitten-milling mystery, shall we?'

'Fingers crossed,' Sam murmured as they crunched across the snow-encrusted frontage, leaving footprints as they went, past the fountain with its tasteless cherubs, each now with a white cap of snow on its head, and on towards the great oak front door.

28

It was Archie who let them in. 'Hey, Sam. Hey, Phoebe. It's really good to see you. You should come and see us more often. Isn't the snow brilliant? I can't believe it's stopped already. Dad...' he called over his shoulder. 'They're here.'

'Well, let them in then.' Rufus appeared in the hallway behind his son. 'Good afternoon. Come in, come in, out of the snow. It's a cold old day.' He pecked Phoebe on the cheek, shook Sam's hand and smiled at Lily, who was looking at him wide-eyed. 'Hello, beautiful.'

They followed him into a magnificent high-ceilinged room with pale cornices and a huge inglenook fireplace where a roaring fire crackled away, spitting sparks into the chimney and chucking out warmth. A fire guard protected it from every angle, Phoebe was relieved to see. Since she'd had a little one, she saw the world through the ultra-safety-conscious eyes of a mum.

It had always been a welcoming room, but it was even more welcoming than she remembered. As she looked around, she realised it wasn't just the fire that made the room so warm; the décor had changed too since the old lord had died. Light-coloured modern blinds had replaced the heavy old brocade curtains, and the dark wood furniture was gone. The room had a different vibe altogether than she remembered. It had been transformed from dark Victoriana drabness to modern country living.

Emilia's touch, no doubt. It certainly worked. It looked beautiful. They'd been here at a New Year's Eve party the year before last and she hadn't noticed the changes then. They must be more recent.

Before she had time to comment, Emilia herself appeared carrying Francesca. ''Ello. It is such pleasure to see you.' Her voice still had a Germanic accent. 'Sit down, please. I will make coffee. Ja? Or is it tea for afternoon?' She looked at Rufus for confirmation.

'It's whatever our guests would like,' he said. 'We have both. Which would you prefer? I'll get it.'

They settled on tea and Rufus disappeared to make it.

Phoebe had worried it might be awkward being here, but it wasn't at all because the two little girls quickly became the focus of attention.

'What age is beautiful Lily?' Emilia asked, cooing over the baby.

'She's nearly six months,' Phoebe told her proudly.

'Chesska is nearly eighteen months old. A big gap now but not very much in the future.' Emilia beamed. 'They will become friends when they know they are next-door neighbours.'

'I hope they will,' Phoebe said, even though she thought the chances of the two little girls mixing in the same circles were probably remote.

'They will have Archie to introduce them,' Emilia said, clearly not oblivious to Phoebe's train of thought. 'He will be the link.'

On the other side of the room, Archie rolled his eyes. 'I expect animals will be the link. Lily can invite Chesska to see the neddies. And then Chesska can invite Lily to have a tea party in the bluebell wood. Girl stuff.'

'Why is this girl stuff? Do you not like tea and scones?' Emilia turned towards Phoebe. 'You settle argument for me, please. Does this word rhyme with gone, like skon or is it skone, like bone.'

'It rhymes with bones, old, dead bones, bleached white by the midday sun,' Archie chanted gleefully, and they all laughed because it was clear he wasn't at all interested in pronunciation, just the shock value of old dead bones. Phoebe was glad he wasn't yet quite as mature as he seemed. She missed the young mischievous Archie who had regularly sneaked across the fields from Beechbrook House to see the donkeys at Puddleduck Farm without telling his father.

Rufus came back in with a tray on which was a teapot and five cups and a plate of delicious-looking pale golden scones.

'I caught the end of that conversation and I can confirm that it's definitely *skon*, as in gone.'

Everyone shook their heads as Rufus put the tray on the table with a little clunk.

'Somebody help me out here,' he added, and glanced at Sam, who put his hands up in mock defence.

'Don't ask me. I just like eating them.'

Rufus chuckled. 'Very sensible. I couldn't agree more. And these are homemade.'

'Oh, wow.' Phoebe's mouth watered as the scent of warm, freshly baked scone hit her nostrils. 'They smell amazing. How do you have time with a little one?'

'I am not a veterinarian,' Emilia replied promptly. She

pointed to a jar on the tray. 'It is family effort. Rufus make this lavender jelly.'

'Really?' Phoebe glanced at him curiously. 'I didn't know you made jelly – er – jam?'

'Strictly speaking, it's lavender jelly and I don't personally make it.' He shot her a wry smile. 'Emilia means that it's made from our lavender. We experimented with some food-grade lavender last year. We thought we'd branch out, if you'll excuse the pun. I know strawberry jam is traditional but lavender also goes really well with *skons*. *Skones*,' he amended as Archie opened his mouth to object.

It did go really well, as they found out a few minutes later, having also had the discussion of cream or jam on the scone first. No one agreed on that either, but it was all very good-natured banter.

Even Chesska liked the lavender jelly, it transpired, and Lily, who they'd just started weaning onto solids, happily ate a tiny piece of buttery golden scone.

After they'd finished their impromptu afternoon tea, they talked about lots of other things. The animals at Puddleduck Pets and how the rehoming was going. Phoebe told them about the dog field, which Rufus said was a brilliant idea. This led naturally on to the subject of Chloe and Spot, who Archie had told them were confined to the kitchen when they had guests round.

'They don't mind. They came riding with me earlier. They're both whacked out and really filthy. You can come and say hello to them before you go if you like? We're going back out to play in the snow before it melts.'

'I'd love to,' Phoebe told him, knowing he was too polite to say overtly that he was in a hurry to disappear, but knowing he must be longing to get outside again.

The chatter was so easy and natural as they played with the children on the thick golden carpet of the big old room that Phoebe almost forgot why they'd come round. It wasn't until Archie asked them if anyone had ever responded to the lost kitten photo that she was jolted into remembering.

'Um, no. Natasha would have told you, love, but... there was something I wanted to ask you. All of you, actually. This is going to seem a little random but I want to know if any of you recognise this picture. Hang on. I'll find it.' She rummaged in her bag and pulled out her phone and scrolled through.

It didn't take long. Her photo gallery contained a mixture of photos of Lily and photos of animal ailments so the picture of Mr Smarmy Ski Jacket that she'd got Eddie to send over stuck out like a thorn bush in an English country garden.

She turned the phone round towards Archie. 'Does he look familiar at all?'

Archie studied the photo for a few seconds before frowning and shaking his head. 'I don't think so. Why? What's he got to do with our kittens?'

'He's a local breeder. That's all.' Phoebe showed Rufus. 'I don't suppose you recognise him, do you?'

'No. I certainly didn't buy Emilia's kittens from him. They came from a woman on the other side of Southampton. I did a fair bit of research before I got them, and she had a good reputation.'

Emilia's face shadowed and Phoebe felt a little guilty that she'd brought up the subject. Especially as it was clearly a dead end. 'Can I look?' she asked, getting up from the floor where she'd been playing with Chesska.

'Of course.' Phoebe passed her the phone and was surprised when she did a double take.

'I know this man. Pfff. I do not like him. He is bully.'

Phoebe's heart started to beat extra fast. 'How do you know him?' She hoped to God that Emilia hadn't arranged to buy more kittens from him – or if she had that it wasn't too late to renege on the deal.

'He is boyfriend of Carmel. I often hear him shout at her when he comes to the house to collect her. I tell her, you must not let a man talk to you this way. He is not good man.' She pursed her lips.

Phoebe couldn't imagine any man having the audacity to shout at Emilia. Even when she'd been working as Archie's live-in nanny she'd had the bearing of a haughty princess. Phoebe hadn't been surprised at all when she'd discovered that Emilia was actually related to the Prince of Liechtenstein and had a title of her own.

'Who's Carmel?' Sam asked.

'Carmel is our cleaner,' Rufus answered him. 'What's all this about?'

Phoebe's head was now spinning as she remembered the discussion the Dashwood family had had at Christmas. It had been Maggie who'd mooted the idea that Emilia's kittens may have been stolen by someone who regularly visited the house.

It had seemed odd that two lots could have been stolen, but now it made total sense.

'How long has Carmel been your cleaner?' Phoebe looked at Emilia and the younger woman frowned.

'She has been helping me since Chesska arrived. This is a big house to clean.' There was a defensive note in her voice.

'Of course it is,' Phoebe said quickly, shooting an anguished glance at Sam, who looked as though he was also now putting the jigsaw pieces of this mystery together. She willed him silently not to answer Rufus's question.

They couldn't just go accusing the Holts' cleaner of being a kitten thief. Even if it did suddenly seem like a terrible possibility.

It would be awful for Emilia to think that her beloved kittens might have ended up in a kitten mill and were now being subjected to a life of misery as enforced brood cats.

Thankfully, Sam had understood Phoebe's anguished look and he had switched his attention to Lily, who'd been on the floor but had just put up her arms for a daddy cuddle.

'One of Phoebe's clients had concerns about him being a reputable breeder, that's all.' Sam had put on his most reassuring voice. The one he kept for his most nervous riding pupils. *All is well; there's nothing to fear.*

Rufus nodded silently. Luckily he'd been distracted by his daughter too. She'd been trying to get his attention. 'Need pee, Daddy.'

'Come on then, princess, let's go and find your potty.'

Thank goodness for kids and their bladders, Phoebe thought as Rufus took Chesska out of the room.

Emilia wasn't looking much more reassured, but not for the same reasons as Phoebe.

'I wouldn't buy a teacup from this bully,' she said huffily. 'He is not nice person.'

'No.' Phoebe blinked. 'Why does Carmel go out with him?'

'Pfff. I do not know. I suppose maybe he flatter her. He has big car. Big wallet too.' She raised her eyebrows. 'Some women are impressed by these things. Ja?'

'What's his name?' Sam asked.

'I call him Mr Slimy Balls,' Emilia answered. 'But his correct name is Duncan.'

'Does he have a surname?' Phoebe asked idly.

'Jukes. His name is Duncan Jukes.'

So Natasha hadn't been too far off the mark then.

Emilia lost interest in the conversation as Rufus came back through the door with Chesska, and Phoebe decided it seemed like a natural time for them to go home too.

Archie diverted them into the kitchen to see his two dogs and Phoebe stroked the little grey lurcher's soft head and the black and white patched terrier, both of whom wagged, yawned and blinked sleepily at her. Archie was right about them being worn out and filthy. They looked like two dogs who'd had an excellent morning's run. And now they'd be playing in the snow with their young master. They'd definitely landed on their paws at Beechbrook House.

'Don't leave it so long next time,' Rufus said as they all trooped back out to the front door.

'We won't. And you do know you're welcome at Puddleduck any time, don't you? All of you,' she told him. 'We'd love to see you.'

'Thank you.'

His eyes were warm, and as Emilia and Chesska came up to stand beside him and Archie stood on his other side, Phoebe had the impression when she looked back of a perfect little family.

She waited until they were driving back down the long drive once more before she glanced at Sam.

'Thanks for not saying anything. I was so torn. Half of me wanted to demand they interrogate Carmel and ask her about those kittens and the other half of me knew we couldn't just go jumping to conclusions.'

'I know. I felt exactly the same. We need to find out more before we go diving in. But my gut tells me we're on exactly the right track. Duncan Jukes must have taken those kittens. It's too much of a coincidence.'

'I can't bear the thought of Emilia's beautiful cats being used as breeding machines, though, Sam.'

He took his hand from the steering wheel and touched her knee. 'Slowly slowly catchee monkey. The last thing we want to do is to scare him into shutting operations down and getting rid of all his cats. We still don't know how Oscar got away.'

'No, I was thinking it might be wise to warn Emilia not to say anything to Carmel about her boyfriend being a cat breeder. Just in case he realises we're on to him. I'll message her later and say thank you for the tea. I've still got her number. In fact, better still, I'll phone her and make it crystal clear that she shouldn't breathe a word. I'll tell her it's part of an ongoing investigation and therefore top secret.'

'Which is close enough to the truth anyway.'

'Mmm. The truth is I haven't got a clue what to do next though.' Phoebe told him about Maggie's Plan B. 'We need to stay on the right side of the law, but Maggie's right. We also need to get into that garden and see what Duncan Jukes keeps in that shed of his. I just have no idea how we're going to manage it.'

'We'll work something out,' Sam said confidently.

29

Emilia sounded pleased when Phoebe phoned to thank her for their hospitality and she agreed not to say anything to Carmel about the possibility of her boyfriend being a cat breeder.

'Pfff. She does not listen to any criticism of Mr Slimy Balls, so I do not mention his name!' she muttered.

Phoebe wondered whether to tell her the usual expression was Slimeball, but she decided against it. Mr Slimy Balls was so much more evocative an insult.

Luckily Emilia didn't seem to have made the same connection between Carmel's boyfriend having a cat-breeding enterprise and her own missing kittens. But then she probably wasn't aware of the dark underworld of kitten-milling operations.

Maggie was outraged when Phoebe and Sam took Lily and Roxie to see her at the bungalow on Sunday afternoon and told her what was going on. The snow had all but gone now, only the odd sprinkling in sheltered corners evidence that it had ever been there.

'The audacity of the man. Do you think the cleaner's in on it too? Or is she just being used as a pawn by Mr Slimy Balls?' She'd agreed with Phoebe that this was a much better insult than the proper English expression.

'Emilia seemed to think Carmel was a nice girl, but I guess we don't really know.'

Phoebe paced up and down Maggie's kitchen, which was filled with the meaty smells of mince and gravy simmering in a pan on the stove. Pacing around Maggie's kitchen was getting to be a habit.

She glanced into the saucepan as she passed. 'Why are you cooking mince? Have you given up being vegetarian? Or is that for Eddie?'

'It's for the dogs,' Eddie told her from his position at the table. 'I'm not a big meat eater these days...'

'I've been banned from boiling tripe in the kitchen,' Maggie interrupted him. 'He doesn't like the smell.'

'I don't blame him,' Phoebe said as both she and Sam screwed up their faces in distaste at the memory.

'Lightweights, the lot of you,' Maggie said, but she was smiling. Phoebe was pretty sure she didn't much like the smell either and the dogs certainly wouldn't be complaining about getting Sainsbury's Taste the Difference mince instead.

'Give it a stir while you're up there, can you, Phoebe?' Maggie added. 'In fact, you can probably turn the gas off.' She currently had Lily on her lap and in between the adult chatter she was communing with her great-granddaughter. 'You're not a lightweight, are you, my darling? I bet you wouldn't mind a little bit of stinky tripe cooking!'

'Gah,' Lily shouted. 'Gah. Goh Gah. Gra!'

'Precisely,' Maggie said. 'I couldn't agree more.' She glanced at Phoebe. 'Her first word's going to be Great-Gran, I'd say.'

Phoebe didn't disillusion her. She checked out the mince which was cooked and switched off the gas before turning back towards them all. 'The question is, what do we do next? It's still all just circumstantial, isn't it?' Phoebe counted things off on her fingers.

'We know Slimy Balls was planning to resell the Puddleduck kittens that he said were for his sister – although we can't prove that because we didn't get a screenshot of his advert. And even if we had, it wouldn't stand up – he could argue they were different kittens, just similar looking.'

She sighed. 'We know Oscar was living somewhere else – and very likely fathered some kittens, but we can't prove that definitively either. And we can't prove any definitive link between him and Slimy Balls either. He might not have had him at all.

'And we know he had the opportunity to steal Emilia's kittens but we can't prove that either. Even with the DNA test it's not 100 per cent without the mother. Arghhh.' She made a frustrated gesture with her hands.

'One thing we do know for sure,' Sam said, 'is that he's a breeder with dubious practices. He lets kittens go before they're old enough to leave their mother and without being vaccinated. But that's not going to land him in jail. More's the pity.'

'Carmel's the key to all this,' Maggie said firmly. 'She's going to know a lot more about him and his nefarious activities than anyone else so we need to get Carmel on side. Or not – as the case may be. And in order to do that we'll need to tell Emilia what we think is going on.' She looked at Phoebe. 'You're the best person to do that. She trusts you, doesn't she?'

'Yes, I think she does. But then what do we do?'

'We decide whether Carmel's loyalty lies with her boyfriend or her employer. That's what we'll do, isn't it, darling?' She bounced Lily up and down and she squealed in delight. 'That's the way forward.'

'And then what?' Phoebe asked.

'Give me a chance. I haven't got as far as that yet.' Maggie shot her a look.

'I know what we can do.' Eddie spoke for the first time in a while. He'd been looking at the sports pages of a newspaper that was lying on the kitchen table.

They all looked at him.

'We can have a sponsored walk,' he said, nodding his head in agreement with himself. 'They're good fundraisers.'

Phoebe blew out a breath, remembering what Maggie had said about her husband turning off his hearing aids when he didn't want to participate in a conversation. Had Eddie even been listening at all?

* * *

During the latter half of January, the plan for the proposed Mission Cat Rescue inched forward. Phoebe went to see Emilia and told her everything they had found out so far. Emilia suggested immediately that they tell Rufus everything too. Then they could all decide on the best way to proceed. Maggie got involved with these discussions too. As she was fond of telling Phoebe, her middle name was 'devious' and she didn't have to stay whiter than white like Phoebe did, because she didn't have a vet practice to run and a reputation to worry about.

Sam didn't get as involved as either of them, although he listened to Phoebe's updates with interest. It was impossible to get too involved with anything else or even give it much headspace when he was still so hands-on with Lily.

Phoebe had gone back to work full time and that was

working out well, but his plan to go back to Hendrie's on Wednesdays and Thursdays while Maggie and Eddie and Jan and Louella helped out with Lily wasn't working out quite as well.

Life kept throwing up curve balls. Ma had a flu bug for two of her Wednesdays, and then she passed it on to his pa too, so that scuppered a third one.

Louella had had to cancel one of her days too, thanks to car trouble.

Sam had picked up the slack every time. It was much easier for him to juggle commitments than it was for Phoebe to try to arrange cover for her appointments. Puddleduck Vets was more than busy enough for three vets, especially as Seth was only supposed to be part time.

Maggie and Eddie were fairly reliable Saturday babysitters, but they couldn't do every one so Sam had put most of his plans on hold. He'd already ended up having to cancel two appointments he'd made to go and talk to Marjorie Turner at Brook Riding School, and his plans for setting up any private tutoring at Puddleduck were firmly on the back burner.

Every time he brought Ninja into the stable at night and rugged him up, with Lily watching from her buggy, buttoned up warmly in her hat and coat, he felt guilty.

Not so much for his daughter, who loved these excursions, but for his thoroughbred cross, who was growing flabbier and more unfit by the day.

'We'll get back into exercise one of these days,' he told his horse. 'I promise.'

Ninja would blow softly on his hands and accept a treat with gentlemanly grace, but it didn't alleviate Sam's guilt.

It didn't help that the latter half of January had been beautiful. There had been no more snow but crisp cold mornings with clear blue skies greeted Sam every time he went outside. Frost sparkled across the Puddleduck fields and spiders' webs strung across bushes, glittered like little silver masterpieces.

Forest rides had become a distant memory. Sam missed the peace of the forest. The time to think when it was just him and his horse. Puddleduck Farm was rarely peaceful. The comings and goings of clients to the vet or the comings and goings of Natasha and the visitors and volunteers meant there were aways people around.

In a bid to help out Phoebe, Sam had also agreed to be chief overseer of the dog field. What this meant in reality was that he kept an eye on who was coming and going and made sure that it matched with who was *supposed* to be coming and going, according to the booking website.

This was possible because hirers had to put their car registration on the booking forms as well as to say how many dogs they were bringing. People were fairly good and respected the other field users. Sam hadn't yet had to sort out any disputes.

He also restocked the coffee and tea supplies that were in the shed, emptied the honesty box, cleared the field of dog toys if any had been left out, and locked up the gate every night.

The worst bit was making sure the field stayed dog poo free. There was a lidded dustbin just inside the entrance which had to be emptied daily. Sam was used to clearing donkey and horse manure from the neddie field but dog poo was in a league all of its own. A very smelly league. It was a horrible dirty job that Sam would never have let Phoebe do.

Sometimes, when he was carting bin liners from the dustbin to be disposed of, Sam consoled himself with the thought that although much of his life these days seemed to consist of clearing up poo, it was all done in the name of love.

He'd often thought the same thing when he was changing

Lily's nappy. Love wasn't about flowers and chocolates, although he had taken Phoebe for a wonderfully romantic meal out on Valentine's Day and the house was full of roses.

Love wasn't the big romantic gestures you made when you were trying to impress someone. Love was a series of daily acts, carried out dozens of times; it was cleaning up after people you adored. Doing stuff they didn't like. Without fuss. Without complaint. That was what love was really about.

* * *

Sam finally got the chance to go to Brook Riding Stable to see Marjorie about the possibility of resuming some teaching in the third week of February.

It was a cold frosty Saturday. Maggie and Eddie were looking after Lily. Phoebe was working. And in between work, no doubt she'd be plotting with Maggie about Mission Cat Rescue. They'd got Rufus on board now and they had a plan, which was all a bit hush hush. Phoebe had told him that even she didn't know all the details. Apparently Maggie thought it was better that way.

Which probably meant something nefarious was going on. Sam knew he'd find out more on a need-to-know basis, which suited him fine. He adored Maggie, but she had always been a maverick rule breaker and age hadn't slowed her down. If anything, it had made her slightly more reckless.

He and Phoebe hadn't discussed any more of the detail about setting up an indoor school at Puddleduck. Sam had got as far as pricing up some of the practicalities, and as he'd suspected the costs were astronomical. The expenditure of building a suitable construction, that's if it even made it past the planning permission stage, was eye-watering. A decent floor surface was much more than even he had anticipated. It ran into thousands, not hundreds, and then there was the whole matter of electrics.

They would need floodlights if the school was to be used out of daylight hours, through the winter, which was of course the beauty of an indoor school. People worked in the daytime, so evening availability was key.

All of this was before you even thought about the annual rates that would be payable, once it was actually up. Insurances, health and safety; the list was endless. It would take years of private riding lessons even to make a dent in the amount he'd need to borrow. No self-respecting bank was going to stump up that amount of cash.

He was trying not to feel despondent about it all. The dream had been fun while it lasted. The one thing he could do though was to resume teaching at Brook Riding School. It was a less lofty ambition but it was much more doable. So he'd given Marjorie a call about this and she'd suggested he come over for a proper chat.

As he drove through the forest on that Saturday morning, which was frost-silvered and beautiful, Sam felt his heart lighten.

He arrived just as the ten o'clock hack was about to go out and he walked into a buzz of activity. It felt great to be back in the yard amongst the smell of horse. The sensory overload of Sam's happy place was all around him. The jingle of tack and the creak of leather, the clatter of ponies' steel-shod hooves on concrete as they milled about, the white clouds of breath, both human and horse, rising into the cold air and the buzz of chatter from six or seven excited riders, their coats and riding jackets bright splashes of colour.

Marjorie was in the yard speaking to one of the ride leaders, identifiable by her fluorescent-yellow high-vis vest, and Sam waited until the hack had trooped out of the yard in a clip-clopping line before he went over to talk to her. After the mass exodus of ponies and riders it was suddenly peaceful. Now there were just the sounds of birdsong in the air, the scrape of hooves on the concrete yard, as a left-behind horse stamped his disapproval, and the distant sound of a car horn on the road.

'Hi, Marjorie. Is now a good time?'

'It's perfect.' Her face creased into a smile. It was hard to tell how old Marjorie was. She'd always been one of those ageless people who looked the same however many years went by. She had grey hair which she kept coiled up in a wispy bun on the back of her head, weather-beaten skin from being outdoors most of her life and kindly button brown eyes. Although because he hadn't seen her for a while Sam fancied she looked a little more tired than usual, and maybe a little more stooped.

'It's good to see you, Sam. How's the little one doing?'

'She's a joy,' Sam said. 'And hard work.'

'Ah, they are, Sam. Horses are easier than little ones.' He realised suddenly that he didn't even know whether Marjorie had children of her own. They never discussed anything personal really; their conversation revolved around horses and students who came to ride, and occasionally segued into dogs or money. Sam had kept Ninja at part livery for years before he'd moved him across to Puddleduck Farm.

Marjorie must have picked up his questioning glance. 'When my Peter was small, I remember thinking, when will this end? And when he was grown up I remember looking back and thinking that his childhood had gone by in a flash, and that those times were some of the happiest of my life. Enjoy it, Sam. It'll go really quickly.'

'Thanks.' He hesitated. 'I don't think you've ever mentioned

Peter before...' He left the unspoken question in the air, thinking she could pick it up if she wanted to – or not.

'There's not usually a lot of time for chitchat around here,' Marjorie continued as she beckoned him through to the office.

He followed her, his eyes making the adjustment from the brightness of the February day outside to the relative gloom of the concrete-floored barn. Marjorie rubbed her hands together as she strode over to her desk, which was, as always, strewn with papers.

'Peter lives in Arizona. He went there on his gap year, met a girl, and never came back.' Marjorie's voice was light. 'I'd had high hopes when he was small that he'd love horses and grow up and help me with this place.'

'But he didn't,' Sam finished softly.

'Well, he did and he didn't. Peter's middle name is "adventure". He grew up loving horses, and he met a horse-loving girl, who'd been brought up on a ranch in Arizona, and guess what happened?'

'They settled down there.'

'You've got it in one. I can't say I really blame him. Where would you rather settle, Sam? On a thousand-acre ranch in Arizona, with scorching summers, or in a riding school in the damp New Forest?' She stamped her feet on the wooden floor of the unheated building.

Sam took a breath. 'That would be a hard one,' he said, even though he knew that deep down he'd probably have gone with the New Forest himself. But then his middle name wasn't 'adventure'.

'Anyway, you didn't come here to talk about my family. You came here to talk about doing a few riding lessons again, didn't you?'

'If that's possible. I'd love to. I've really missed this place.'

'And if you're sure you can spare the time, Sam, then I'd love to have you. We don't see so much of the young Lord Holt as we used to, but we've still got a few of your old clients left, I believe.'

30

At Puddleduck Vets, Phoebe was about to take a call regarding a rabbit. Marcus was covering reception.

'The woman isn't a client, but she said you came highly recommended. Her name's Mrs Samuels. It sounds like it might be a call-out. Although I'm not sure whether it's a wild rabbit or a domestic one. Would you like to speak to her or shall I ask her to call back another time?'

'No, it's fine. I'll talk to her now. Thanks.' Phoebe frowned as Marcus unmuted the phone and handed it to her. She hoped she wasn't about to deal with another owl in the shed situation.

'Hello, Phoebe Dashwood speaking, can I help you?'

'I really do hope so. I've got a question about a rabbit that I've – er – befriended...'

'What's the question?'

'There's a lot of myxomatosis around here and I was wondering if he could be vaccinated against getting it. Your receptionist said it might be possible.'

'Yes, it's definitely possible although we don't usually vaccinate wild rabbits. Is this your rabbit? Or a wild rabbit?'

'He's not mine exactly. But he comes into my garden a lot, and I'm worried about his safety.'

'OK.' Phoebe took a breath. 'The main difficulty I can foresee is catching him.'

'I can catch him, no problem. Don't worry about that.'

'I see. So – er – do you want to bring him in to us?'

'Truthfully... I'd much rather you came out here. I think it would be less stressful for him. I'm happy to pay for a call-out...'

'Are you sure?' Phoebe quoted her the cost.

There was a pause before she said, 'Yes, that's fine. Could you possibly come this afternoon? I'm in Totton.'

Phoebe put the phone back on mute, aware that Marcus was listening to this one-sided conversation. 'She'd like me to go out this afternoon. She's about half an hour away. Do I have any other calls?'

Marcus shook his head. So Phoebe arranged for Mrs Samuels to be her first client after lunch, letting out a sigh as she disconnected.

'I hope it doesn't turn out to be a wild goose chase, or should I say wild rabbit chase?' Marcus raised his eyebrows. 'Did she say she'd trapped him already?'

'No. But she said it wouldn't be a problem. That will be interesting to see.'

'Yeah.' Marcus drummed his fingers on the desk. 'I don't suppose I could tag along, could I? I'm not on shift this afternoon.'

'Of course you can. If you want to. But surely you've got better things to do than chase around after wild rabbits in your time off.'

'That sounds intriguing.' Max appeared in reception behind them. 'What are you two up to?'

Phoebe told him.

'Are we supposed to treat wild rabbits? There's definitely legislation around that.'

'I'm not entirely sure whether this one is wild or domestic. She was a little bit cagey about it. I'm also not sure if we're going to be able to catch it anyway. So this whole thing might be a waste of time.'

'Take some gloves,' Max advised. 'Gauntlets would be good.'

'Gauntlets! Why?'

'Because if he's been near any wild rabbits he'll be covered in fleas. Wild rabbits are a bit like hedgehogs. That's one of the ways myxy is carried. It's a horrible disease. It's nice of her to want to vaccinate him.'

'It is,' Marcus said. 'Presuming she hasn't got him locked up in some hutch in a shed. It's back to the whole keeping wildlife in captivity because you can't afford a pet thing, isn't it?'

'Is that why you want to come?' Phoebe glanced at him. 'We're not going out to lecture her, Marcus. That's not our job.'

He put up his hands, palms forward. 'I wouldn't dream of it. But we can give her some friendly advice about the dangers of keeping wild animals as pets. Can't we?'

'If you mean in a very gentle, non-judgemental manner, then yes. But nothing heavy, Marcus. Promise me. Or you're not coming.'

'Sure thing, boss. No lecturing.'

Phoebe decided he meant it. 'OK. And if this rabbit is hopping around in the garden, I might well need a hand to catch it.'

'I'll get two pairs of gauntlets then,' Marcus said. 'As well as the myxy jab.'

The address Mrs Samuels had given them turned out to be on a run-down housing estate just on the edge of Southampton.

'I'd have thought this place would be closer to the Marchwood Practice than us,' Phoebe said to Marcus as she followed her satnav's instructions around several horseshoe-shaped roads that wound around the estate.

'Yeah, it probably is. But Marchwood's prices have gone up a lot since Seth sold the practice. Have you noticed? We're about a third cheaper.'

'Are you saying we're too cheap?'

'No, I think it's more they're too dear. Although you could go up a bit, boss. I'm sure no one would complain.'

'Mmm. We'll see. I don't want to rip anyone off.'

'I can't imagine you ever doing that,' Marcus said with such sincerity it warmed her.

The houses on the outskirts of the estate looked like newbuilds but not particularly upmarket ones, Phoebe noticed as she pulled up outside number seventeen, which was on the furthest edges of the development and backed on to fields.

'Do you reckon these are the cheap houses they had to build in order to get planning permission to put up the rest?' Marcus asked as Phoebe turned off the engine.

'It does look like it.' Phoebe surveyed their surroundings. The owner of this house didn't look as though she had much money to spend. That was for sure. An ancient mustard-coloured Mini with a mismatching pale yellow passenger door was parked on the road in front of her.

'It's going to be another owl in the shed, isn't it, boss?'

'Let's not jump to conclusions just yet,' Phoebe said, even though she was pretty sure he was right.

A few minutes later they'd rung the doorbell and were let in by a woman who looked old enough to be a pensioner, albeit a very sprightly one. She had greying hair drawn back tight in a ponytail from an age-spotted, lined face and she was wearing faded denim jeans and a tatty old rainbow-coloured patchwork jacket.

Phoebe introduced herself and Marcus.

'I'm Connie Samuels – Connie.' She frowned. 'I didn't realise there'd be two of you. I hope this isn't going to cost me more.'

'Not at all.'

'Then follow me.'

The house smelled faintly of lavender, which reminded Phoebe of the afternoon tea they'd had with Rufus.

She realised, as they walked down a narrow hall that opened out into a bright and rather lovely blue and yellow kitchen, that there were little bags of what must be lavender, pinned over some of the doorways.

'It's something my old gran taught me,' Connie said, noticing her looking. 'It's a great way to scent a room naturally. As long as you like lavender, that is.'

'Yes.' Phoebe smiled. 'So do you have any other pets? Besides... er...' She hesitated, realising she hadn't asked her prospective patient's name.

'I haven't given him a name. I thought if he had a name I might get too attached – that probably sounds daft, and as it happens, it hasn't worked. I am attached. But to answer your question, no, I don't have any pets these days. Too costly on a limited income. That's why it was so nice when this wild one and I became so... well acquainted.'

Phoebe and Marcus exchanged glances as Connie opened the back door of her spotless kitchen and beckoned them outside.

The house had been a surprise – the pristine inside making a pleasant contrast to the rather tatty outside – but the garden was even more of a surprise.

An off-white stepping-stone-style footpath ran down the

middle of a patch of green lawn towards a neat laurel hedge. To the right of that was a semicircular weeded flower bed filled with evergreen shrubs and several blue and white pots grouped together, awaiting spring occupants. Clusters of snowdrops encircled an apple tree at the far end. They reminded Phoebe of family groups huddled together, their tall green stalks adorned with winter white bells pealing out music no human ear could hear. There were also purple velvet-petalled crocuses that had braved the winter frosts, nestling in the longer grass around the edges of the garden.

Amongst the shrubs were two lavender bushes and there was a well-stocked bird table just left of the centre of the lawn. In the left-hand corner closest to them was a small pond, covered with lilies and edged by another rockery, and when Phoebe glanced across she saw a frog leap into the water with a small splash. Somewhere nearby a blackbird sang his heart out.

It was an idyllic little spot and looked well-tended, even in its winter bareness. Phoebe imagined it would look wonderful in spring and summer.

Connie was obviously a fan of wildlife. Her garden was a shrine to it, but there was no sign of a wild rabbit. There was no shed either, Phoebe was relieved to see.

'I'll call him.' Connie's voice interrupted the peace. 'But if you two wouldn't mind standing back a bit. He's quite shy.'

They did as she said, and Connie stepped across to the low hedge, put two fingers to her mouth and gave a low whistle.

At first nothing happened, but a few seconds later there was movement in the sprawling molehill-dotted field that lay beyond the hedge. 'Wow, do you see?' Phoebe breathed to Marcus. 'He's right out there across the far side.'

Marcus nodded. He looked as astounded as Phoebe was feeling as the dot of a smoky-grey rabbit began to lollop across the field towards the little garden. He wasn't in a hurry. Every so often he stopped by a molehill to sample a patch of grass, but slowly but surely he was heading their way.

Connie didn't have to whistle again. Although she did crouch down a little as the rabbit got closer to the hedge. 'Come on then, lad. Come on, little rab.'

Phoebe and Max watched as the rabbit arrived on the other side of the hedge, then ducked down and came through what must have been a gap near the ground. A few seconds later it was in the garden.

The rabbit paused a few feet away and sat back on its haunches for a second, scenting the air, nose wrinkling, as if it had sensed danger.

'He knows you're here,' Connie said. 'Please don't move until I've caught him.' She crouched and held out a piece of orange carrot. 'It's OK, my lad. They're here to help. Come and get your carrot now.'

The rabbit barely hesitated before he hopped closer and began to take more pieces of carrot from her hands.

Phoebe had never seen anything like it in her life. It was heartwarming how much trust the little fellow had in a human.

Then Connie, still moving very slowly, bent down and picked the rabbit up. 'Where would you like him?'

'Just where you've got him is perfect,' Phoebe said. 'I'll be as gentle and quick as I can.'

She unlatched her vet bag, took out the ready-prepared vaccine and went slowly across the grass. The rabbit barely flinched as she gave him the necessary dose while Connie continued calming him gently with her voice.

To her relief, there weren't any obvious fleas, so hopefully they were in time with the preventative vaccine.

Phoebe stepped back again, giving Connie a few more moments with the rabbit before she released him.

They all watched as he ignored the other pieces of carrot on the grass and shot away swiftly through the hole in the hedge, and back to the safety of the field beyond.

For a few moments no one spoke.

The sun had just come out, bathing the garden in a wash of afternoon light, and Phoebe wondered if Marcus felt, as she did, that they had just witnessed something very special in that winter garden.

She cleared her throat. 'I really hope this doesn't affect your relationship with him in the future.'

'I hope so too,' said the old lady. 'But to be honest, it's more important to me that he's safe. It's not a good disease to get. Manmade too. I guess you vets know that. We humans introduced it to keep down the population. And it's decimated them.' She paused. 'As if we don't do enough harm to our wildlife. Flattening them on our roads, shooting them in their own environment, taking their habitat.' She gestured towards the field. 'That will all be houses soon. They've just got the planning passed for Phase Two.'

There was sadness in her voice.

'Not all humans are anti-wildlife,' Marcus said gently. 'Look at what you've done today.'

Connie glanced at him and her blue eyes were very bright before she blinked rapidly.

'It was a very small thing to do.'

'You remind me of my grandmother,' Phoebe said. 'She's been a voice for animals for as long as I can remember.'

'What's her name?'

'Maggie Crowther – Crowther-May now. She started an animal sanctuary. You two would get on well.'

'Is that Puddleduck Pets – the same place you came from?'

'Yes, it is. We're always looking for volunteers. If you ever had any spare time.'

'I'll think about it. You'd better come back in. I need to wash my hands. And pay you.'

They went back in and Connie and Phoebe washed their hands in turn, but Phoebe refused to take any payment.

'Make a donation to Puddleduck Pets if you want to.'

Marcus got out one of the Voice for Wildlife posters he'd brought with him and handed it to Connie. 'We started a campaign last year – to warn people of the pitfalls of keeping wildlife as pets.'

'And is that what you thought I was doing, young man?'

'No.' Marcus blushed and backtracked. 'OK, yes. You're right. I did at first. But that was before I met you. You'd be a great person to head up our campaign. It needs someone like you.'

'Someone like me being…?' She looked at him keenly.

'Someone who's passionate. Someone who really cares. Someone knowledgeable.' His face was the colour of beetroot now, but he wasn't stopping. He was on a roll. He nodded vigorously. 'And someone who maybe has a bit more time on their hands. Everyone at Puddleduck Pets is snowed under with looking after the animals, and the paperwork side of it all just gets pushed to one side. We need someone like you. Please say you'll think about it.'

Gosh, how far he's come, Phoebe thought as she watched this little exchange. Marcus would never have been so forward when she'd first met him and now he was clearly hell-bent on co-opting Connie Samuels to head up the Voice for Wildlife campaign.

She was about to tactfully remind him that Connie might

not appreciate this full-on sales pitch when she realised the old lady was nodding.

'Do you know what? I think you might be right. It sounds like a great project. Can I get some more details? How much time would it take?'

In the end they didn't leave for another hour. By which time Connie had confided she'd been a poet in her youth and had often written funny poems about animals.

'I used to read them out at local pubs sometimes. Back in the days when Pam Ayres had just started up and everyone wanted to be a performance poet.'

'Wow. So you don't mind public speaking?' Marcus exclaimed in delight.

'Not if it's in a good cause. No.' Connie's eyes shone. 'And I can't think of a better one than animals.'

She showed them some of her poems, which ranged from mildly humorous to sweetly poignant, and she promised to come over to Puddleduck Pets and talk to Maggie.

'We can firm up the arrangements, once you've had a chance to think about it all,' Phoebe told her. 'I don't want you to feel pressurised.'

'I don't,' Connie assured her. 'I feel inspired. Thanks again.'

Marcus was jubilant as they began the journey back to Puddleduck Farm. 'I wasn't being too pushy, was I? She was keen to do it, I could tell.'

'She was.' Phoebe navigated their way out through the maze of roads that made up the housing estate. 'Although I am glad we gave her a cooling-off period, so to speak.'

'Yes. But it just goes to show. You never can tell about people. You were right about the fact we shouldn't jump to conclusions.'

'Hmmm.'

Marcus cleared his throat. 'Although there is one thing that's still bothering me.'

'Oh? What's that?'

'When we were talking earlier about prices. I think you might have got the wrong end of the stick.'

'Go on...'

'Yeah. I was kind of recommending you put your prices up, rather than give up charging anything at all.' His eyes glinted with humour but he said it with such a straight face that Phoebe snorted with laughter.

And then they were both laughing so much that she had to pull over for a few moments to recover.

31

'That sounds absolutely brilliant,' Sam told Phoebe later that night, when Lily was in bed, having had a goodnight kiss from both of her parents, and Phoebe had just told him about her afternoon. 'Do you think she'll really do it?'

He hoped she would. It would be one less demand on Phoebe's time.

'I think she actually might. She was really lovely. And it would take the pressure off Maggie. It would be really good to get someone involved who can give some time to it. Do you remember when we were first talking about the Voice for Wildlife campaign, I envisaged someone being able to go out and do talks. I think Connie would be perfect for that. She was a performance poet in her youth, apparently. She's really eloquent. It's a shame she hasn't made any money out of it. She showed us some of her stuff. It's very amusing.'

'I'll look forward to seeing some of that, and I guess not everyone can be as successful as Pam Ayres. Especially with that rural Berkshire accent she uses. Does Connie have an accent?'

'Not that I noticed. But she was talking about successful

poets and saying how rare they were. She repeated some quote.' Phoebe screwed up her face. 'Something like, "There's no money in poetry. But then there's no poetry in money either." I'm not sure if it was hers or if it was someone else who said it originally.'

Sam googled it on his phone. 'It was Robert Graves according to Reddit. He wrote war poems apparently.' He hadn't heard of Robert Graves, although he was sure he should have done. 'Anyway, you're right. It's absolutely brilliant. Fingers crossed she comes to see Maggie. It sounds like they'd make a great team.'

Roxie had sauntered across to see what all the excitement was about and Sam leaned down to stroke her soft head. The dalmatian leaned into his fingers. Roxie treated him as her number one human these days, but that was probably because he spent a lot more time with her than Phoebe did.

'Anyway, enough of me,' Phoebe continued. 'How was your day? Did you go and see Marjorie?'

'I did, and she's more than happy for me to start doing some teaching when the weather's a bit warmer. She said one or two of my former students still go there riding.'

'But I thought you wanted to start teaching from here? What's the point of starting it up again at Brook? I thought you were just going to speak to her so you could make sure you weren't stepping on her toes.'

'I'm planning to do both. Marjorie's doing less, not more, so I don't think I'll be stepping on her toes. My plan is to work there as well as set something up here. But I don't think building an indoor school here is viable, Pheebs. At least not until I'm more established. An outdoor school could work though. It would be relatively cheap to do. There's just the lighting and the all-weather floor. Now, that is definitely doable. And there's room.'

'That sounds great. Yes, it's sensible. You've been doing your homework.'

Sam clicked his tongue. 'I'm looking at it as a long-term sustainable enterprise.' He hesitated. There was something else he wanted to talk to her about too. Something else he'd been investigating. He wondered if this was the right moment to raise it.

Phoebe's mobile rang and he saw her glancing towards it and paused.

She looked at him. 'Sorry. I need to get this.'

The call turned out to be Max wanting to ask her advice on a call-out he was doing, and by the time they'd finished speaking it was late, and the moment for the conversation Sam had been planning to have had passed.

He'd been slightly relieved. There would be a right time. And although, strictly speaking, he didn't believe in fate intervening, he was happy to accept that tonight wasn't it. Sam had always trusted his instincts.

* * *

Meanwhile, the daily routines of life went on. February was much milder than January had been. Clumps of bright yellow daffodils began to appear in the sunnier corners of Puddleduck Farm and the grass had started to grow in the dog field. Despite all the activity of people and dogs walking on it daily – the dog field was turning out to be a great money earner – it wouldn't be that long before it would need its first mow of the season.

Most excitingly of all, Lily began to crawl. This made life harder work as she no longer stayed in one place. But it was also a joyful time for Sam and Phoebe who constantly told her how clever she was. Roxie wasn't so impressed, as the baby crawled determinedly after her, but the young dog soon learned to move smartly out of her way, or to jump up onto sofas. Snowball was already adept at staying out of their little one's way.

Roxie also spent more time outdoors, either with Sam when he took Lily out for her daily walk, or wandering around Puddleduck Pets with Natasha, who always had dog treats in a bumbag around her waist.

Connie Samuels had met up with Maggie, and as Phoebe had suspected, the two ladies had swiftly become very good friends. They had a great deal in common. Connie and Eddie had talked about the Voice for Wildlife posters and they'd decided that some of these might work well in verse. The relevant poems would be printed alongside photos of the relevant animals – a fox or a hedgehog or a bird of prey.

> *Foxes and hogs*
> *Are not like dogs.*
> *They're best off outside,*
> *Roaming free.*
> *It's the countryside*
> *Where their homes should be.*
>
> *Birds of prey*
> *Need to be free.*
> *Not caged up*
> *In an aviary.*
> *It's the countryside*
> *Where their homes should be.*

'They're not literary masterpieces, are they?' Maggie had remarked to Connie with a wink. 'But I can see where you're coming from.'

'I think they're brilliant,' Eddie had contradicted her. 'We're not trying to write literary masterpieces. We're trying to get a message across.'

Connie had just laughed and said she was immune to criticism, having once been a performance poet.

'Back in the day, disgruntled punters threw eggs if they weren't happy with a performer. But apparently today you're more likely to get used teabags or old cabbages. Eggs are too darn expensive to waste on throwing at people. It's a sign of the times.'

Mission Cat Rescue was still very hush hush but would apparently take place at the same time as the sponsored walk that Eddie had suggested as a fundraiser.

Both were scheduled to happen in the middle of March. When Maggie had told her the timing, Phoebe had been worried.

'But don't we need to rescue those cats now?'

'It's more important we set everything up properly, my darling. We're keen to make sure Duncan Jukes can't just simply start over again. It's no good us rescuing the cats he has now if he simply goes out and gets more.'

'Yes, I suppose that's true.'

'There are things that need to be set up first,' Maggie continued. 'You'll just have to trust me.'

The timing of the sponsored walk also gave everyone who wanted to participate enough time to raise sponsorship.

Eddie had suggested it would be a good idea to have tee-shirts made up which could be sold to participants in advance and worn on the day. They'd ordered some sunshine-yellow tees from a website, which did them really cheap, including a design of your choice.

When they arrived, Phoebe realised why they'd been so

cheap. There wasn't much sunshine about them. They were a hideously bright duster yellow. She had suggested they use the Puddleduck Pets logo or even The Puddleduck Pooch and Mooch one, but she'd been overridden by Maggie and Eddie.

'They're going to say, "I'm a Fabulous Fundraiser",' Maggie had said firmly. 'We might want to use them for other things in the future, so I don't want us to pin things down with names too much.'

Phoebe noticed she and Eddie had exchanged meaningful glances when she'd said this, so she hadn't argued too much. They were up to something, that much was obvious, but she knew better than to object too much.

Maggie had also assured her several times that Mission Cat Rescue would be entirely legal.

'We're not breaking any laws,' Maggie had said, looking ever so slightly smug. 'And if you want to check, you can ask Lord Holt. Rufus and Emilia are totally on board with what we're going to do. And, as you know, the lord of the manor can't possibly be seen to get involved with anything dubious. It would be a scandal.'

'It would,' Phoebe had agreed, her suspicions having been slightly allayed. Although she did phone Tori to see if she knew what Maggie's masterplan was. If Rufus was involved in it then he was bound to have told his best friend, Harrison.

'I'm as in the dark as you are,' Tori told Phoebe. 'But Harrison also swears blind they're not doing anything illegal. The cats will be rescued, and it's all perfectly above board. I'll be coming on the sponsored walk, by the way. I've got two hundred pounds in sponsorship so far.'

'Oh my God, that's brilliant. I'd better get my act together.'

Although she was working flat out most of the time, Phoebe had never been happier. She was pretty sure Sam was happy too. Getting their mums and Maggie involved in Lily's childcare was going great. Louella and Jan loved spending time with their granddaughter, although Phoebe was aware that when things didn't work out and they couldn't make it, Sam tended to pick up the slack a lot more often than she did.

He'd started teaching at Brook again, which she knew was his happy place, and he'd got some quotes for the lighting and fencing for the outdoor school. So when they were relaxing one Friday night in the front room after supper and Sam said he had something to show her, Phoebe assumed it would be to do with this.

He had a brown A4 envelope in his hands, and he withdrew a plastic folder that contained some kind of document, which he removed from the folder and laid across his lap, before gently smoothing it out with his fingers. He blinked a couple of times and cleared his throat.

'Phoebe, my darling, I... I heard a radio programme when I was on my way over to Brook recently and it was about a change in the law to do with couples who lose babies.' He broke off, his Adam's apple bobbing. 'Blimey, this is harder than I thought. Look... I hope this is OK with you. I probably should have told you about it first but, oh God, it's easier just to show you.'

He handed the document over to Phoebe with hands that shook slightly so the paper shook too.

Alarmed now, Phoebe took it. She dipped her head to read.

Certificate of baby loss
Issued on behalf of the secretary of state for health and social care.

Phoebe felt a frozen stillness in her heart as she read the rest of the document.

Name of parent: Phoebe Dashwood
Name of other parent: Sam Hendrie
Name of baby: Jack
Sex of baby: male

'Oh my gosh,' she said, a tiny shiver running along the back of her neck as she registered fully what she was looking at, and her eyes blurred with tears. She blinked them quickly away.

He was beside her in an instant. 'I've upset you. I'm so sorry, darling... I...'

'No. No, you haven't, at all... Oh, Sam. This is... it's amazing. Proper acknowledgement that he existed. That he was here. I didn't know we could even do this.'

'Apparently we couldn't until recently. It's only possible because of a change in the law. It's something mothers who have lost a baby have been campaigning for.' His eyes held hers. 'It proves our babies existed. Officially, I mean, and not just in our hearts. They can be honoured and recognised.'

He took her hand. 'I know how much we both grieved for Jack and I didn't want to bring it all up again by telling you about the certificates, but I also thought this might help us to get some closure.'

'It does. It really does.' She squeezed his hand. And then she raised the certificate to her lips and kissed it. 'Jack was really here. Just because we never got the chance to meet him, it doesn't mean he didn't exist.'

There were a few breaths of silence in the room broken only by the ticking of Maggie's old-fashioned clock that still sat where it had always sat on the mantlepiece, before Sam spoke again.

'Formal acknowledgement.'

He had tears in his eyes too, Phoebe saw. This was massive

for Sam. He would never have done anything like this when she'd first known him. He'd have been all stiff-upper-lipped and macho. He would never have been able to acknowledge and act on something like this.

'I sometimes feel that I'm not up to the job of being a parent,' he added. 'I feel like I'm letting her down. And you...'

'I've had those exact same feelings, Sam. About not being good enough. About letting you guys down. Maybe that's just normal for everyone. Everyone who really cares anyway.'

Roxie, aware of the emotion in the room, went from one to another of her humans, offering a comforting paw.

'Dogs are amazing,' Phoebe said, smiling through her tears. 'It's OK, darling. These are happy tears, not sad ones.'

'Thank you, Sam.' She moved into his arms and for a moment they both hugged each other tightly, their tears falling onto the document that honoured their son. 'Thank you so much.'

32

By the middle of March, Phoebe, Sam and Tori had all reached their £500 sponsorship targets for the walk. Marcus and Natasha had gone even further and had raised £1,000 each. Jenna and her husband and Max and India were walking and had a lot of donations. Even Connie had got some hefty sponsorship, and several other volunteers were walking for Puddleduck Pets too. It was turning into a fabulous fundraising effort, and Phoebe was thrilled.

The sponsored walk route was a 10k trek around the New Forest. Natasha and Marcus had worked out the flat circular route, which was partly through the forest and partly on wide sandy tracks and had apparently taken their dogs round it a couple of times to make sure it was doable for even the slowest walker in about two hours. Their meeting point was a forestry commission car park that wasn't far from the Beechbrook estate, and the route would take them along the very outer edges of Rufus's land.

Not everyone was taking a dog. Maggie had said she was going to leave Buster and Tiny behind. 'It's a bit too far for

Buster, these days, and Tiny's getting lazy in his old age. He'd rather be asleep on the sofa.'

Phoebe and Sam were taking Roxie. Louella and James had volunteered to look after Lily, as some of the paths weren't very buggy friendly. Tori had said her mum was looking after Vanessa-Rose too.

'Rufus has got Harrison doing something or other on the estate,' she had told Phoebe. 'I think it might be linked to Mission Cat Rescue, but he was a bit vague.'

'Harrison isn't walking then?'

'No, he said he does enough walking at work, but he did give me quite a big donation towards my target, so I've let him off the hook.'

The day of the sponsored walk was forecast to be unseasonably warm with an 80 per cent chance of sunshine. And the forecasters were right; it began with a blue sky and sunshine.

'We're so lucky,' Phoebe said to Sam as they waved goodbye to Lily, who was happily playing with Granny Louella, and took an excited Roxie on her lead out to the car. 'It wouldn't have mattered if it was wet, but it's much nicer to have sunshine.'

'Absolutely.' He caught her hand. 'It's lovely to be doing something together. It's a pity we couldn't bring Lily.'

'She can come along when she's a bit older.'

There were already lots of cars in the car park when they arrived. And as people began to get out and Phoebe caught more and more glimpses of the yellow duster tee-shirts, she realised most of them were filled with people here to do the sponsored walk.

Archie and Emilia, also both proudly in yellow, waved at her from where they stood beside Rufus's Land Rover. There was no sign of Rufus and they hadn't brought Chesska, so maybe she was with her dad, but Archie had brought Spot and Chloe along and they were all sniffs and excited wags.

Tori had just got out of her car too, and was heading over. She had her camera strung around her neck, Phoebe saw. She'd promised to take some photos for marketing and do a write-up for *New Forest Views*.

'I'm going to do some impromptu pics as we walk, but I'll take a few more formal shots before we go.' Tori's green eyes flashed with enthusiasm. 'I'd better get started, I think. It'll be like herding cats, trying to get this lot into one place.'

She was right. It took at least five minutes to get the sponsored walkers into a group that she could fit into one shot.

'Tall people at the back, short ones at the front,' she bossed. 'And I want to see your lovely tee-shirts. Can everyone unzip their coats, please?'

That took another few minutes, but finally they were ready and Tori took several photos of them all against the backdrop of the ancient old oaks and beeches.

By ten o'clock, Phoebe had counted at least twenty-seven heads. It was very heartwarming. The only disappointment was that Maggie and Eddie hadn't arrived. Phoebe had just got a text saying not to wait for them. They'd needed to see to something but would catch them up.

It was time to go. Natasha and Marcus set off at a brisk pace along the wide sandy path that led away from the car park. 'Don't worry, no one will get lost,' Natasha assured Phoebe and Sam. 'Most people have got a map, and a couple of the volunteers have agreed they'll stay at the back to make sure stragglers know where they're going.'

'The beauty of this walk,' Marcus added, 'is that it curls back around on itself a couple of times. It's like two great big figures of eight. So if anyone gets tired they can drop out or have a rest in their cars for a break, or even stop for lunch halfway through. But it's not that far, so I doubt many people will.'

Sam and Phoebe fell into step beside Tori and Emilia and Archie and there was a lot of chatter about babies, and then about Archie's horse-riding escapades, and finally about what he was doing at school.

'Is it still OK for me to come and do some more work experience in the summer?' he asked Phoebe. 'I've definitely decided I'm going to be a vet.'

'Of course it is. You're always welcome. Just let me know the dates so I can make sure we have something exciting to do.'

'At least I think I'm going to be a vet,' Archie added thoughtfully. 'My Plan B is to work with lions on safari in Africa.'

'Crikey,' Sam said. 'That sounds exciting.'

'It will be. Have you ever treated a lion, Phoebe?'

'No, I can't say I have. Although I'll tell you who may have done.' Phoebe shielded her eyes and looked around them. 'Do you see that lady over there with Max? The one with the red coat and dark hair?'

'Yeah. I see her. Who is she?'

'Her name's India. She's Max's girlfriend. She's a vet and she specialises in exotics. She's seen pythons and all sorts. She might have treated a lion.'

'Wow. That's so cool. Do you think she'd mind if I interviewed her? I've got to do a piece for our school mag.'

'I don't think she'd mind at all.'

'I'll ask her now.' Archie zigzagged away across the path, avoiding dogs and walkers, and a few moments later Phoebe saw him tap India's shoulder.

'He's so confident now,' Phoebe said to Emilia.

'He's never been that backwards in going further,' Emilia said and frowned. 'Is that the correct expression?'

'No.' Phoebe explained what it was and Emilia rolled her eyes. 'I can never get my mouth around your English expressions. They do not make proper sense to me.'

'Me neither,' Sam said, and they all laughed.

It was ages since she and Sam had walked together in the forest, Phoebe thought, even if they weren't alone. She glanced at his profile as they strolled side by side in a steady rhythm with Roxie trotting along not far from them. There were a few other dogs and she recognised some that had been rehomed from Puddleduck Pets. Once again she felt warmed that so many people had turned out for them.

The forest was alive with spring. It had swapped its cloak of winter drabness for one of vibrant green and yellow. Everything was in bud or new leaf. Bright green ferns uncurled into the woodland and splashes of early bluebells were visible so that it looked as though a beautiful lilac carpet wound itself between the trees. The air smelled of earthiness and woody green freshness. The chatter of walkers and the clomp of their walking boots was all around them.

After about forty-five minutes of walking, the group had split up into fast walkers who'd already disappeared into the distance and been swallowed up by the trees and a long tail of slower walkers stretching out behind them. Phoebe, Sam, Tori, Emilia and Archie were somewhere in the middle-to-end section.

Phoebe realised they couldn't be that far from Rufus's land. She could hear the sound of a distant chainsaw. Maybe that's what he'd got Harrison doing today. Chopping down trees. Oh well, he was probably happier doing that. Harrison had never been a great socialite.

'I thought Maggie was coming today,' Tori remarked, 'but I didn't see her at the start. Is she OK?'

'Yes, she's fine. She texted to say she and Eddie had something they needed to do but they would definitely see us on the walk and not to wait for them. She didn't want to hold us up.'

'That's good news then. How's the Voice for Wildlife campaign going?' Tori asked. 'Did you want me to do any more features to tie in with dates? Easter bunnies maybe?'

Phoebe told her about Connie and the wild rabbit, and she gasped. 'That sounds amazing. Should I put that in the mag? Actually, on second thoughts, maybe I'd better not. We probably shouldn't be encouraging people to befriend wild rabbits.'

'No, it's a shame, but I think you're right. No more cute photos.' Phoebe had told Tori in the end about the woman whose husband had been prompted to buy her an African pygmy hedgehog after reading the feature about them in *New Forest Views* and Tori had been horrified.

Now, Phoebe turned towards Emilia. 'Are we very close to Rufus's land, do you know?' The sounds of a chainsaw were getting louder.

'I do not know,' Emilia said. 'But maybe...'

'I think we're pretty close to the back boundary,' Tori said. 'Hey? Maybe it's Harrison making that godawful racket.' Tori shook her head in exasperation. 'And there's us all trying to have a nice peaceful country walk on a Sunday afternoon. You'd think they could have held off until tomorrow.'

Phoebe was about to joke that they'd have to put in an official complaint when they came out into a clearing alongside some newly felled trees.

'I think we've gone wrong somewhere,' Emilia said, looking at the map in her hand. 'We've come off the main path, haven't we?'

Archie looked over her shoulder. 'Yes, it looks like we took the wrong fork a little while ago. Oh, no. Shall we turn back?'

'Just a minute,' Emilia said. 'Let's go and see what's going on here.'

The path they were on had narrowed and ran close to the back gardens of some posh-looking houses which had high wooden fences. It looked as though some workmen had been felling trees close by. There were a couple of warning signs up about the dangers of log felling and the strong smell of freshly sawn wood.

'We've definitely wandered off route,' Sam said. 'We must have somehow missed the warning signs further up the path too. Looks like those guys did as well.' He pointed through the trees towards another small clearing.

A group of sponsored walkers, identifiable by their duster-yellow tee-shirts, were standing in a cluster watching someone in a high-vis jacket saw through the trunk of a big tree. As he did so, someone else detached themselves from the cluster and came trotting down the path towards them.

Phoebe saw to her amazement that it was Maggie. How had she got up here ahead of them without her noticing?

The old lady was gesturing by putting her palms up in front of her that they stop where they were, and they all did as they were bid.

'I think you'll be out of range there,' Maggie said, giving them a beaming smile. 'But it's better to be safe than sorry. He's only got one more tree to go apparently, but it's a big one. Dogs on leads would probably be safest too.'

Archie called Chloe and Spot and snapped on their leads and Sam put Roxie's on too. Then they all looked back at the tree feller.

'He's a bit close to those garden fences,' Sam said, frowning. 'I hope his tree's going to fall the right way. Otherwise it'll be in one of those gardens.'

'Oh, I think he knows what he's doing,' Maggie said cheerily. 'He's had plenty of practice.'

'It *is* Harrison,' Tori said, her eyes widening in surprise as they all paused to watch. 'Blimey. He is a bit close. But yes, you're right, he does know what he's doing.'

'Timber!' yelled Harrison, and they all watched in expectation as the tree began to topple.

'It's not falling the right way,' Archie shouted. 'Look at that.'

'It's going to hit that garden fence.' Sam's eyes were wide.

Then there was a frozen moment of shock as the huge old beech tree came down in what seemed like a slow-motion horror movie before it smashed across the fence with an almighty crash, splintering it like matchwood.

33

For a few moments no one moved. And then it seemed as though everyone was moving at once. Dogs were barking, someone was shouting, and there were people in yellow duster tee-shirts all over the place. There were far more of them than Phoebe had noticed before, and, to her shocked eyes, they seemed to be on both sides of the demolished fence. They were running in and out of the garden, which was clearly visible now the fence had gone, with what looked like cat baskets, filled with cats.

She must be having some sort of hallucination. As her stunned brain tried to catch up with what was happening, she saw there was a long wooden building in the garden. An outbuilding of some sort. Maybe a summerhouse but bigger. The end door was hanging off by its hinges and one glass window was smashed. Had that just happened? The rest of the building seemed to be intact.

The people coming in and out of the garden did indeed have cat baskets. Phoebe could have sworn one of them was Rufus.

Where had he sprung from? She was definitely imagining things. This was totally surreal.

'Have you any idea what's going on?' Sam's voice broke through her shock.

'No.' She blinked rapidly. 'Oh my God. Yes.'

'Mission Cat Rescue.' Sam cottoned on at the same time as she did. 'This is Duncan Jukes's house?'

'It must be. But blimey. Surely that wasn't all done deliberately.' Phoebe was galvanised into action. 'We need to help them.'

'I think they've pretty much got it in hand,' Sam said as they both hurried towards the now totally exposed back garden with an excited Roxie, pulling on her lead. The tree was lying in the bottom third of a very long garden. Its heavy trunk had hit the fence but its branches were fanned out on the ground like some enormous decorative garden ornament.

The summerhouse was surprisingly unscathed. It had been just out of range and the tree had missed it by inches, only the tree's uppermost feathery branches were brushing against the door that was off its hinges.

Phoebe peered inside the summerhouse, which was jammed with pens and cages, all of which were now empty, although they'd clearly been occupied until very recently. The sour smell of cat urine and faeces hung in the air.

'It's so lucky that tree didn't go through the roof,' Phoebe said. 'If it had it could easily have injured any of the cats in here.'

'Luck or skill?' Sam murmured, touching the shattered hinges with his fingertips. 'If you ask me, those cats were long gone when that tree hit the fence. And I don't think those branches caused this damage either. Even though it does look like they did.'

'You're saying the cats were already in the cat baskets before the tree came down? But how did anyone get access to the back garden before the fence was down? And where were they all?'

'I suspect we're going to find out any minute,' Sam said as Maggie appeared in the garden beside them.

'What are you two doing? We need some help, getting all these rescued cats to safety. They can't stay here. Come on, chop chop.'

She disappeared around the side of the summerhouse and Phoebe realised Sam was right. There were three cat boxes lined up beyond it. They all grabbed one and hurried after Maggie, back onto the forest path.

There was now a Land Rover with its engine running parked in a clearing in the woods. The back of it was already half full of cat boxes and a chain of people were passing in more. Phoebe recognised Denise Wyatt, Oscar's owner, amongst them. A stocky man in a tweed jacket was by her side. Presumably he was her husband, Ken, the Rottweiler barrister.

'My God, how many cats did they have locked in that shed?' Phoebe asked in horror.

'A lot,' Denise told her grimly. 'Cats and kittens. Thank goodness for freak accidents, or we'd never have been able to liberate them all.'

There was no trace of irony in her voice, but Rottweiler Ken was smiling as he glanced at Phoebe. 'A terrible freak accident.'

Not far from them, Emilia was bent over one of the cat boxes with Archie by her side. 'Minka and Charly. I never thought I'd see you again, my babies.' She poked her fingers through the grille of the box.

'You can say hello to them properly later,' Rufus was saying. 'Come on, we need to get all this lot safely home.'

Emilia nodded. She didn't seem at all fazed at what was

going on, Phoebe realised, and as she arrived beside her, Emilia glanced up guiltily.

'You knew about this, didn't you?'

Emilia had the grace to blush, but before she could reply, a young blonde woman Phoebe didn't recognise, wearing a faded denim jacket, arrived beside Emilia.

'He's on his way back,' she said urgently. 'I think the neighbours must have phoned him when the tree came down because he just texted me to see what was going on. I told him I'd just got here to check the house. He's been away. You need to get the rest of the cats loaded and that Land Rover out of here.'

Emilia nodded, and Rufus swung Emilia's cat basket up into the Land Rover. 'Any more to go in?' He looked around the assembled people, and they all shook their heads.

Rufus shut the doors and then hurried up to the driver's door and spoke to someone, and the Land Rover pulled smoothly away, bumping across the uneven ground until it disappeared between the trees.

Emilia turned towards Phoebe. 'This is Carmel, our cleaner. Carmel, this is Phoebe, our lovely vet.'

Carmel smiled shyly, and Phoebe wondered fleetingly if Emilia tagged everyone she knew with the word 'our' and introduced them as a member of staff. Maybe that's what everyone did when they had staff and a title. She berated herself for being so cynical.

'Carmel's on our side,' Emilia told Phoebe quickly, misinterpreting her expression. 'Carmel has been helping with Mission Cat Rescue. She let us know when Slimy Balls would be away.'

'He must never find out,' Carmel said quickly. 'I think he would kill me.'

'You did turn off the CCTV before you let anyone in?' Emilia asked, and Phoebe glanced back towards the garden, noticing for the first time that there was a camera on the summerhouse. There had been another one on the back gate, which had come down when the fence had been smashed, but that one lay broken on the ground. Some fragments of it were scattered across the path. The security must have been pretty tight then.

'Yes.' Carmel nodded vigorously. 'When he checks he will find that it mysteriously cut out around ten thirty this morning.'

'Excellent. We'd better stop talking.'

'Yes. I'm going to leave before he gets back.' Carmel hurried back into the garden and disappeared.

The rest of the people in the clearing who'd been helping with the cat baskets were now chatting, the adrenaline of a few minutes earlier evident in their voices.

'Well, that was exciting…'

'Thank goodness the cats were all safe.'

'Do you think we should get back to the walk? We can't get our sponsorship if we don't finish.'

As Phoebe glanced around, she realised she knew most of them. As well as Maggie and Eddie, and the Holts and the Wyatts, there were a few of her dedicated volunteers.

She was about to thank them all for their help with what had clearly been a meticulously planned operation when she saw a furious figure negotiating the felled beech tree that now lay in his back garden and stomping his way towards them.

'What the hell's been going on here? Who's responsible for this bloody fiasco?'

He was so angry he couldn't say any more. Rage was coming off him in almost palpable waves and his face was beetroot red as he stomped around over bits of broken tree boughs, occasionally stopping to kick one out of his way. He paused beside a window of the summerhouse. Then he looked inside, did a double take, and looked again. 'Where are my bloody cats?'

Rufus stepped forward. 'Allow me to introduce myself. I'm Lord Rufus Holt.' He held out a hand in a gesture of appeasement. 'I'm afraid this is down to me. My man's been tree felling. Slight miscalculation.'

'Lord Holt – er...' Clearly nonplussed, Duncan Jukes stopped in his tracks. He shook his head. 'But my cats. I had cats in there. Expensive cats...'

Emilia stepped forward. 'Oh, good gracious alive. I think I did see a cat or two. Yes, maybe three or four cats now I can think of it. They ran into the forest after the tree came down. We did not realise they were yours.' She smiled sweetly. 'This is terrible tragedy. Ja?'

'There were a lot more than three bloody cats. You let all of my cats run into the forest. You didn't catch *any* of them.' He shot her a furious glare. Lady Holt's presence clearly didn't faze him anywhere near as much as Lord Holt's had done.

But other people were now speaking too.

'I saw a cat. It went that way.' A woman in a yellow tee-shirt pointed into the forest.

'No, it went that way,' someone else contradicted. 'It ran into the bushes. Those gorse bushes, I think.'

'No, that was a rabbit. The cats all went that way.' A tall guy in a deerstalker pointed in yet a different direction.

'I think I saw a white cat in your neighbour's garden. Did you have a white cat? It might have been fluffy.'

'Did any of them have a red collar? I think I saw one in a red collar.'

'I definitely saw a cat climb up a tree.'

'We may need to get the fire brigade out.' That was Maggie. 'No. Hang on a minute.' She shielded her eyes and glanced upwards. 'There it is. Did you have a grey cat? It's up there. Oh, no, sorry. I think that may be a squirrel.'

She laughed delightedly and Duncan Jukes must have suddenly recognised her because his face turned even redder.

'You! You came to my house. This is your doing. You're all in on this, aren't you? The lot of you.'

'I didn't chop down the tree.' Maggie gave him her best outraged look. 'I'm just on a sponsored walk.' She opened her coat, flasher style, to show him that her tee-shirt said 'I'm a Fabulous Fundraiser'.

Other walkers began to follow suit. They all opened their coats to show off their tee-shirts in tandem. 'Look, see. We're all on a sponsored walk,' came a chorus of voices. 'We were just passing.'

'We're raising money for animals.'

'Yeah. Homeless dogs and cats. It's a very good cause.'

'You're going to wish you'd never messed with me. I'm going to make your lives hell. Every single one of you. I'm going to sue you from here to kingdom come.'

'I don't think you are.' Rottweiler Ken strode across to Duncan, his hands in his pockets, his back very straight.

He wasn't as tall as Duncan but what he lacked in height he made up for in solidness and sheer straight-backed demeanour. He had an air of impressive authority which seemed to bristle into the air around him. The slightly carnival atmosphere of a moment before changed and stilled as he squared up to the corrupt cat breeder.

'You need evidence to sue and I think you'll find there are dozens of witnesses who'll testify that nothing more than an unfortunate tree-felling accident has occurred here today.'

'And I think you'll find the truth will come out when I check my CCTV.' Duncan was still angry but now he looked smug too. His face was set in a sneer.

Rottweiler Ken gave the slightest of nods. If he'd looked

scary before, he looked twice as intimidating now. 'I'll see you in court then. Believe me, I can't wait.'

There was a fraught little silence as everyone around them seemed to take in the implications of there being CCTV and one or two of them started to disperse.

Phoebe saw Rufus and Emilia exchange glances and Emilia gave the slightest shake of her head.

Then, Rufus, who'd been watching the proceedings with interest, stepped forward. 'I was going to offer to pay for the damage to the fence, but I'm quite happy to go to court if that's the route you'd prefer to take.' He didn't wait for a reply but turned on his heel. Emilia and Archie and their dogs went with him.

Sam caught hold of Phoebe's hand. 'We should probably get back to our sponsored walk.'

She nodded and glanced at Maggie, who gave her a very obvious wink.

'Yes, we won't be able to collect our sponsorship if we don't finish it, will we, love?'

'Hear, hear,' said Eddie, coming forward and rattling a collection box at Duncan. 'It's for all animals. Cats as well as dogs. You obviously love cats, sir.' He coughed. 'It's not too late to donate!'

34

Phoebe and Sam found out a lot more as they finished the sponsored walk. Maggie and Eddie walked the last bit with them, and they slowly filled in the gaps about what had happened as they strolled along sandy paths through the early spring forest.

'Carmel's been brilliant,' Maggie said. 'We couldn't have done it without her. Emilia had a long chat with her about the kittens and about what we thought was going on and in the end she was able to confirm everything. She knew Duncan had cats but she had no idea he had a full-scale breeding operation going on in the garden.

'She didn't realise he'd taken Emilia's either. She trusted him totally. She was mortified when she found out he had and that she'd inadvertently helped him by telling him about them. Luckily Emilia had taken enough photos of both sets of kittens for Carmel to be able to identify them in the summerhouse.'

'Poor little things,' Phoebe murmured. 'It doesn't bear thinking about.'

'I know. They were being used for breeding, poor little

beggars. But they'll be safe now.' Maggie shook her head. 'They'll all be safe now. We'll find them all good homes.'

'That was very brave of Carmel. Slimeball won't be happy if he realises she helped us.'

'She's leaving him. So hopefully he won't. She said she'll leave it a few days so he doesn't get suspicious before she tells him. They don't live together or anything. In fact he won't even know her address any more because Emilia's offered her a live-in position at Beechbrook.'

'That sounds sensible.' Phoebe paused. 'Do you think there will be any comeback on us? What if he turns up at Puddleduck Pets and recognises them?'

'He's hardly going to report cats as stolen when he stole most of them in the first place. Besides which, my darling, we won't have all of them at Puddleduck Pets. That lovely Jade Foster has said she'll take a few. And the Cats Protection League will take some too. We're hoping that some of them might still have microchips which will prove who their original owners were. They can all be returned.'

'Yes, that's true. He wasn't expecting any of them to ever be found, was he? Did we ever work out how Oscar had escaped?'

'No, but Denise told me that Oscar used to go in and out of their tiny bathroom window if they left it open, and they must have opened the windows in that hellhole sometimes. Maybe that's how he got out.'

'I guess we'll never know.' Phoebe sighed. 'I can't, hand on my heart, say I totally approve of your unorthodox rescue methods, but I'm really glad you got them out.'

'And that's why I didn't tell you all the details, my darling.' Maggie winked. 'Besides which, we'll need you to do your part too. There are twenty-seven assorted cats and kittens currently waiting up at Beechbrook House for a vet check from our friendly local vet.'

'I'll get Max and Seth to help me out. We can go up straight after the walk.'

'Duncan Jukes seemed pretty certain he'd got CCTV footage.' Sam joined in with their conversation. 'Is he likely to send the police up to Beechbrook House?'

'He hasn't got any footage,' Phoebe reassured him. 'Carmel turned it off apparently.'

'She turned it off before she opened up the back gate and let us into the garden,' Maggie confirmed. 'Like I said, we couldn't have done it without her. And she certainly wasn't going to incriminate herself, was she? Anyway, I can't see the police heading up to Beechbrook House with a search warrant on Duncan Jukes's say-so, can you? That's a *Sun* headline if ever I heard one.'

'Good point,' Sam said, smiling. 'Harrison's gone right up in my estimation too. How on earth did he get that tree to take out the fence without managing to touch any more than the end door of the summerhouse?'

'Years of practice, I should think,' Phoebe said, but she felt the same. Harrison had gone way up in her estimation too.

They arrived back at the cars about fifteen minutes later and Sam went home with Roxie to look after Lily and tell Louella and James what was going on. Phoebe, Seth and Max headed to Beechbrook House.

Fortunately, the three vets discovered none of the felines were in such bad shape that they'd needed to be put to sleep, although some would need ongoing medical treatment for a while. Quite a few had the feline herpesvirus that Oscar had had. Phoebe, Seth and Max examined each one in turn and prescribed the relevant treatment.

'The only problem with Maggie's slightly unorthodox method of rescue is that we don't now have any evidence to prosecute the bastard,' Seth said when they'd finally finished and were back at Puddleduck Vets, which Phoebe had opened up especially.

'Even if we did, he'd probably just get a slap on the wrist,' Max said, looking across at Seth. 'Even when they are proved guilty the worst that happens is a slap on the wrist and a fine. They just wait for the dust to settle and start up again.'

'I hate the thought of that happening,' Phoebe said. 'But I'm not sure what we can do about it.'

* * *

Another week of March had come and gone by the time Phoebe discovered the Mission Cat Rescue team had thought of this too. It had been one of the reasons the timing of the rescue had been so critical. Carmel had been waiting for Duncan Jukes to go away on a four-day business trip during which she'd offered to house sit.

Carmel hadn't just switched off the CCTV on the occasion of the tree felling; she'd done it a couple of days earlier too. She'd done it for just long enough to take some video footage of the whole cat-breeding operation under Rottweiler Ken's instructions of exactly what they needed. As she'd had legal and unrestricted access to the house and garden at the time, and she hadn't broken any laws to get it, the footage should be valid as evidence.

They'd also now been able to establish which cat had been the mother of their kitten Freda and had the DNA evidence to prove it. Rottweiler Ken hadn't been joking when he'd told Duncan Jukes he couldn't wait to see him in court. Exploiting cats might not be too heinous a crime in the eyes of the law, but if you added in theft and fraud, things got a lot more interesting. Particularly if you were a hotshot barrister with an axe to grind.

To Phoebe's relief, Carmel had also given her erstwhile boyfriend his marching orders without any comeback and had moved in with Rufus and Emilia to be their live-in housekeeper. She'd offered to be a witness for Ken Wyatt too.

As Denise told Phoebe when she brought Oscar in for an appointment one Friday afternoon, revenge really was a dish best served cold. Duncan Jukes was going to regret the day he'd stolen the Wyatts' cat and Emilia's kittens very much.

35

By the end of March, all of the cats and kittens whose original owners couldn't be traced had gone to new homes. Rufus and Emilia had their four back, although they were adults now and they'd all been in to Phoebe's surgery for castration and spaying.

'None of them will be parenting another litter,' Emilia had said firmly. 'And we have enough space for four. We just have to hope for no fights.'

Luckily, the two females, Mia and Lucy, preferred to spend a lot of their time outside on the estate, hunting mice and other hapless wildlife that ventured too close to the house while Minka and Charly, the boys, were fond of indoor living at the manor. They could often be found curled up on easy chairs that were in patches of sunlight or on warm windowsills, snoozing in the sun.

Denise and Rottweiler Ken had taken Freda's mum in and had called her Shadow because she liked to follow Denise everywhere she went. Oscar, Freda and Shadow had also been in to Puddleduck Vets for ops. Thankfully, Oscar was fully recovered now and back up to his normal weight.

'So all's well that ends well,' Phoebe said to Marcus and Jenna as they opened up the practice one sunny morning. 'I still can't believe there was a kitten-milling operation going on right under our noses.'

'I guess they can be anywhere,' Jenna said with a sigh.

'And our job is to make sure the public know not to buy kittens or puppies from people who aren't reputable breeders,' Marcus said. 'Or any animal, come to that.' He glanced round at the Voice for Wildlife posters up in the surgery. 'We can get another poster up about that, can't we?'

'I'll organise it,' Phoebe said. 'Connie can spread the word too. Maybe she can do a poem.'

'Cats and kittens...' Jenna began and paused. 'Hmmm, what rhymes with kitten?'

'Mitten,' Marcus said with a grin. 'Or how about smitten... Don't get smitten with a cute little kitten. Unless you've met their mum and dad and, er... it's not just a passing fad. Hmmm. This poetry lark is harder than it looks.'

Jenna raised her eyebrows. 'You started well, but maybe we should leave it to the experts.'

They all smiled as the first client arrived, a woman with a collie coming in for a booster.

Another day had begun. And it was the usual mix of routine calls and thankfully no emergencies.

Not long before midday, Marcus called Phoebe out to reception. 'There's a guy outside who'd like someone to look at an exotic pet. I was going to get Max but he's busy. Would you be OK to take a look?'

'What kind of exotic pet is it?'

'Some kind of bear, I think he said.'

'A bear!' Phoebe looked at him in disbelief. 'Are you seriously telling me there's a man with a bear outside?' She moved to the plate-glass window of the surgery and looked out into the yard beyond. 'I can't see anyone.'

'He said he'd wait until we gave the OK before he brought him in. He didn't want to upset any of our other patients. He said it was quite small.'

'How small exactly? I mean, is it in a crate or what?' Phoebe had visions of someone with a koala bear in a crate sitting in the car park. 'What kind of bear is it?'

Jenna appeared from one of the consulting rooms. 'A water bear, I think he said. I spoke to him earlier too.'

'So why has no one told me before?' Phoebe sighed. 'What's a water bear, anyway?'

'A bear that likes water?' Marcus ventured.

Jenna shrugged. 'Don't ask me.'

Phoebe shook her head. They both seemed to be being particularly obtuse today, but luckily the surgery was empty of other patients. She turned back to Marcus.

'OK, I'll see him. What's wrong with this bear anyway? Did he say?'

'Injured leg,' they both said in unison.

At that moment the door opened and a teenager in jeans, tee-shirt and a back-to-front baseball cap appeared. He had nerdy black glasses and a nervous grin and he was carrying a green holdall, which he heaved up on to the reception desk.

'Leaping lizards, that's heavy. I hope it was all right to come in. I'm actually quite worried about Paddington.'

'You're the client with the bear?' Phoebe asked. This was getting more surreal by the moment. 'He's not in there, is he?' She hoped not; the poor creature could be suffocating. 'Can I take your name, please, sir?'

'Albus Clutterbuck. It's great to meet you. I've heard you're the best. Top of the pops.' His nervous grin had morphed into earnestness and Phoebe felt for him.

'OK, well, Mr Clutterbuck, if you'd like to bring Paddington through to...'

Before she could finish, Albus unzipped the holdall and whipped out a navy hoodie, swiftly followed by several grubby-looking white socks and what looked like a pair of boxers which he piled on to the reception desk haphazardly, before he located what he was looking for.

'Phew, I thought I'd lost him for a moment. Sorry, that's my laundry.' He bundled the clothes back into the holdall and hooked out some kind of flat round container which he thrust towards Phoebe.

Phoebe hoped it was clean laundry. It hadn't looked very clean. But she resisted the urge to comment and took the container.

It was a petri dish. How curious. She frowned and leaned forward to see whatever it was she was supposed to be looking at.

'Paddington's a tardigrade,' Albus continued.

'I see.' Phoebe racked her brains. What was a tardigrade? She'd heard the word somewhere, but couldn't quite bring it to mind. She had the feeling she was being wound up, but she wasn't quite sure enough to call it. 'Which leg is injured?' she asked Albus, putting on her most serious voice.

'I dunno, but he's definitely limping.'

There was a snort from behind her. Jenna seemed to be having some kind of sneezing fit, which she was trying desperately to suppress by cupping her hands over her nose.

Marcus also seemed to be finding it a struggle to contain himself. He had his head down but he was spluttering.

Now Phoebe was sure this was a wind-up. And two could play at that game. Or four in this case, because Albus was almost certainly in on the joke. 'I'll need to fetch my microscope,' she murmured. 'Oh dear, these specialist cases can be expensive. Particularly if we need surgery. Is Paddington insured?'

'Um...' Albus looked at her askance, opened his mouth to say something and then shut it again.

Marcus, who'd been sitting at the desk throughout the exchange, began to speak too, but Phoebe held up a hand. 'Hold that thought. I won't be a second.'

Maintaining both her stern face and her sense of dignity, she disappeared into the back room where she googled tardigrade and discovered it was a microscopic eight-legged animal, commonly known as a water bear. She took a deep breath and shook her head in bemusement.

What on earth had got into her usually sensible and hard-working staff? Suddenly she noticed the date on her phone: 1 April. Oh my goodness. So that's what they were up to. Now she'd got over the shock, she had to admit it was quite good as April Fools went. Not that she had any intention of telling them that just yet. Oh, no!

Now, it was payback time.

She found her TTL loupes, a purpose-built magnifying glass, which resembled a pair of glasses with two old-fashioned lenses stuck on the eye pieces, and headed back to reception. Before she opened the door, she leaned against it listening. There was a low buzz of chatter, which hushed as she went in wearing the glasses and a perfectly straight face.

She strode through reception, walked straight through it to the outside door and then locked it. She didn't want any real customers coming in for a moment. Then she went back to reception. 'Pass me the petri dish, please, Mr Clutterbuck.'

The teenager complied and Marcus began nervously, 'But boss, there's not actually anything to, er...'

Phoebe hushed him with another wave of her hand as she leant over the dish, which was empty apart from a little black mark, which she guessed had been made with a pen, on the white background. Surreptitiously, she loosened the lid before she let the dish slip out of her hands onto the surgery floor with a clinking sound. The lid and the dish parted company.

'Oh, my goodness,' Phoebe gasped. 'I'm so sorry. Our patient appears to have escaped. We need to look for him. Everyone, on their hands and knees, quickly, please.'

Albus's eyes grew wider behind his geek glasses. Jenna's face dropped, and Marcus just looked stunned.

Trying not to laugh herself, Phoebe clapped her hands. 'Come on, everyone. Chop chop. We need to search every corner. He can't have got far. Poor Paddington. We need to find him. On your hands and knees, please.'

None of the April Foolers were sure enough of her to take the risk that she might not be serious.

Marcus and the teenager both frowned before obeying her and getting down on the floor. Jenna bit her lip nervously and busied herself searching the top of the reception desk, moving pens and papers and a stapler to one side.

Phoebe, who was very good at keeping her emotions hidden, thanks to years of practice with clients, let them hunt for a good couple of minutes before she looked at the clock. It was one minute to midday. Finally, she relented.

'I've got him,' she shouted. 'He's over here on the weighing machine. Phew, I was lucky to spot him. It's only because there's a white background I managed to see him.'

The two guys got up off the floor in relief, and Phoebe took off her loupes and grinned at them. 'April Fool, right back at ya.'

Albus and Marcus broke into nervous laughter.

Jenna shook her head. 'Oh my God, you had me going there. I seriously didn't know if you were joking or not.'

'Ditto,' Marcus said.

'Leaping lizards.' Albus looked at her in admiration. 'That was a superb backfire. When did you guess?'

'When you said he was limping.' Phoebe smiled sweetly at them all. 'That was a step too far... if you'll excuse the pun.' She paused. 'Is your name really Albus Clutterbuck?'

'No, it's Ethan Drake. I'm a friend of Marcus's.' He whipped off the geek glasses and held out his hand.

Phoebe shook it. 'Ethan's studying drama at uni.' Marcus introduced them properly.

'A little more work to do then,' she teased, 'but I'll give you a B.'

They all laughed some more and Phoebe went across and unlocked the reception door again.

'Timewasters, the lot of you!' she muttered as she came back to join them. 'What if we'd had an actual emergency?'

'We wouldn't have done it if there'd been any clients about,' Jenna said hastily.

'Absolutely not, boss.' Marcus straightened his back. 'Sorry.'

'You're forgiven. It was quite funny as April Fools go.' Phoebe smiled at them. 'It was even funnier watching you all hunting for Paddington, though.'

When she told Sam about it over supper that night, he rolled his eyes. 'I can't believe you kept a straight face.'

'Neither can I, to be honest.'

'I'd have loved to have seen them all crawling around hunting for an imaginary tardigrade. What is a tardigrade anyway?'

'It's a microscopic eight-legged animal which can apparently survive in outer space and would very likely survive the apocalypse. At least that's *National Geographic*'s description of them. I looked them up earlier. They're often referred to as water bears so it was quite a clever joke actually.'

'Of course it was if Marcus was behind it. Why are they called water bears?'

'Because under a microscope they look like an eight-legged panda. Not that they'd actually got one in that petri dish.' She laughed. 'So how was your day, Sam? Anything exciting to report?'

'No April Fools around here, but yes, it was quite exciting. Ma texted to tell me about a wedding fair that's happening next weekend at the Rhinefield House Hotel. It's all day Saturday and Sunday. She was wondering if we fancied going along to it. Apparently Pa's happy to babysit if we don't want to take Lily, and Louella is keen to come along too.'

'That sounds like excellent fun. Maggie would love it too.' Phoebe nodded happily. 'It's about time we started planning, isn't it? I'll ask Tori too. You don't mind, do you, being surrounded by females at a wedding fair?'

'The more the merrier as far as I'm concerned.' Sam's eyes were warm. 'I can't think of a better way to spend a Sunday. Even if it's just to give us some ideas for our big day it would be good.'

'I think we need to set a date first.' Phoebe felt her heart skip with excitement. 'Get it firmed up. That is exciting. Oh, Sam, I know we've had some ups and downs this last year, but we've survived, haven't we?'

'We could survive anything. We'd be right there alongside the tardigrades in the apocalypse, I reckon.'

Phoebe laughed. 'Let's do it. That's the first thing we can buy at the wedding fair. Save the date cards. I'll get the diary. Let's set the date now. I think it's in the front room.'

A few moments later, she was back with the desk diary they used for appointments they both needed to know about. 'We've got time to plan a wedding this year if we crack on, but it's also got next year's calendar in too, if we decided we need more time.' She met his eyes.

'Cool. I found a half bottle of bubbly in the fridge too. It must have been left over from Christmas. We could have a toast.' Sam indicated the half bottle of Moët on the table, condensation glistening on its curved green glass.

'A toast to what?'

'Whatever you like. To planning a wedding, to surviving the apocalypse or just to us if you like.'

Phoebe nodded. 'How about a toast to our future? To our future as a family at Puddleduck Farm.'

'That sounds good to me.' He removed the gold foil and cage from the top of the bottle and eased out the cork, aiming carefully towards the floor, so it didn't break anything as it sprung out. Then he quickly poured the pale gold fizz into two flutes and handed her one. They both raised their glasses towards each other in the soft warmth of the Aga-heated kitchen.

They spoke together, in total synchronicity.

'To our future as a family at Puddleduck Farm.'

* * *

MORE FROM DELLA GALTON

Another book from Della Galton, *A New Arrival at Duck Pond Cottage*, is available to order now here:

https://mybook.to/NewArrivalDuckPond

ACKNOWLEDGEMENTS

Thank you so much to Team Boldwood – you are amazing. Thank you to every single one of you who works so hard to bring my books to my readers in paperback, audio and digital.

As always, my special thanks go to Caroline Ridding, and Cecily Blench and Jennifer Kay Davies, and to Alice Moore for the gorgeous cover.

Thank you to Rhian Rochford for her veterinary knowledge. Thank you to Jordan Hall for his veterinary knowledge about exotic animals. Huge thanks to Cara Wallace whose knowledge about African pygmy hedgehogs was invaluable, and for her pictures of Bumble and Honey. Also to Sarah Dempsy for her help and her gorgeous African pygmy hedgehogs. Thank you to Mel Flower for her help with the practicalities of setting up a dog field. The Puddleduck Pooch and Mooch was very much based on her brilliant dog field, Fieldtastic. Thank you to the Dunford Novelists for their perceptive comments. And to Jan Wright for hers.

Thank you to Gordon Rawsthorne for being my first reader and all of his comments about cars.

Thank you, perhaps most of all, for the huge support of my readers – without whom it would be pretty pointless writing novels. I love reading your emails, tweets and Facebook comments. Please keep them coming.

ABOUT THE AUTHOR

Della Galton writes short stories, teaches writing groups and is Agony Aunt for Writers Forum Magazine. Her stories feature strong female friendship, quirky characters and very often the animals she loves. When she is not writing she enjoys walking her dogs around the beautiful Dorset countryside.

Sign up to Della Galton's mailing list for news, competitions and updates on future books.

Visit Della's website: www.dellagalton.co.uk

Follow Della on social media:

- facebook.com/DailyDella
- x.com/DellaGalton
- instagram.com/Dellagalton
- bookbub.com/authors/della-galton

ALSO BY DELLA GALTON

The Bluebell Cliff Series

Sunshine Over Bluebell Cliff

Summer at Studland Bay

Shooting Stars Over Bluebell Cliff

Sunrise Over Pebble Bay

Confetti Over Bluebell Cliff

The Puddleduck Farm Series

Coming Home to Puddleduck Farm

Rainbows Over Puddleduck Farm

Love Blossoms at Puddleduck Farm

Living the Dream at Puddleduck Farm

Happy Ever After at Puddleduck Farm

A New Family at Puddleduck Farm

The Duck Pond Cottage Series

A New Arrival at Duck Pond Cottage

Summer Secrets at Duck Pond Cottage

BECOME A MEMBER OF THE SHELF CARE CLUB

The home of Boldwood's book club reads.

Find uplifting reads, sunny escapes, cosy romances, family dramas and more!

Sign up to the newsletter
https://bit.ly/theshelfcareclub

Boldwood

Boldwood Books is an award-winning fiction publishing company seeking out the best stories from around the world.

Find out more at www.boldwoodbooks.com

Join our reader community for brilliant books, competitions and offers!

Follow us
@BoldwoodBooks
@TheBoldBookClub

Sign up to our weekly deals newsletter

https://bit.ly/BoldwoodBNewsletter

Printed in Dunstable, United Kingdom